DOCTOR WHO

THE SPACE AGE
STEVE LYONS

BBC

Published by BBC Worldwide Ltd,
Woodlands, 80 Wood Lane
London W12 0TT

First published 2000
Copyright © Steve Lyons 2000
The moral right of the author has been asserted

Original series broadcast on the BBC
Format © BBC 1963
Dr Who and TARDIS are trademarks of the BBC

ISBN 0 563 53800 7
Imaging by Black Sheep, copyright © BBC 2000

Printed and bound in Great Britain by Mackays of Chatham
Cover printed by Belmont Press Ltd, Northampton

Prologue

History is being remade constantly.

You can't see it from your point of view. You drift through the fourth dimension, unable to change direction or even see where you're going. But other beings are different. They see the whole of the tapestry that is Time. They pull at a thread here, create a new detail there, and they don't care what their interference does to the rest of the fabric. Why should they? Do you care when you shoo away a butterfly, with all the consequences that might entail?

Something – perhaps somebody – does care, at least enough to darn the holes. The changes are not lost but they are subsumed, worked into the grand design. The overall picture is preserved by the sacrifice of a billion unimportant details.

Your life could be reworked from start to finish and you wouldn't even notice.

On a grey beach beneath a grey sky tinged with sunset red, in that area of the fourth dimension that you would think of as 1965, one of history's favourite stories is in progress. But the ending is about to change.

He is nineteen years old. She is eighteen. He wears a black leather jacket and T-shirt, and stiff blue jeans into which he has rubbed dirt to make them seem worn. She is clad in a simple powder-blue top, darker blue skirt and a sensible long coat that her parents picked out for her. His hair is black and untidy, his eyes green and wild, his chin rough with stubble. Her blonde hair is tied into a ponytail and the lines around her weary eyes age her beyond her years.

His name is Alec Redshaw. Hers is Sandra McBride. They think they are in love, and it's the best and the worst thing that has ever happened to them.

'Strange, isn't it?' says Sandra, drawing her coat tight in response to the cold breeze that haunts this grey evening. 'Everything's so quiet now. The beach looks so small.'

'Yeah,' says Alec. 'Well, that'll change soon, won't it?'

'Did you have to put on that filthy gear?'

'It's part of me, baby.'

'You mean it's part of that bloody gang you've sold your mind to.'

'I didn't think you'd come,' says Alec, clumsily changing the subject.

'I didn't want to. I'm supposed to be looking after the kid.'

The kid – Ricky – glances up at this, but quickly loses interest. Sandra brought along a comic book to keep him quiet, but it lies discarded beside him. The lurid four-colour world of science fiction has sparked his imagination, and he is building alien castles in the sand.

'But you came. You came here for us.' Alec seizes Sandra's arms passionately.

'No, Alec,' she protests, pulling free. 'I don't want this. You forced me to come here. You wouldn't leave me alone.'

'I had to talk to you without those big apes hanging about.'

'They'll find out. They'll catch us together and you know what they'll do to you.'

'I don't care. I love you, Sandra.'

'No you don't.'

She walks away from him. For seconds, he just stares after her, astonished and hurt. He doesn't know what to say. But she turns back first, swallowing hard. 'No, you're right. I owe you more than this. Oh, Alec, I spent hours practising what I was going to say to you. Just – just listen to me, will you? Just let me get the words out.'

'I love you,' he repeats.

'No. You love the idea of getting at my brothers.' Sandra's voice pleads with him to accept what she is saying, to put an end to this madness for both their sakes. 'But this isn't some stupid game, Alec, not to them. They meant what they said. They're even more into this gang thing than you are. They'll do something crazy before they'll let me swing with a rocker.'

'I don't care.' Alec sounds more sullen than defiant.

'Well, maybe I do.'

He won't give up. The thought of her makes his spine tingle with excitement. If he's honest, then she's right – that's partly because of the danger that comes with her. But he craves that thrill too much to let it go, even if his pride would allow it. 'They'll get theirs,' he mumbles. 'No mod's gonna dare raise his head in this town after the weekend.'

'There you go again. Is that all you can think about?'

'They've asked for it – and there's rockers coming from all over the country to make sure they get it. It's gonna be like Brighton all over again. We'll put this place on the map.'

'You think that's going to make things better? Fighting!'

'It'll show your brothers, won't it? I'll go out with any bird I want, and they can't stop me.'

'Don't you understand?' cries Sandra, exasperated. 'This is why I can't see you again. You're nineteen years old, Alec. You've got a job, and your own flat, and yet you spend your nights riding around on a stupid motorbike, looking for fights. I get enough of this at home. I wish you'd just grow up, the lot of you!'

Her anger is spent, then, and a moment of awkward silence passes between them. Sandra breaks it when, in avoiding Alec's eyes, she sees that her young charge has strayed. 'Ricky, come back here!' she shouts, with a little more snap than she intended.

'Look, can't we lose the kid brother?' complains Alec in what is supposed to be a conciliatory tone.

Sandra, in turn, is icy. 'No. In fact, I'd better get him home. He's only three. He's supposed to be in bed by eight o'clock. My parents'll kill me.'

'They won't know. They're at this lame dance, aren't they? They'll be out for ages.'

'You said no one was going.'

'None of our lot'd be seen dead there.'

'It'll be a disaster then, won't it? They'll probably break early.'

'They won't. They'll sit around with the other oldies and gas about the state of youth today.'

'At least they're trying to sort this mess out!'

'Yeah, sure. They'll get both sides together in the town hall, and we'll all kiss and make up and listen to some fogy on the piano and forget that music's moved on in the last hundred years. This ain't the "good old days" any more.'

'What a shame,' says Sandra acidly. 'In the "good old days", we might have been an item.'

The capsule was designed not to affect the picture, but it does. You see, its pilot lost control, and now the capsule tears through the cloth. Such a small hole. But, as always, it isn't the size of the impact that matters. The danger is that a fire might start, that its flames might spread to the furthest corners of the tapestry.

The capsule lies, broken, on an English beach. You could see it if you were to go there now. It doesn't matter when you're reading this. The capsule is still there, will be there, has always been there. At the same time, it isn't there, hasn't been there for many years, can't be there. Time will edit it from your life and smooth over the discrepancies. But not yet.

Time reaches out, engulfs the capsule and draws it in. It anchors the capsule to a part of itself, incorporating it into the picture. The metaphor changes now, as the pilot is forcibly introduced to an alien perspective. He is adrift on a great river, unable to move his capsule against its tide. Seconds pass him by, and the pilot feels a form of motion sickness.

To Alec and Sandra, it is as if their world were taken apart. Their minds, unable to cope with such a concept, delete the memories of it to leave a nagging trace of vertigo and the sick, unreal feeling that things aren't as they should be.

The world has been reassembled, but one tiny thing is

different. One minute detail in the tapestry. The broken capsule lies on the grey beach, and Alec and Sandra know it has been there all their lives and yet they have never seen it, never reacted to its presence before.

Their own concerns are forgotten in the rush to fit something so big, so strange, so utterly beyond their experience, into everyday frames of reference. The object is metallic and egg-shaped, but it has been ruptured. It sports a jagged hole, and Alec cannot help but imagine that some technological horror has been hatched from it.

Sandra's theory is perhaps born from the comics she reads to Ricky. 'Some sort of flying saucer,' she breathes. She jerks forward as if pulled in two directions, but the only forces acting upon her are her own conflicting emotions.

Alec tries to hold her back, but she shrugs him off again. 'It's a flying saucer, Alec. It's crashed here. Someone might be hurt. We've got to see.'

Alec shakes his head and suffers the destruction of his bold self-image. He wants to justify his fear, warn Sandra of the possible danger, but shame has stolen his voice.

'Keep Ricky back,' says Sandra, as if the boy were little more than an afterthought. 'I'm going to see what that thing is. I'll be careful, I promise.'

Ricky sits, cross-legged, in the sand a little way behind them. He has seen the capsule too, and his eyes are wide and bright with wonder.

Sandra hesitates for a moment. 'If anything happens,' she says, 'don't come after me. Get someone from the hall. Tell them what's happened.'

She grits her teeth and steps forward at last. She walks slowly, arms wrapped around herself as if the wind were harsher than it is. Alec thinks to turn around, to check where Ricky is, but he can't take his eyes off her. His lungs inform him that he isn't breathing. He exhales slowly, and aches with the effort. He needs a cigarette, but he can't move to reach for the packet.

Sandra approaches the capsule. She skirts around it gingerly. She draws closer. She peers into the jagged hole.

And a new fear hits Alec. Fear for her safety. The fear takes control.

He doesn't remember telling his feet to move. His legs feel numb, but he is running towards her all the same. He has to be with Sandra, to protect her, despite the danger to himself. There is no excitement attached to such a proposition now. Just dread. But he has no choice.

She turns to him and her face is ashen, but, thank God, she isn't panicked. She is unhurt.

'There's something in there,' she whispers. 'I think it's alive.'

The fire takes hold.

Chapter One
City on the Edge of Wherever

'Now that –' Fitz Kreiner whistled '– is what the future *should* look like.'

The city, he reckoned, was about a mile long and three miles away, although it was difficult to judge scale across the expanse of parched land. Its surfaces were uniformly silver and metallic, and its boxlike buildings and towering, apparently freestanding spires looked as if they were huddling together for protection. The buildings rose to varying heights, often great. There was no pattern to them, except that the tallest building was situated at the very centre of the city. A radio mast increased its apparent height so that it dominated, and provided an illusory symmetry to, the skyline.

Narrowing his eyes, Fitz made out a series of elevated roadways, which described great loops across the city at all levels. From this distance, it looked as if silver ribbons had been cast over the buildings, to freeze in the act of uncoiling.

'How many fingers am I holding up?'

Fitz turned, with a frown that became a pitying smile as he saw what his travelling companion was doing. 'No?' said the Doctor. 'Then how about... Look! Look over there.' One arm flailed outward as if unco-ordinated, to point vaguely into the distance. The Doctor's expression of hope was almost childlike, as was the speed with which it sagged as the arm flopped back to his side, forgotten. A second later he was hopeful again, as he rummaged inside his bottle-green velvet jacket and muttered to himself. He produced a gold fob watch, held it in front of Compassion's eyes by the few remaining links of its chain, hesitated and returned it to its pocket. 'No, perhaps not.'

He cut an incongruous figure in his old-fashioned clothes,

1

wing collars protruding haphazardly from beneath a lazily tied cravat, his hair long and windblown despite the absence of wind. They probably all did, thought Fitz: three strangers alone in a strange place. He rarely appreciated that any more, rarely thought about how far he was from home. Doing so produced a thrill in his stomach that was one part fear and three parts excitement.

And one part something else. Something was wrong.

The Doctor had been pacing around in tiny circles, head cocked, eyes half closed. His lips moved, but no sound emerged. Suddenly he stopped, turned back to Compassion, leaned over her and bellowed, 'Daleks! Cybermen! We're under attack! Snap out of it, woman!' He emphasised each beat with a downward stroke of both hands.

Fitz started at the sudden outburst. Compassion moved only her eyes, and they moved slowly and showed no interest when they finally did alight upon their target. The Doctor straightened and withdrew, thoroughly disappointed.

'Doctor.' Fitz's problem was becoming more pressing. 'I can't breathe.'

'Really?' The Doctor bounded up to him, all enthusiasm again. Fitz couldn't help but feel that he was more curious than concerned. He clapped his hands on to Fitz's shoulders, lowered his head and moved it in so close that Fitz recoiled from the invasion of his personal space. The Doctor gazed up at Fitz's nose and mouth with a raised eyebrow. 'Everything looks to be in working order to me. Oxygen going in where it should, carbon dioxide coming out, yes, yes, that is the right way around for human beings, isn't it? Yes, of course it is.'

'I mean, I'm finding it difficult to breathe. It's an effort.'

The Doctor let him go, seeming to lose interest. 'Ah yes, well, I have told you about the effects of smoking upon the lungs, of course.' A thought visibly occurred to him. He licked a finger, then held it up and looked at it. 'And the air is a little less rich in oxygen here than you're used to. Don't worry, it's perfectly safe. I'm sure you'll get used to it.'

'That's easy for you to say.'

'Try not to think about it, that should help.' Spotting a particularly dull purple weed at his feet, the Doctor dropped to his haunches and examined it, his face suggesting that it was the most beautiful and interesting flower in the universe. 'I'm worried about her,' he said, as he produced an eyeglass, screwed it into place and poked at the hard earth around the weed.

'Huh?' said Fitz, still more concerned with the fact that his chest hurt.

'Compassion. She was so emotional, so full of life, when she first changed. So unlike her. I thought it would be all right. But since then, she's become... distant. Aloof. And now, to just withdraw like this, so completely, so suddenly...'

'She was never all that chatty though, was she?'

'It's more than that. She won't respond at all – even out here. I can feel her in my mind. She's still in there somehow, but she won't talk to me.'

The Doctor's mood had changed again. He seemed to have forgotten about the plant. He was staring into nowhere, and the burden of years had settled upon him. The glass fell from his eye, landing neatly in his hand as if it had planned its own course. 'I have to wonder where it will all end,' he said. 'Should I be doing something?'

'She isn't complaining, is she?'

'Perhaps she can't. Perhaps by the time she knew, really knew, what was happening, it was too late. If only I could get through to her, find out if she's happy...'

'Was she ever?'

Fitz had never known how to relate to Compassion. Feeling uneasy with her, he had responded by trying to prick her cold surface, to reach the person beneath. He hadn't found anything. And then the change had begun.

He didn't really understand what had happened to her, how the hard-wired technology of the Remote and the telepathic

3

influence of the Doctor's ship had combined to rebuild her from the inside out. If she really had become little more than a machine now, a substitute TARDIS in which he and the Doctor travelled, then that would almost suit him. It would help him, he hoped, to adjust to what she had become; to forget what she had once been. Except that, now he had stepped out of the pocket dimension that existed somehow, impossibly, inside her, he saw Compassion as she used to be. Red hair, freckles, heavy bone structure, apparently a normal human girl in her mid-twenties. She even wore normal casual clothes, although Fitz shivered at the realisation that she had used her chameleon circuit to change them. He had no idea what they were made of now. The clothes or the woman herself.

Compassion turned her eyes towards Fitz, and he gave her an embarrassed half-smile of acknowledgement, feeling guilty about his discomfort, unsure if she would notice or care.

'So much going on,' the Doctor muttered, 'but it's all beneath the surface. Buried.' Then, with another alarming change of demeanour, he sprang excitedly to his feet. 'An interconnected root system,' he announced as if he had just made the greatest discovery in the world. 'Yes, yes, these plants extend much further below the ground than it appears. They seek each other out under the soil. They nurture each other; they're almost a self-sustaining system.' He put his hand to his mouth for a second, then lit up with another joyous realisation. 'They don't draw anything from the atmosphere.'

'Is that relevant?'

'Details, Fitz,' boomed the Doctor, a zealous gleam in his eyes. 'Small, beautiful details.' He spread his arms theatrically. 'Open your eyes to the wonders around you.'

'Well, pardon me for not caring about some weed, but I was looking at that bloody great –'

'City!' The Doctor had whirled around, to follow Fitz's line of sight. He reacted as if seeing the city for the first time. His expressive eyebrows knitted into a frown. 'Yes, well, that is interesting, isn't it? "The future", you said? Hmm.'

'Well,' said Fitz lamely, 'as I always used to imagine it.'

The Doctor started forward, then glanced back at Compassion. He scurried over to her, and placed his hands on her shoulders as he had on Fitz's a moment earlier. He stared intently into her eyes and spoke slowly and clearly. 'Can you hear me, Compassion? Fitz and I would like to explore the city. The city!' he repeated with emphasis, waggling a hand in the appropriate direction. 'Will you come with us? Can you still walk?'

He pouted, then took a few steps away and turned back hopefully. Compassion didn't follow. She didn't move at all. Her eyes rotated slowly in their sockets as she scanned her surroundings with total detachment. She ignored him completely.

'You won't get through to her,' said Fitz. 'She's in a world of her own.'

'We can't just leave her.'

'Why not? She's got defences, hasn't she? She's a walking TARDIS now.'

'If she was walking,' the Doctor rumbled, 'there wouldn't be a problem.'

He was torn for a moment. His face betrayed hunger at the enticing mystery of the still-distant city, but guilt as he regarded his erstwhile companion. Fitz could tell how difficult it was for him to think of Compassion as no more than a vessel, something to be left behind until it was needed again. But he guessed that hunger would eventually win out, and he felt a tingle of satisfaction when the Doctor proved him right.

'It couldn't hurt, could it?' It was almost a plea. 'To leave her alone, just for an hour or two. After all, if we left now we'd spend the rest of our lives wondering where on earth we were.'

'Her senses extrude into other dimensions now,' said the Doctor, his hands working furiously as they tried in vain to illustrate the concept. 'She might be aware of you and me and this whole planet, but it's only a small part of what she's experiencing.'

He had returned to the subject of Compassion several times during the trek, interspersing his hypotheses with observations about anything that caught his eye, from a pool of stagnant water to the black, stunted, skeletal trees that dotted the bleak plain. Resisting all attempts to engage his interest, Fitz had passed the time by studiously not thinking about breathing. His lungs felt like overworked bellows on the verge of collapse. But, when he had complained of dizziness, the Doctor had peeled back his eyelids, stared into his soul and assured him that the symptom was imaginary. His nerves demanded a cigarette, but his lungs vetoed the idea.

Every so often, the Doctor's whirlpool mind threw out the name of a planet that might conform to the conditions they had observed here. There was always one thing that didn't fit, though. It was usually the city.

Spotting something in the distance, the Doctor changed course and speeded up eagerly. He didn't consult Fitz at all. By the time they reached the object, it had been revealed as a vehicle. Its tubular framework reminded Fitz of a motorbike, but chunky, rounded panels had been welded on to it, more than doubling its width. Its saddle was long enough to seat three, one behind the other, and so sunken that it was almost a cockpit. The vehicle was constructed from a thin and lightweight but sturdy metal, silver in colour but streaked with red paint and brown dirt. The foremost panel of its bodywork curved upwards and backwards, reminding Fitz of nothing more than a shield. Somebody had painted a red skull-and-crossbones motif on to it, but their artistic skill had been wanting.

'I suppose we're meant to be intimidated,' he remarked, regarding the lopsided design, 'but all it says to me is "Watch out – this bike's in the hands of a two year-old."'

The Doctor swung a long leg over the side of the vehicle, rested his foot on the seat and leaned over the dashboard. A pair of handlebars jutted out of it, but otherwise it seemed to Fitz that everything was controlled by three rows of identical, unlabelled buttons.

The Doctor pressed a button – just one, as if he knew exactly what he was doing despite the lack of clues – then frowned and tried again. 'No power,' he reported. Without looking down, he added, 'And have you noticed that there's blood on the seat? Human. Dried. About two weeks old, I'd say.'

'Human. I thought so,' said Fitz, as casually as possible. 'We *are* in the future then.'

The Doctor looked puzzled, as if he'd been caught unawares in the middle of an entirely different train of thought. Or several trains, more likely. 'Whose future?'

'Whose do you think? Mine!'

'Ah. I picked you up in 1963, didn't I? In that case, Fitz, you're right: the technology to create this vehicle certainly didn't exist then. Not on Earth, at least.'

'What I mean,' said Fitz, as the Doctor hopped off the vehicle, 'is that it's from Earth's future, isn't it? Specifically, Earth's future. It was made by humans.'

'Oh no, no, no, we aren't on Earth. The conditions are all wrong. Look at the horizon, for example. Far too close. The curvature of this planet must be quite steep. Give me a hand with this, will you? I want to turn it on to its side.'

Fitz tried again, feeling less clever by the second, as he reluctantly slipped his hands beneath the vehicle and helped the Doctor to heft it up and over. 'I know we're not on Earth – I'm just saying this thing was made there. It's what motorbikes will turn into, isn't it?'

'Look at this.' The Doctor waved a hand vaguely across the vehicle's newly exposed underside. It had three small wheels, laid out in a triangular pattern with two at the back of the chassis. They had spokes and tyres, which surprised Fitz as it seemed almost too normal. The tyres were thick, but their tread had almost worn away and they were beginning to shred.

The Doctor was more interested in the silver disc that sat

between the tyres. 'An antigravity generator,' he explained. He fingered a wire that, had the vehicle been upright and moving, would have trailed along the ground. 'Yes, I see how this should work,' he announced, with breathless fascination. 'It runs on wheels in its own environment – the city, I expect – and absorbs energy of some kind – static, perhaps? – through the ground. With enough of a charge, it can power the antigravity disc and fly – for a time, at least. Or it can leave the city, as this one did.'

'It didn't get far, though.'

'No, it didn't, did it? An old Earth motorcycle, you say? Hmm. Perhaps, perhaps. You'd be surprised how many coincidences of design concept there are throughout the universe, though. So, somebody came out here, perhaps from the city –' The Doctor used one hand to trace out an imaginary path. 'But ran out of power before he or she could get back.'

'Then met something,' Fitz realised with a prickle of fear, 'which left blood on the seat.'

'Indeed.'

'Something dangerous,' Fitz prompted, concerned that the Doctor wasn't treating this potential threat seriously.

'That's certainly one of the possibilities.' The Doctor cast around as if searching for clues. Then his habitual, slightly one-sided grin spread across his face and, with positive glee, he announced, 'Perhaps these gentlemen can tell us more about it.'

Fitz turned, alarmed, to see that six animals were approaching. They were some distance away yet, but he could see that they were quadrupeds, with dusky brown hides and long, mournful faces. They looked not dissimilar to camels, albeit without the humps. A human – or at least, humanoid – figure sat astride each one.

'Yes, I think they probably can,' said Fitz through clenched teeth. 'In fact, if we're really lucky, they might even show us what happened.'

'Oh, do you think so?' said the Doctor, with infuriating happiness.

* * *

At Fitz's urging, they had moved on. Still the Doctor strolled casually, his hands clasped behind his back. His gaze roved his surroundings and only occasionally rested on the animals and their riders. They had changed course slightly, to intercept the strangers.

As they drew closer, Fitz made out more details. The humanoid figures wore hooded cloaks, of the same colour and presumably the same material as their mounts. As a consequence, he couldn't see their faces. But he could see the rough-hewn, stone-bladed axes that they all had strung to the sides of their animals. Not for the first time, anxiety speeded his pace. But the Doctor seemed unconcerned, and Fitz only ended up having to wait for him.

'They're going to kill us,' he said. 'You do realise that, don't you?'

'I try not to prejudge people,' said the Doctor.

'That's because you don't have my experience of being picked on by gangs. You learn to sense when they're looking for trouble.'

'And, by reacting to that sense, you risk creating a self-fulfilling prophecy. You know, we'd all get along much better if we'd just take other beings as we find them.'

'Well, I find that lot coming towards us with big axes.'

'That doesn't mean they aren't capable of civilised discourse.'

Fitz looked longingly at the city, still a few hundred yards away. Even that held no guarantee of protection, but he might have felt safer if it was closer. He had expected to be able to make out more detail by now, but its surfaces still appeared as smooth and blank as first impressions had suggested.

He looked back at the riders, hoping to see that somehow, miraculously, they weren't as close as he'd thought; that he and the Doctor had a chance of reaching shelter before they were cut off.

The leading figure pulled his axe free from its restraints and wielded it menacingly by its stout, black, wooden handle. Two other riders copied his actions, and Fitz felt blood draining from his face. He pulled at his companion's sleeve urgently. '*Now* can we run?'

The Doctor thought for a moment, then nodded vigorously. 'I apologise, Fitz. I think your plan may have been the best one after all.'

The leader of the riders let out a deep, rattling war cry.

The Doctor and Fitz ran.

They didn't get far. As soon as they began to flee, the riders spurred their mounts to greater efforts. Fitz tried not to look at them as they galloped closer with frightening speed. He concentrated on the city, but the distance between him and it seemed to expand with every step he took. Not for a second did he imagine he was going to make it.

The riders were upon them and, for frantic seconds, things happened too fast for Fitz's brain to register them all, let alone react. He twisted and ducked at random, but found his path blocked by animal hide wherever he turned. An axe swooped by his head and he threw up his arms reflexively. Something hit his left shoulder. He grunted with pain, expected it to get worse, then registered the fact that the blow had been a glancing one, struck with the flat of a blade. He was on his knees anyway, although he didn't remember falling. He caught a few flash-frame images of the Doctor whirling beneath a concentrated onslaught, coat-tails flapping, hair streaming wildly. Then the Doctor fell heavily beside him and sprawled in the dust, even as Fitz scrambled back to his feet and realised that, by luck alone, he was staring at an opening. He kept his head down as instinct propelled him through it. He was past the savages and running before his judgement kicked in and told him there was nothing he could do for the Doctor anyway. Nothing but find help.

He was running towards the city. Which was another lucky break.

He willed his muscles to pump more furiously and his feet to fall more swiftly, almost too swiftly, his gangly body always one misstep away from falling. At first he could hear hoof beats behind him, but blood and panting filled his ears until he didn't know if the sound was there or not. He didn't dare take his eyes off the ground, couldn't risk slowing even enough to glance back. The savages may have ceased their pursuit – or they may be at his shoulder, axes raised, about to chop him down.

He crossed the perfectly straight threshold of the city like a sprinter breaking the finishing tape. His footsteps clanged on metal, although in truth this surface felt no harder than the earth over which it was laid. Too late, the realisation hit him that his race wasn't won yet. There was nobody around, nobody to help him. Despair gaped in his stomach. Pains shot through him. His body had pledged itself to support him this far, but now it demanded its promised respite. He had to slow down, for fear of his legs either buckling or carrying him into a wall.

He turned at last, and was relieved to find no mad axemen behind him. He stumbled to a halt, looked again, and saw three of them. They were lined up on their animals, a few hundred yards back, glaring in his direction. Fear spurred spongy muscles into a final effort, as Fitz staggered around the corner of one building and then another, hoping his pursuers would forget him once he was out of their sight.

He collapsed against a metal wall. Despite the sunlight, it felt cool against his back. He closed his eyes and let the wall support him as he concentrated on steadying his breathing and swallowing the rising tide of acidic bile that stung his throat.

All the thoughts that had been lost to the overriding imperative to save himself crashed back into his mind. The savages couldn't see him, but he couldn't see them either. Would Compassion be safe, alone on the plain? What if they were sneaking up on him? But they had seemed shy of the city. The Doctor had been right. He didn't notice the rarefied atmosphere any more, even as he gulped down great lungfuls of it. What if they had good reason to fear the city? He needed to find help. All the time he'd spent with the Doctor, he ought to be more used to running. What if nobody lived here? Only three of the savages had chased him. Was this some kind of trap? What might the other three be doing to the Doctor?

He levered himself away from the wall. His legs protested at having to bear his weight again so soon, but he stumbled forward anyway, deeper into the city, calling for help. The buildings threw his voice back at him and gave it an eerie, ringing quality.

The city wasn't as perfect as he had first thought. Once upon a time, though, it had been. Even now, the flat walls with no seams, no rivets and no sharp edges made Fitz feel as if he'd been shrunk down and set loose in a maze hammered out of a single sheet of stainless steel. He couldn't actually identify the smooth, silver metal from which every building was constructed. It absorbed the sunlight and cast no reflections. Many of the smaller buildings had no windows at all; the larger ones were studded with them, but they were all black and he couldn't see through them. A hint of ozone mingled with the musty smell of neglect, despite which the city showed signs of habitation. Scratches on the walls, scuff marks on the ground. Dust had settled on the road, only to be kicked up again.

Two narrow grooves ran the length of the pavement on which Fitz now walked, effectively splitting it into three sections. As he paused to get his bearings, he heard the clunking of disused gears beneath him, and suddenly the pavement's mid-section lurched into motion. It carried him for a couple of yards or so, before he decided that this was too freaky. He hopped off the conveyor belt backwards, and jumped at a whooshing noise behind him. He whirled around, to find that he had stepped into the entranceway of a building and that its door had opened for him. When nothing came through it, Fitz stepped back and the door closed; he stepped forward and it opened again. Cautiously, he put his head through the doorway. The inside of the building was surprisingly well lit, considering its black windows and the lack of a visible light source. But it was an empty metal shell; he could see through to its back wall and right up to its roof. The dust on its floor lay undisturbed.

Fitz walked in the road after that, following it until it bifurcated. One fork curved upwards, so he followed the other one, nervous about leaving ground level just yet. Above him, the road looped back on itself to provide higher-level access to a row of buildings.

He approached one of the narrow spires, intrigued and worried to note that a hole had been gouged out of its side at about eye level. A tangle of silver wires was exposed. As Fitz drew closer, it spat electrical sparks at him and he withdrew quickly.

A nearby wall provided more evidence of vandalism. Huge, crooked letters spelled out the legend ROCK N ROLL RULES in black spray paint. Overlapping the bottom of that in a smaller, neater, red was the claim SANDRA IS A TRAITOR. A less careful hand had added, AND A SLAG. This last painter had misjudged the size of his canvas, and the final few letters were squashed together at the wall's edge. The paint looked as if it might have been recently applied. Fitz thought about running his fingers over it, to see if it was still wet.

Then a faint whine attracted his attention. He looked up to see something – a vehicle of some kind, he couldn't see what – zipping along one of the elevated roadways. It was some distance ahead of him, and a good way above his head. Even so, it reminded him of his reason for being here. His strange, gloomy surroundings had somehow dulled the urgency of the situation. But the Doctor was still in peril.

'Help!' he cried. 'Help!' He ran forward, waving his arms to attract the driver's attention. He knew, though, that it was hopeless. The vehicle passed from his sight and Fitz stopped, dismayed and desperately aware that time was passing.

'How may I assist you, sir?'

His heart leapt. He spun around, wondering how somebody

could have sneaked up on him. The answer was, nobody had.

Almost without noticing, he had crossed an open square. At its centre, just behind him now, stood a fountain bordered by four benches. It was fashioned from silver metal, of course, and designed to be functional rather than ornate. However, it wasn't working.

Approaching him from across the square was a robot. It was a clunky, unwieldy thing: bottle green in colour, about six feet tall and roughly humanoid except that its surfaces were too flat, its lines too angular. Its base section was moulded to give the impression that it had two legs, but they were forever joined. There were tiny wheels beneath the robot's 'feet', and it rolled along on these. Its chest was too bulky for the rest of its torso; a small, blank screen was set into it, with columns of what looked like small tuning knobs to each side. The robot's arms were broad and inflexible. It held them away from its body, but they turned inward at the elbow and extended out in front of it. The clawlike pincers at the end of each arm came a couple of inches shy of meeting. The robot had no neck. Its head was a perfect cube, with only two features: a square speaker grille where the mouth ought to have been, and a transparent strip that ran the width of its 'face' at what should have been eye level. A dim, yellow light shone behind this strip. A slender but perfectly straight wire extended from the top of the robot's head, to a length of about a foot. Strange though the idea seemed, Fitz could only guess that it was an aerial.

While he had been staring at the robot, it had almost reached him. Gliding to a halt in front of him, it said, 'You indicated that you require help. How may I assist you, sir?' With each word, a bead of brighter yellow light raced from left to right across its eye-strip. The robot had a cultured voice and studied enunciation. It reminded Fitz of English butlers in old films.

'My friend,' said Fitz, feeling awkward about explaining himself to a lump of metal. 'He's under attack. People with axes, out on the plain. You've got to help him.'

'I do apologise, sir, but I am unable to leave the city. Nor do I have offensive capabilities.' There was no regret in the robot's tone, no emotion or inflection at all. Each time it said 'sir', it was with the same careful pronunciation and identical emphasis, as if it could access and play back only a single recording of each word in its vocabulary.

'You must be able to do something!'

'I suggest you enlist the aid of the city's human inhabitants.'

The word 'human' fired up hope in Fitz's heart. 'There are humans here? Great! Where do I find them?'

'It is only midday, sir. Most of the inhabitants choose not to rise until early afternoon.'

'They're still in bed? But the buildings around here look empty.'

'Indeed, sir, this sector is uninhabited at present.'

Fitz realised that the robot wasn't going to offer assistance; it would respond only to a direct request. 'Take me to them.'

'To whom would you like to be taken, sir?'

'I don't know. Pick somebody. Anybody. The closest human being.'

'Very well, sir. However, I must warn you that the resources of the city are spread thinly. If I am to abandon the task of removing paint from the walls in this sector, then it will be –' the robot paused, and Fitz heard a distinct whirring sound inside its casing – 'two point four days before I am able to return to it.'

'Yes, yes,' said Fitz, exasperatedly. 'That's fine. I don't care. Just find someone for me.'

'Very well, sir. Follow me if you would.'

The robot rolled past Fitz and out of the square. In order to follow it, he had to reduce himself to a slow walk, which soon defeated his patience. 'Can't you go any faster?'

'Alas, sir, I cannot.'

'Then give me directions and I'll go on ahead.'

'That will not be necessary, sir.'

'Why not?' asked Fitz, suspiciously.

'I perceive the rapid approach of eight inhabitants.'

'What?'

'I perceive the rapid —'

'Yes, yes, I heard you.' He waved the robot into silence. Concentrating, he made out the approaching whine of engines. 'I can hear them too. They're coming here?'

'I think we may assume so, sir, given that I reported your presence and location to several inhabitants as per my standing instructions.'

Fitz went cold. Much as he had wanted to find someone, he didn't care for the idea that someone had found him instead. Suddenly, he was sure that uninvited visitors weren't welcome in the city. He was being illogical, he told himself, reading meanings into the robot's dispassionate pronouncement that couldn't have been there. But what if the savages had come from the city in the first place? 'Are they friendly?' he blurted out.

'I do not understand your question, sir,' said the robot.

Then the whine turned into a throaty roar, and they appeared: eight of them, as the robot had discerned, on eight futuristic motorcycles similar to the one that Fitz and the Doctor had examined. The bikes were battered and dirty, their riders equally so. They were all male, Fitz noted: grimy, unshaven and all in their mid-thirties, a little older than he was. Some wore normal T-shirts and jeans, but they were tattered and filthy. Like the savages, they had also stitched together clothes from animal skins. Not cloaks, though. Their garments were tied to them with cords or chains, the overall effect being of a primitive type of armour. They seemed somehow out of place in the city, providing the first real colour that Fitz had seen here.

They roared down the narrow street in formation, until the first four bikes peeled off and passed Fitz, two to each side. He didn't have time to recover his wits and think about fleeing. He heard the squeal of tyres being forced around behind him, even as the back four bikes stopped in front. He wanted to say something, but the words caught in his throat.

Surrounding him now, the eight men dismounted. Some drew weapons. Knives. Or, rather, twisted scraps of metal – but they were wielded in such a way as to leave no doubt as to their function. Fitz found himself shrinking against the side of his robot guide, for all the good it would do him. 'What I mean is,' he muttered hoarsely, 'are they going to kill me?'

'I could not possibly comment, sir,' said the robot, as callused hands seized Fitz's arms, wrenched them behind his back and placed a sharp blade at his throat.

Chapter Two
A Visit from Outer Space

Alec inspected his reflection in the patch of wall that Sandra had diligently polished. He ran his hand through thick, black hair that had started to tangle with dirt, making his scalp itch. He pushed it back from his forehead and wondered how much further it was going to recede. The bristles on his chin had started to form a scraggly beard. He had been pacing the complex into the early hours again, and his eyes were red-rimmed. He hated being woken up. The jarring shock left his brain feeling fuzzy and his eyes aching on the inside.

'Are you going to admire yourself all afternoon?' mumbled Sandra from somewhere beneath a pile of dyed fur blankets. 'They'll be back soon, you know.'

'I know,' sighed Alec. He plucked his leather jacket from its hook and forced his arms into it. The jacket was battered and faded, and its stitching was coming loose. It was tight around his shoulders and he couldn't fasten it. He wore it only on special occasions, when he wanted to display his roots. 'It'll be another false alarm, though. Or a mod trick.'

'Or it might be exactly what we're waiting for.'

'Even if he is from the future, I bet he can't blast off again. They never can.'

'Just go and find out, will you?'

Alec sighed again, but the sigh turned into a yawn. He rubbed his eyes, teasing dribbles of water from them. He had to get his head together, but it seemed too much of an effort.

Everything seemed too much of an effort these days.

'I might stand down,' he said, to see how Sandra reacted.

'It's up to you,' she said, as if she didn't care.

'I'm sick of being the responsible one. I'm getting too old.'

'You're only thirty-eight.'

'There's not many here that are older. Anyway, it's how I feel.'

'Just go and see what's happening.'

'Aren't you coming?'

'I'll follow you up in a minute.'

Alec looked at the pile of blankets for a while, but it didn't move. He breathed in deeply to stifle another yawn, then let the door swish open for him and stepped through it.

His personal servo-robot swung around to face him. 'Good afternoon, sir. May I be of assistance?'

'Send a message up to the bar. I want a shake ready. Heavy on caffeine.'

'Very good, sir.'

Alec strode along the corridor, the robot trundling beside him. 'Any progress on the stranger?'

'As I predicted, sir, your men reached him first. Would you like me to show you?'

'Just tell me what they're doing.'

'They are escorting him across the city, sir. I believe they are heading towards the bar, but they are taking a circuitous route presumably to avoid other occupants.'

'ETA?'

'They should arrive in approximately six point two minutes, sir.'

'Good,' said Alec with a brisk nod. Another door opened for him at the end of the corridor, and he marched through it. The servo-robot stayed behind, as it had been programmed to do.

As he approached the bottom of the gravity pit, he felt a tingle of anticipation. He quelled it with a thought. It was the only way to avoid disappointment. But he couldn't help thinking about the stranger. He had seen him only briefly: a blurred image relayed in monochrome from one maintenance robot to the tiny chest-mounted screen of another. He had looked surprisingly normal: a few years younger than Alec, tall and thin, untidy brown hair, narrow face, pointed nose. He had been dressed in blue denim jeans and jacket, but the material had looked new and clean.

Surprisingly normal. And yet his was the first new face that Alec had seen in many years.

Upon realising that the bikers weren't about to kill him, Fitz had found his tongue. It hadn't done him much good. Despite his protests, he had been ordered on to the back of one of their vehicles. Now he clung desperately to the huge, sweaty man in front of him as the bike jetted along an elevated roadway at a speed that whipped its rider's greasy hair back into Fitz's face and made him fear to look down.

Three more bikes rode in front of him, four behind. Even if Fitz had been brave enough to attack his rider, perhaps unseat him and seize control of the vehicle, he would still have been surrounded, unable to escape. As it was, the point was academic.

The formation rocketed towards a sharp bend. Fitz watched in horror as the three leading bikers missed the turn and shot over the edge. He tightened his grip on the huge, sweaty man, anticipating his use of the brakes. But the bike didn't slow. The road slipped out from beneath Fitz and he yelled as his heart and stomach leapt in opposite directions.

With a heavy clunk, the bike abruptly ceased its forward motion. That in itself should have been enough to fling its occupants over the handlebars, but somehow the expected push never came. The bike plummeted downwards, then slowed as if it had been caught on a blanket of hot air. By the time Fitz remembered the antigravity disc on its underside, the vehicle had landed on its still-spinning wheels on a ground-level road and was roaring forwards.

He was still hyperventilating when it rolled to a halt and he was surrounded by men with home-made knives again. He flashed them a wan smile. 'Yeah, all right, I'm coming. You'll have to give me a minute to unlock my muscles and remember how to stand up.'

The huge, sweaty man tore himself free from Fitz's grip. He turned around in the saddle and gave his passenger a hefty shove. Fitz toppled over the motorbike's side panel and landed hands down on the hard, metal road.

Fitz didn't get much of an impression of the street outside the building. He was too busy blowing on his skinned palms ruefully as he was manhandled to his feet and past at least four guards. By the time he had been bundled through the sliding entrance door, though, he was taking an interest in his surroundings again.

The door was set into the left-hand end of the longer wall of a rectangular room. Paint had been plastered over the walls, in random splashes of colour. At least two of the futuristic motorbikes had been disassembled, their parts strewn untidily across the floor. Dozens of tyres had been thrown hither and thither like scatter cushions. There were a few thin-framed metal chairs, mostly twisted out of shape and upended.

Six or seven people – men and women both, all dressed in the same manner as Fitz's captors – sat or lay on fur rugs or tyres. The intensity with which they stared at him belied their studiedly casual poses. As Fitz was prodded along the length of the room, more eyes glared out from a series of six booths to his right. Each booth contained a small table, without legs but fixed at the far end to the exterior wall. The partitions that separated the booths were moulded into two-seater benches, one on each side, allowing four people to sit around each table. There were no windows and no lights, but, as with the building he had looked into before, Fitz could see perfectly well.

He realised now what the room reminded him of: a milk bar from his own time. The counter stretched for most of the length of the room to his left. Behind it, a row of unlabelled metal boxes was attached to the wall. A robot, identical to the one he had encountered outside, stood immobile, waiting to serve.

He saw only one other door. It was ahead of him and to the

left, in the opposite corner to the one through which he had entered. A jukebox stood against the far wall, a bright yellow liquid bubbling through the arch-shaped glass tube that trimmed its edge. The colour bled out on to the walls and floor. As Fitz watched, it shifted lazily across the spectrum, slowly settling into an almost sickly green.

A man stood in front of the jukebox, arms folded, regarding Fitz coolly. Green light played with one side of his face and cast the other into shadow. The man was heavyset and unshaven, and wearing an ancient leather jacket that was several sizes too small for him.

A final shove from Fitz's captors sent him stumbling forward and almost falling over the debris. They had delivered him, he guessed, into the presence of their leader.

'I don't know you,' said the man slowly.

'Looks like we're even, then,' said Fitz.

'I'm Alec. I'm in charge here.'

'Fitz Kreiner.' Fitz extended a hand, but the man called Alec didn't take it.

'We haven't seen you in the city before, Fitz. Where have you come from?'

'Another city. Far away.'

'There are no other cities. Only this one survived the war.'

Fitz was aware of movement, behind and around him. Alec's people were closing in. Those who had been seated stood up, a threatening air about them.

'That's what we thought too,' he said, trying to keep his voice even. 'Then our instruments detected you. I've come a long way to find you. In fact, I could do with a drink.'

Alec turned away, giving no reaction to the lie. Fitz wondered if he could get past him and through the back door while he wasn't looking. Could he outrun the mob behind him? Would the door lead outside or only further into the building?

Alec punched a button on the jukebox, and Fitz heard the sound of a vinyl record being dropped into place behind the glass. Then Alec picked up a black, wooden stick that had been leaning against the side of the machine.

Fitz tensed as his interrogator took three measured steps towards him. The jukebox struck up a discordant electronic hum, to which it added a deep, reverberating drumbeat that never quite settled into what Fitz, with all his musical experience, would call a rhythm. The liquid in the tube turned a deep, bloody red, which he hoped was an unfortunate coincidence.

He was about to run, despite having missed the most opportune moment to do so, when Alec casually tossed the stick to someone behind him. Fitz barely had time to look over his shoulder before the weapon cracked against the backs of his legs. His knees buckled involuntarily; he swallowed an oath as they hit the floor. Someone grabbed his straggly hair and yanked his head back.

'Don't lie to me,' warned Alec through clenched teeth. 'We've explored as far as the air will let us. There are no other cities on Earth.'

'OK, I'll tell you the truth,' croaked Fitz, his eyes beginning to water. His mind worked furiously; the mention of Earth had not been lost on him. 'Jesus! It's just difficult to explain, you know? I didn't think you'd believe me.'

'We know about flying saucers.'

'You do?'

'Of course we do. What do you think we are, primitives?'

At a curt nod from Alec, Fitz was released. He stayed on his knees and blew out a faint sigh, pretending to be relieved. 'That's just the point,' he said, 'we don't know anything about you. We thought Earth was deserted. We didn't think anyone had lived here since the war.'

'So, why did you come here?'

'There was an accident.'

'You crashed your saucer?'

'Quite badly, actually. It went up in flames. I'm surprised you didn't see the smoke.'

Alec nodded thoughtfully. 'You're not the first to crash here. We think the bombs changed something about the atmosphere or gravity of the planet.' He spoke the words as if he had no idea what they meant; as if he had just read them in a book once.

Fitz felt a smile pulling at his lips, but he didn't show it. This time, it was working. He was reeling them in. He let his imagination roam. 'You could be right. All I know is, we were taking supplies to the colony on Mercury. On the way back out, I tried to trim our flight time with a slingshot around Earth. I thought I'd misjudged it, but maybe it was something more than that. Anyway, we hit the atmosphere and I lost control.'

'How many in your crew?'

'The others didn't make it,' said Fitz automatically. Alec narrowed his eyes suspiciously; the treacherous robot had probably reported the details of its conversation with the newcomer. Anyway, the Doctor still needed help, and Alec's people were all Fitz had. 'But we had a passenger on board,' he added quickly. 'A doctor. He's still alive – at least, I think so. We were attacked outside the city.'

Alec nodded sagely. 'Not many crash survivors get past the cannibals.'

'Cannibals? God, I didn't know it was that bad! Can you do anything for him?'

'He'll be dead by now.'

'He might not be. He's very resourceful. But he might still need help.'

'A doctor, you say?'

'That's right. Well, more of a scientist really. He just calls himself…'

Fitz's voice tailed off as an almost tangible current of anticipation rippled around the room. Alec reached behind the jukebox and yanked its plug out of the wall, stilling its unearthly wail and extinguishing its light. A few seconds later, he broke the silence by asking, in a throaty voice, 'Where did you last see him?'

'Ah. I lost my bearings a bit on the way here. I think –'

'We know where you entered the city.'

'Right. Well, it was near there. We'd almost reached the city when the cannibals –' Fitz grimaced as he spoke the word. 'The cannibals attacked us.'

'Take Leopard Group out and search for him,' said Alec, to someone behind Fitz.

The eight men who had brought him to the milk bar filed back out in silence. Once they had gone, the remainder of its occupants returned to their own business. The low buzzing sound of conversation helped Fitz to feel a little less intimidated. He risked climbing to his feet. 'You're looking for a scientist, then?' he said to Alec, with strained congeniality, hoping he hadn't just landed the Doctor in deeper trouble.

'A good Technician could save our lives,' said Alec solemnly.

'Oh. Well, I'm sure the Doctor will do what he can for you. He's like that.'

'Chances are he's dead. We'll probably have to make do with you.' Fitz didn't act fast enough to conceal his expression of worried surprise. 'You piloted your own saucer,' said Alec, raising an eyebrow. 'You must have some technical know-how.'

'Yeah,' bluffed Fitz, 'a bit, I suppose. We had someone else to do the repairs, though.'

'You wanted a drink?'

Alec leaned against the bar. The future man joined him, his smile not quite disguising his nervousness. Alec scrutinised him closely. Despite his affected air of nonchalance, there was something about Fitz Kreiner: a quiet intensity, which suggested that there was more to his story than he had revealed. Still, he may prove useful, especially if his friend was a Technician. Alec had to play this carefully.

'Thanks,' said Fitz. 'What have you got? I need something strong.'

'The usual,' said Alec, studying Fitz for a reaction.

'And what is usual for Earth these days?' asked Fitz, perhaps too carefully.

Alec ordered two plain shakes from the serving robot. It acknowledged him with a dutiful 'Very good, sir,' then pivoted to face the drinks machine. As always, it had to rotate the entire top half of its body so that its pincers could make contact with the buttons.

'You must tell us what it's like in outer space,' said Alec.

'Of course,' said Fitz, 'but I've got a lot of questions to ask you too.'

'Will someone come looking for you?'

'They'll have written us off by now. How did you survive the war?'

'Long story. How many people escaped?'

'Well, it was before my time, of course.'

'Really?' Alec's surprise was more evident than he would have liked. 'How old are you?'

'What I mean is,' said Fitz, 'it happened when I was a kid. I remember the evacuees from Earth coming to my world, but that's about all.'

He was lying, but Alec didn't know why. What did Fitz Kreiner know about the universe that he didn't want to reveal?

'What year is it?' Alec asked.

'Nine hundred and twelve,' said Fitz without hesitation. 'By the Imperial Calendar.'

'Who won the war?' asked Alec. 'Rockers or mods?'

At that moment, there was a brief commotion at the front door. Six members of Eagle Group burst into the milk bar, and Alec was pleased to see that the first three held a struggling teenager between them. He had almost forgotten about the group's mission this morning, but it seemed to be his day for opportunities.

'Davey!' he greeted his new prisoner, turning away from Fitz and allowing a feral grin to cross his face. 'Davey, Davey, Davey. How nice to see you again.'

'Excuse me, sir,' said the servo-robot behind the bar, 'you have not collected your drink.'

Irritated, Alec plucked the proffered metal cup from its pincers, slammed it down on to the bar and forgot about it. 'I have a few questions for you, Davey.'

Davey responded by unleashing a torrent of curses and furiously trying to shake his captors' grips. 'Such language, Davey,' said Alec with mock disapproval. 'Looks like you've copped yourself an attitude since I last saw you. Well, you'd be... how old, now? Of course! Nineteen. Nineteen years old. One of the big boys now, eh, Davey?'

'Bigger than any of you scummy rockers!' spat Davey. 'All hiding in here together. Why don't you come out and fight like men?'

The words sounded pathetic coming from someone whom Alec couldn't help but think of as a child. Even now, Davey was slight of stature and delicate of feature. His skin was smooth, his hair blond and neatly trimmed. He was wearing the uniform of Alec's lifelong foes: the silver tunic with its pattern of black and white squares scattered at random across the fabric, sometimes overlapping. The tunic covered Davey from his neck down to his ankles, with no seams or fasteners. On his feet, he wore a pair of silver moon boots.

'I hear you've got brains as well, Davey. In fact, I've been hearing a lot of things about you lately. You've been excelling yourself.'

A sneer twisted Davey's face. 'You don't know nothing.'

'You've grown into a bit of a swot, haven't you? Especially at science.'

'So, that's what your cowardly ambush was all about! Hate to disappoint you, Alec, but you've got the wrong man.'

Alec didn't want to believe him. Davey seemed cocksure, unafraid, but it could be a bluff. He tried to match his prisoner for confidence. 'Even if you're not the Technician, you'll tell me who is.'

'In your dreams! You won't get a word out of me, greaser!'

'Take him over there,' instructed Alec, nodding towards the cubicle that was furthest away from the front door. Davey didn't bother to struggle as he was hauled across the room. His face wore a triumphant, mocking smirk. Alec set his lips into a thin, straight line, determined that he wouldn't be provoked to either anger or despair.

'You're two down,' he noted as he took Kenny, the group's leader, aside.

'Captured,' Kenny confirmed with a nod. That was better than the alternative.

Alec groaned. 'How did you manage to lose two?'

As Kenny reached into his animal-skin jacket, his long, thin face betrayed his concern. 'We went for the kid as soon as he showed himself, like you said. But there was trouble. His pals had something new.'

'Again? I don't get it!'

'We got hold of one of them. I think we got problems, boss.'

Alec felt his stomach sinking as Kenny produced his catch. He had seen nothing like it before, but he recognised it from his dreams. For years, he had been driving his Technicians to produce something like this. They hadn't come close. Now his worst nightmare had been realised. The other side had beaten him to it.

He was looking at a gun. It was compact but, Alec was sure, no less powerful for that. He couldn't guess how his enemies had produced even the white plastic from which it was moulded. How advanced were they? The weapon had no trigger. Three buttons were set into its handgrip, and Alec guessed that they would fire it at varying intensities.

'Is this what I think it is?' he asked, almost voicelessly, knowing the answer. His people knew it too. They had crowded around him, silently awe-struck. And fearful.

Kenny nodded mournfully. 'It's a ray gun,' he said.

* * *

The campsite was a simple affair: a few blankets stitched together and stretched between trees for shelter; a few metal tanks to collect rainwater. The Doctor sat cross-legged on the ground, chin in hands, as the plain-dwellers built a fire using wood from the black trees. They crowded around it, feeding off its heat. Then they filled a pot from one of the tanks and hooked it to a precarious wooden frame, so that it hung over the flames. And the elderly man with the thinning hair, the ruddy complexion and the wart on his nose – the man the Doctor had come to think of as the head chef – approached him with a hungry look in his eyes.

'Fire's ready,' he wheezed. 'Time to prepare the meal.'

The Doctor bounced to his feet. 'Excellent! Now, let me show you how to do this.' He scooped up the purple leaves that the plain-dwellers had collected for him. 'Now, in its natural state this weed is highly toxic, as I'm sure you know. But this –' He scratched at a leaf, staining his fingers purple as he teased a viscous, violet substance from beneath its veins. 'This sap is a concentrated source of essential nutrients. It's still rather poisonous, I'm afraid, but we can deal with that.'

The head chef watched, fascinated, as the Doctor squeezed the sap into the pot. A hint of violet shimmered across the water's surface and a blackcurrant aroma wafted outwards. 'You shouldn't need more than five or six leaves for a pot this size. Just enough to colour the water a bit. Here, you try.' He handed the leaves over, then stepped back and watched benignly as, concentrating hard, the head chef copied what he had been shown. The rest of the plain-dwellers – twenty or so, in all – strained to see, open-eyed with wonder.

The joy of discovery, thought the Doctor, there's nothing quite like it.

Something pushed at his back, and he turned and beamed at the camel-like creature that was nuzzling him affectionately. He tickled its chin, confirming as he did that it had no nostrils. It didn't appear to breathe at all. Another mystery.

Thirty minutes later, they all sat in a circle, drinking from metal bowls that warmed their hands. The Doctor was pleased to note that, in addition to its nutritional properties, his improvised drink had a pleasant fruity taste.

The sound of engines didn't disturb them at first. The motorbikes were just eight spots on the horizon. But, as they drew closer, an air of nervousness descended. 'Mods or rockers?' wondered one man quietly. Someone else asked if it mattered either way.

'City folk,' deduced the Doctor. 'You don't like them much, do you?'

'No good comes from the city,' hissed one of the women.

'But aren't you from the city yourselves?'

'We scorn it! We want nothing from its technology.'

The Doctor nodded, then raised his eyebrows and looked directly at the woman, his eyes wide with innocent charm. 'I see. But you have brought these bowls with you, and tanks to collect rainwater in and what other trinkets I wonder?'

'We use only what we are forced to use,' snapped the man who sat next to him in the circle, 'and we would not need this much if the city would only set us free.'

The head chef intervened, calmly but forcefully, brooking no further argument. 'Thank you, Doctor, for helping us come one step closer to breaking the city's shackles.'

The Doctor bowed his head graciously. He couldn't help but notice that the head chef was at least twenty-five years older than anyone else here. Doubtless life on the plain was difficult. But then there were precious few youngsters either. Most people were in their thirties.

By the time the visitors – rockers, it had been concluded – arrived, the plain-dwellers were on their feet. They formed a living, defiant barricade, but they were frightened all the same. The Doctor watched calmly as one of the riders dismounted. It didn't take long for the burly rocker to pick him out of the crowd. 'You,' he grunted. 'We've come to rescue you.'

'Have you? That's extremely generous of you. Who from?'

'These savages,' said the rocker, his thick lips folding into a sneer. 'These cannibals.'

'Cannibals?'

'A label attached to us long ago,' the head chef growled.

'You still eat your own dead,' the rocker spat.

'Well then,' said the Doctor brightly, 'I don't appear to be at risk.'

'Our leader requests your presence.'

'Oh, does he indeed?'

'He already has Fitz Kreiner for company.' The rocker's hand hovered over the makeshift knife that had been thrust through one belt loop of his filthy jeans.

'Oh, I do beg your pardon,' said the Doctor, clapping a hand to his forehead. 'I'm being terribly slow. You want me to infer that, if I don't go with you, you'll harm my companion. Oh, well then, yes of course I'll come.' He pivoted around, took a few of the plain-dwellers' hands at random and shook them vigorously. 'I'm dreadfully sorry, but I have an engagement that I can't seem to get out of. It was very nice meeting you all and I'll drop in again if I can.'

'Hey, watch it!' snarled the rocker, as the Doctor backed into him.

'Be careful, you almost dropped this,' said the Doctor, handing his knife back to him and rubbing his hands together enthusiastically. 'Now, will I be riding with you?'

Fitz's drink was thick, milky and bland. It left a taste of flour on his tongue. He took a long swig of it anyway, and left the metal cup against his lips for a while to disguise his keen interest in the milk bar's other occupants.

The rockers were leaving him alone for now, but they might turn nasty again at any time. His best bet, he decided, was to make a run for the back door while he could. Now he only had to convince his legs.

The prisoner, Davey, had been dragged back before Alec, and the jukebox was playing its tuneless electronic music again. Its drumbeat vibrated through the metal floor, and seemed to drive both parties into an increasing state of agitation.

'Admit it!' demanded Alec. 'You've messed with the Brain.'

'Who needs to?' scoffed Davey.

'Don't lie to me. We've all seen what's happening. The city's in a mess!'

'Your lot should be at home then. I thought you liked living in pigsties!'

'You idiot. Don't you realise the Brain keeps us alive?'

'I haven't been near it. None of us have. If there's anyone stupid enough to mess with the Brain, he'll be a rocker!'

'It's the mods who've got all this new technology all of a sudden.'

'And wouldn't you just like to know where that comes from, eh?'

So, thought Fitz, this is Earth's future after all. This is how it ends. War. Devastation. Nuclear bombs, no doubt. They'd even altered the atmosphere. And even now, with armies reduced to handfuls of survivors in the sole remaining city in the world, the fighting didn't stop. He wondered how far forward in time he'd travelled.

'Typical rocker,' said Davey with disdain. 'You tamper with the Brain but you're too thick to know what you're doing, so you screw it up and blame us.'

There had been rockers in 1963, of course. Not that Fitz had had anything to do with them. Just another crazy fad: disenfranchised teenagers trying to feel superior by dressing the same way and acting the same way and sharing the same tastes. They had always made Fitz nervous: he had thought them one dangerous step away from a different kind of uniform. He had made himself feel superior by being an individual.

He hated the idea that such attitudes still existed in the far future.

Alec slapped Davey's face. As the sharp sound reverberated around the room, Fitz realised that this wasn't the time for contemplation.

Davey leapt at Alec, fists flailing, but immediately there were four rockers on top of him.

Fitz edged his way cautiously along the counter.

'Take him downstairs,' ordered Alec. 'We'll see what he has to say when he gets hungry.'

Fitz swore under his breath as a struggling and spitting Davey was carried past him and through the back door.

'Hey, 'Lec!' called a blonde-haired woman in her early thirties, who was sitting on the floor against the counter. 'What does it matter what the mods do now? We've got us a spaceman!'

Fitz squirmed as all eyes turned towards him again.

Then, from outside, cutting across the din from the jukebox, came a series of staccato explosions, like gunshots, with an electronic ring. *K-chow! K-chow! K-chow!*

Somebody leapt to the front door and pressed his eye against what must have been a spyhole. 'Mods!' he cried. 'A dozen of 'em, with those ray guns.'

Fitz turned, took two steps towards the back door and collided with Davey, who pushed him aside, yelled 'Mods for ever!' and charged head down back into the milk bar.

Fitz dived behind the counter as Davey's erstwhile captors pursued him. Crouched in shadow, he strained to hear what was going on, but everyone was shouting and the jukebox kept pumping out its drumbeat and that infernal screeching. He glanced towards the back door in time to see Alec disappearing through it, along with a four-strong escort.

'Pardon me, sir,' said the serving robot, disregarding Fitz's frenzied attempts to wave it into silence, 'but, if you sit there, then I shall be unable to perform my duties.'

On his hands and knees, he squeezed past its metal base and scrambled towards the far end of the counter. He peered around it and confirmed what his ears had told him: that the milk bar was emptying. The rockers – those who hadn't fled – were spilling out on to the street to face their enemies. Soon, no obstacles remained between Fitz and the open door. Beyond it, though, was a mass of writhing bodies, and he could still hear the intermittent bark of electronic gunshots.

He had a good chance of escaping in the confusion. He also had a good chance of being caught in the crossfire.

But how long could it be before Alec caught his breath and sent someone back for him?

Fitz broke cover and raced for the door.

Immediately, a rocker loomed before him.

The rocker hadn't seen Fitz. He had scooped up the ray gun from the counter; he was aiming it, and, in a horrifying instant, Fitz took in the scene.

He saw Davey frozen in mid-run, fear in his eyes, and he realised that the boy had fought his way past all but one of the half-dozen or so remaining rockers – and that this last one was about to shoot him. And kill him.

Kill him.

Fitz turned his run into a shoulder charge, hitting the rocker as he fired and barging him into the first partition. His shot went wild, the gun's yellow beam leaving a scorch mark on the counter. Fitz recoiled, his thoughts still trying to catch up with his actions, and then Davey had hold of his arm and he was pulling him through the door and out into the mêlée.

Suddenly, mods and rockers were fighting all around him, the sides identifiable by their differing styles of dress. Davey used his slight form to his advantage, dodging and weaving through the combatants, but Fitz was less agile and more concerned with what was going on behind him. He found himself separated from his would-be rescuer and hemmed in. He turned from one side to another, and gasped as he found himself staring into the snarling, crazed face of a rocker. A rocker with a knife.

A sharp pain ripped across his chest and the world tunnelled around him. As his attacker fell away, attacked in turn from behind, all Fitz could do was stare at the livid red line that cut through shirt and flesh alike. He could feel his strength draining from him.

He was dragged out of his trance by Davey, and towards a line of motorbikes. They were similar to the one on which Fitz had been brought here, but cleaner and without the extraneous extra panels. Indeed, they had been stripped down almost to the point of becoming skeletal frameworks of tubes. Their saddles had unusually high backs, and to the front of each vehicle was bolted a cluster of headlamps and wing mirrors. The mods were retreating, Fitz realised. He didn't know what else to do except stick with Davey – but then Davey jumped on to the back of someone else's bike.

Fitz clamped a hand over his wound, and felt blood trickling through his fingers. He ought to tell somebody, get help. 'Davey...' he gasped.

'Jono,' shouted Davey, 'let the scrawny guy on your scooter, would you? He's with us.'

The stout, moustached man who must have been Jono struggled on to his scooter and glowered back at Fitz, who clambered on to the saddle behind him, uncertainly. He experienced an unwelcome sensation of *déjà vu* as the bike leapt forward, and he clung to its rider and screwed his eyes shut. The knife wound was a scalding line across his chest. 'I... I've been cut,' he reported plaintively.

'Don't sweat it,' growled Jono over his shoulder. 'You're riding with the mods now.'

'Great,' said Fitz, without confidence. 'I feel much safer already.'

Chapter Three
Living in the Modern World

The Doctor kept up a running commentary as he was conveyed across the city. 'Dear, oh dear, you really ought to do something about this graffiti. I mean, that spelling... I say, now that's an interesting vehicle. A hovercar, isn't it? You must let me examine it. I'm sure I could get it working again... You know, your people really ought to be more careful. Leaving wires exposed like that could be dangerous.'

The rockers braked outside a single-storey metal building, which was dwarfed by the towers around it. The Doctor frowned and wrinkled his nose. 'You appear to have had trouble.' He hopped out of his saddle and past a couple of discarded bikes to examine the building's front wall. 'Scorch marks. Made recently, I'd say, by an energy weapon of some kind.'

He turned to find that the eight rockers had dismounted and formed an intimidating semicircle behind him. He grinned sheepishly, showing his teeth. 'I'm terribly sorry, I didn't know we were in a hurry. Your leader is a busy man, I expect.' Stepping forward, he took the hand of the man on whose bike he had ridden, and shook it. 'Well, it was very nice talking to you – and, by the way, what planet are we on?'

The rockers looked at each other, disconcerted.

The Doctor spread his arms wide, palms upturned. 'I thought it was a simple question.'

'This is Earth,' said one of the rockers, in a low growl.

'Oh no, I really don't think that can be right.' His captors were becoming restless, so the Doctor strode towards the door, which swished open to admit him. He stopped suddenly on the threshold, so that one of the rockers bumped into him. He

36

pivoted, fixed the man with a penetrating stare and asked mildly, 'So, what year do you think this is?'

'Twenty nineteen,' said the rocker, nonplussed.

The Doctor nodded thoughtfully and stepped into the milk bar.

The mods' base was situated in a long, low building, like that of their enemies. Inside, though, it was much more spartan. It was laid out like a café, with square tables neatly arranged in a grid pattern. Two pinball machines sat side by side against the far wall. Still, the counter with its line of shake dispensers and its attendant robot was familiar. The chairs too were identical to those in the milk bar, albeit undamaged.

The mods chattered loudly, exhilarated by what they saw as a great victory. Some headed straight for the back door, but most pulled up seats or sat on tables. Fitz stumbled through them, a hand pressed to his chest as it had been throughout his journey, as if to hold his heart in. Davey was receiving a lot of attention – a lot of handshaking and slaps on the back – and it took Fitz a while to reach him.

'I need a doctor,' he said, directing Davey's attention towards his injury.

'Doesn't look too bad,' said Davey, with none of the grave concern that Fitz felt his predicament merited. 'We can fix that downstairs. Come on. Back in a mo, guys!'

He led Fitz through a back door, across a narrow passageway and into a small, square room, the only feature of which was a circular hole in the floor, which almost touched its edges. Fitz recoiled from the precipice, but Davey walked right past him.

Fitz almost cried out as his new-found friend plummeted away from him.

A second later, Davey drifted back up over the edge of the hole and regarded him with a puzzled look. 'What's up? Don't they have antigrav tubes where you come from?'

The mods were going to give him the same 'crashed

spaceman' routine as the rockers, Fitz realised. That bloody robot had probably reported his arrival to both sides.

'They're obsolete,' he said. 'We ride on beams of coherent light now. It's faster and there's less danger of, ah, collisions.'

Davey grinned. 'The Brain monitors everyone in the tube. If you're on a crash course, you get shunted aside. You don't even notice.'

'Oh, obviously,' bluffed Fitz. 'I mean, it just makes people feel safer, that's all.'

'Come on, let's get you seen to.' Davey dropped out of sight again.

Fitz took a deep breath, closed his eyes and jumped into the hole.

'No one lives above ground any more,' said Alec. 'It's too dangerous.'

'How sad for you,' the Doctor emoted. He maintained a casual posture as he strode alongside the rockers' leader, but he was well aware of the four rockers at his back. Not that he intended to escape – not until he had learned more. It was enough to know that he could. 'And this complex extends beneath the whole of the city?'

Alec nodded. 'Some parts of it have been collapsed, though, to separate rockers and mods. The only way from our living space to theirs is above ground.'

Two children were playing with ball bearings on the floor. At the approach of Alec and his entourage, they scampered off down a connecting corridor.

'Mods and rockers,' the Doctor murmured. 'How quaint.'

Alec halted, and a door slid aside for him obligingly. 'This', he announced, 'is to be your laboratory.'

The Doctor peered through the doorway, but all he saw were a few scattered chairs and a haphazard jumble of components spread across three metal workbenches. He identified a few instruments amid the mess – a microscope here, a broken

thermometer there, a Bunsen burner with its gas hose severed –
but he would hardly have called the room a laboratory.

'That's very kind of you,' he said, 'but I don't think I have
room for another one.'

Alec's smile was toothy and without humour, confirming the
Doctor's instinct that his hospitality was a tissue-thin mask. 'I'm
well aware that your flying saucer blew up as it touched down.'

'Ah,' said the Doctor, sensing Fitz's handiwork.

'I'm offering you a place to live and food to eat, if you'll help
us.'

'And what if I don't want to take sides in your parochial
conflict?'

'You don't have a choice.'

'Threats now?'

'A fact of life in the city, I'm afraid.'

The Doctor wandered into the so-called laboratory, and
inspected its contents with casual interest. 'Yes, I believe you
are. You realise, of course, that the only way to improve things
is to end the war.'

'With a good Technician, I might be able to do that.'

'You humans,' laughed the Doctor. 'I say "end the war", you
talk about winning it. That's the worst way to end a war. Well,
the second worst.'

Anger darkened Alec's face. He reached into his leather jacket
and produced a white, plastic pistol, which looked like a child's
toy. The Doctor had wanted to test Alec, to see how far his
patience would hold and how he would react when it was
exhausted. He had his answers now. The same old answers.
'How frightfully dull,' he sighed despairingly.

To his surprise, Alec turned the gun around and handed it to
him butt first. 'I want you to duplicate this ray gun,' he said.

The Doctor took the weapon and held it gingerly between
thumb and forefinger. 'I think there are quite enough of these
things in the universe already,' he rumbled darkly.

'The mods have them –'

'So, you must have them too. Oh, I understand the principles of an arms race, Alec, just as I understand what it must lead to. Tell me, as a hypothetical question: what's to stop me from turning this gun on you now and shooting my way out of here?'

'There are five of us, Doctor, and only one of you.'

'I might have fast reflexes.'

'You might,' said Alec. 'But I have your friend, Fitz Kreiner.'

The Doctor nodded cheerfully. 'Good. That's what I thought.'

A woman's voice buzzed over a loudspeaker system, its steady monotone punctuated by injections of synthetic excitement. 'Our demonstration of mod superiority was even more successful than anticipated. As well as teaching the rockers a lesson, our task force was able to free Davey. Congratulations to them, and welcome home, Davey.'

There weren't many mods in the recreation hall – most were upstairs, celebrating in the café – but those that were present kept glancing at Fitz from their little groups. Self-consciously, he turned away from the food machine as if he hadn't really been trying to work out its controls. He slipped a hand inside his ripped and bloodied shirt, and checked the spray-on plastic patch that had sealed his wound. It felt strange. But it had stopped the bleeding and taken away the pain, so who was he to complain?

'Don't worry about it,' said a kind voice behind him. 'It'll drop off in a day or two. We'll have to sort out those clothes of yours too, when you've eaten. Hi, I'm Deborah, this is Vince. Davey told us you'd be here. Having problems?'

'The food machines aren't like this where I come from,' said Fitz, abashed. Deborah smiled and reached past him to the object of his frustration. A keypad was attached to the large metal box, and she punched a sequence of numbers into it. She guided Fitz's hand into a small aperture, and something dropped into it: a large white pill in a transparent plastic packet.

'What do you call this?' he protested.

40

'Space-age food,' said Deborah, as if surprised.

'Of course you do.'

She was cute, thought Fitz. Short, black, wavy hair, a smattering of freckles and a button nose that gave her a pixie-like quality. Her eyes sparkled. She was a few years older but a full head shorter than he was. Her regulation silver uniform with its black and white squares clung to her curves in a way of which he wholeheartedly approved.

'I hear you saved our son's life,' said Deborah's companion, derailing Fitz's train of thought before it could leave its station. Vince had a reedy voice and a huge bald spot that was rather premature. His eyes were blue and watery, and he squinted at Fitz as he talked to him.

'I was just in the right place and all that,' said Fitz, not really meaning it. Hoping to ingratiate himself, he added, 'The rockers were holding me prisoner. I don't know what they would have done to me if Davey hadn't come along.' Davey was nineteen, he recalled. Vince and Deborah must have been younger than that when he was born. 'Where is he, anyway?'

'He was called away,' said Deborah, as she extracted another two pills from the machine.

'He had to report in,' said Vince, 'you know, to our glorious leader.'

'He asked us to look after you.'

'It's the most he's said to us in years. We should be grateful.'

'Right,' said Fitz. 'I think I heard them call for him while I was waiting for your doctor.'

Deborah pushed a cup into his hand. It contained a thick white drink, which looked suspiciously similar to the one Alec had given him in the milk bar.

'Preparations continue for tomorrow's attack upon the rockers,' said the loudspeaker woman. 'Our Technician is hard at work producing a new batch of ray guns, and we expect to score another resounding victory. Our leader will commence his briefing at 0700 hours.'

Fitz, Deborah and Vince sat around a collapsible metal table. Simple but functional, like the rest of the mods' living space. They hadn't even thought to decorate the metal walls. Fitz studied his drink and wondered if he could get away with leaving it.

'Is it like this all the time?' he asked.

'How do you mean?' asked Vince, squinting at him again.

'How long have you been at war?'

'For ever,' sighed Deborah.

'But why? What are you fighting for?'

'Because they're rockers and we're mods.'

'That's all?'

'It's always been that way.'

Not as far as Fitz was concerned it hadn't. But he thought it best not to press the point. Rockers he knew about, but he'd never heard of mods before today and he didn't want to betray his ignorance. 'So, why not stop being mods?' he asked tentatively.

'You have to choose a side,' said Vince, earnestly. 'You can't be neutral.'

'We used to be neutral once,' said Deborah, wistfully.

'But not any more. Not in the city.'

'No, not any more.'

'Not unless you become, you know, a dropout. A plain-dweller.'

The couple had drifted off into a shared world of regrets and disappointments. Fitz looked from one to the other, lost for something to say.

The loudspeakers delivered another bulletin. 'Our leader has confirmed that Davey found our missing spaceman at the rockers' headquarters. His name is Fitz Kreiner, and we ask you to welcome him into our community. He has chosen to take our side.'

To Fitz's embarrassment, scattered applause broke out across the hall.

* * *

42

The Doctor had been left alone in the laboratory, but there were two guards outside the door. He had checked. The gun lay discarded on one bench as he sifted through the assorted junk on another. He was looking for a scalpel, but he was frequently distracted.

He found two lightweight, cylindrical containers and unearthed one of them. A hole had been punched into its side, and a black rubber hose – apparently cut from an old tyre – had been jammed into it. The Doctor held the other end of the hose beneath his nose and sniffed at it experimentally.

The door opened, and a woman stepped into the room. She was in her mid-thirties, although her fallen face, dead eyes and stooped shoulders could have tricked the Doctor into thinking her older. Her hair was a darkening blonde, combed neatly back and tied into a ponytail that reached almost to the base of her spine.

The Doctor put down the tank. 'Hello. Have you come to threaten or torture me? It's just that I'm a bit busy at the moment.'

The woman gave him an embarrassed smile, which nevertheless softened her features and radiated warmth. 'I came to say I'm sorry about Alec. He can be a bit rude.'

'He was perfectly polite to me,' said the Doctor generously, 'on the surface. I'm sure he was trying his best.' He offered a hand, which the woman took. 'I'm the Doctor.'

'Sandra. I'm Alec's wife.' She mumbled the words slightly, as if speaking were an effort.

'I see. Have you come to check up on me?' He didn't give her a chance to reply. He walked briskly away from her, sweeping an arm wide. 'This is a very interesting place you have here. Not very efficient, but interesting. Some of your attempts to create – oh, what do you call them? – "ray guns" have taken quite fascinating turns.'

'We're close, then?'

'Oh, no, no, no, not at all. Tell me, Sandra, how many rockers are there in the city?'

'About forty,' said Sandra, shuffling after him, 'just under.'

'And mods?'

'Same again.'

'Predominantly male, am I right? And mostly in your mid-to-late thirties.'

'I suppose so.'

'But there are exceptions.' The Doctor halted at the far end of the room, remembered something and cast his eyes about the workbenches. 'Scalpel. Scalpel, scalpel, scalpel…' That did him no good, so he patted down his jacket until he felt a likely shape, reached into his left-hand pocket and produced a metal comb. 'Well, never mind, this should do.'

Dropping to his knees, he scraped at a patch of flaking metal at the bottom of the wall. Silver particles collected in his palm, and he inspected them with interest.

'Alec does his best,' said Sandra. 'He's led the rockers for years, and he's under a lot of pressure. Especially now.'

'I'm sure he is,' said the Doctor, without looking.

'And we do need your help.'

'I'm not prepared to help you slaughter your enemies.'

'It's the mods who are slaughtering us.' There was no hate, no anger, in Sandra's voice. Moved by her plea, the Doctor shifted his attention towards her. He raised his eyebrows and fixed her with a sympathetic gaze. It was funny how, in this body, that was often all he had to do to earn a confidence. 'Their Technician must have solved the city's secrets. We don't even know who he is for sure, but he's giving them weapons like that ray gun.'

'I see. A shift in the balance of power. You must be very disconcerted.'

'People never used to die. Well, not much. But we've lost two in the last month, and the mods have caught four more.'

'What do you think you're doing?' snapped a voice from the doorway.

The Doctor jumped to his feet, pivoted to face the new arrival and made his way around the benches towards her. 'I do seem to be popular today. Good afternoon, I'm the Doctor. You already know Sandra, I assume. I would shake hands, but I'm afraid they're rather full at the moment.' He waved the comb apologetically. 'Do come in, come in.'

He darted over to the microscope, hoisted it upright and slipped his left hand with its collection of particles beneath it. The new arrival marched up to him, pushed the device back over and nudged the Doctor in the process so that his samples skittered on to the bench.

'Hey!' he squealed indignantly, his face twisting in dismay.

'I said, what do you think you're doing?' the woman stormed.

'What do you think *you're* doing?' the Doctor mimicked childishly.

'My name is Gillian, and this is my laboratory.'

Gillian was about the same age as Sandra, which was no surprise to the Doctor. Her hair, chestnut-brown with lighter streaks, was parted in the middle. It danced on her shoulders. Her mouth seemed somehow too small for the rest of her face, particularly with her lips pursed as they were now. She was a little over average height for a human woman, broad without being fat. The shapeless furs in which she was wrapped accentuated her bulk.

'I thought it was *my* laboratory,' said the Doctor.

'I'm the rockers' Technician. You're my assistant – and Alec ordered you to duplicate the ray gun, not play with my equipment.'

'He didn't order me, he threatened me – and I couldn't duplicate that weapon if I wanted to. Not with the materials and tools you have here.'

'The mods did it, and they only have the same.'

'I doubt that very much.'

'I'll determine that for myself, thank you,' said Gillian primly. 'The first thing we're going to do is take that gun apart and see exactly how it works.'

'Oh, if that's all you want to know, I can –' The Doctor made to pick up the gun, but Gillian reached it first. She clamped her hand down on top of it and glared at him. With an indifferent shrug, the Doctor withdrew.

Gillian produced a paint-spattered screwdriver from a fur pouch and turned the gun over in her hands. The Doctor hovered at her shoulder. 'I see you've been trying to reinvent the oxygen mask,' he said casually. Gillian didn't answer, but the Doctor persisted. 'What you need is a proper demand valve. I can work on that if you like. Why do you want it?'

Unable to find a join in the plastic, Gillian pushed the blade of her screwdriver down the gun's barrel. 'We're supposed to be working on this.'

'You seem to be coping quite well on your own,' said the Doctor.

She looked at him sharply, as if suspecting that he was mocking her. She pushed down hard on the protruding handle of the screwdriver, but the barrel didn't crack. The lips of her tiny mouth curled in frustration, and she removed the tool and brought the gun down hard on the edge of her workbench.

'I think you might want to be a bit more careful,' warned the Doctor. 'That device has an internal energy source, which is probably quite dangerous. Are you leaving us already?'

This last was directed at Sandra, who, until the Doctor dashed forward to intercept her, had been shuffling towards the door. 'It's best,' she said, flashing him a weak smile. 'It was nice meeting you.'

'Oh, please stay,' he begged. 'I need someone to talk to. Gillian here is busy, and I'm supposed to be assisting her, except that she doesn't seem to want my assistance, and anyway wouldn't it be much nicer if you two could work out your differences and be friends?'

'Who –' stammered Sandra. 'Who told you?'

'I thought you did.' The Doctor closed his eyes and knitted his eyebrows as he sifted through his memories. He clicked his fingers. 'Yes, yes, you did – in body language, just a few seconds ago. Now, I can understand Gillian not liking *me* – she doesn't know me yet – but she's deliberately ignoring you. I think the two of you should –'

Something fizzed and crackled on the workbench, and Gillian recoiled with a shriek.

The Doctor flew towards her, flung a protective arm around her shoulders and inspected the damage. There was a livid red bruise on the palm of her right hand. The gun lay abandoned, the screwdriver protruding from a small hole that had been chipped out of its butt.

'You've shorted out the power pack,' cried the Doctor in dismay.

'I suppose you're going to say "I told you so",' moaned Gillian, shrugging off his arm, blowing on her hand and fairly hopping about in pain.

'Yes, I did. You should get that burn seen to. I expect it hurts.'

'No, not at all,' said Gillian through gritted teeth. 'It feels like I've dropped a blob of ice cream on to my hand.'

The Doctor was surprised. 'Really? Energy burns usually hurt.'

'I'll take her to the medical room,' offered Sandra, with visible reluctance.

'No you won't,' said Gillian. 'Mark's outside. He'll take me.'

'If that's what you want,' said Sandra coldly. She reached the door before Gillian, and swept out of the room without looking back.

'I don't need help from any traitor,' swore Gillian under her breath as she followed.

When the automatic door had closed behind both women, the Doctor dashed back to the microscope and stood it up again. Fastidiously, he collected as many of the dropped metal flakes as he could. As he examined them, he nodded and muttered to himself gravely. Then he straightened, and brushed the silver particles distractedly from his hand.

A thought struck him, and he loped towards the door. It

opened for him, and he stuck his head out into the corridor curiously. As he had suspected, there was only one rocker there now. The other must have taken Gillian to the medical room.

It would almost have been impolite not to escape.

The guard's hand moved towards his knife as he regarded the Doctor warily. 'You're not meant to leave the lab,' he said.

'Alec's orders, I know. I don't suppose there's any chance of a cup of tea, Mr, ah…?'

'Tom.'

The Doctor beamed at him. 'Mr Tom.'

'Just Tom.'

'I see. Does nobody here have a surname? Never mind. It would help me think, you see, and I promise not to spill any on the equipment.' The guard looked befuddled, so the Doctor reminded him: 'Tea.'

'We don't have tea.'

'You don't? How utterly dreadful for you.' The Doctor took a step forward. The guard tensed. The Doctor rummaged through his pockets. 'You must be very bored standing out here alone. I wonder if I can – ah!' His face lit up as he produced a silver yo-yo. He dangled it enticingly before the guard's eyes, like a hypnotist's watch. The guard stared at the yo-yo. The Doctor let it drop, and the guard's eyes followed it as it spun towards the floor. In gathering it back up, the Doctor contrived to take another step closer to him.

He cradled the yo-yo in his hands and offered it to the guard, eyebrows raised in encouragement, his lips stretched into their one-sided grin. The guard hesitated.

The Doctor took another step, and the laboratory door swished shut behind him. Suddenly alert, the guard brandished his knife, but the yo-yo shot out and knocked it from his hand.

The guard was still looking surprised when the Doctor stepped into his personal space, applied pressure to a sensitive nerve cluster and rendered him unconscious.

* * *

'You'd like it on Mechta,' Fitz assured Vince and Deborah as they strolled through the complex together. 'The state looks after you. Full employment, a decent health service, they even make sure you've got somewhere to live.'

Deborah surprised him by asking, 'Is it exciting?'

'Exciting?'

'Living in outer space.'

Fitz concealed a sly grin. The couple had swallowed everything he'd said so far, but then a lot of it had been based on truth. It was time for a real test.

'Absolutely,' he said, nodding furiously. 'There's nothing like having your own, um, flying saucer. You haven't lived till you've flown through a black hole and out the other side.'

'What's on the other side?' asked Deborah, eyes wide with interest.

'A negative universe! Space is white there, you know, and the stars black.'

'Wow.'

'We knew there were colonies, of course,' said Vince, 'but we've never seen proof before. Are there... you know, any aliens?'

'Daleks, Martians, Meeps, Xaxxons, you name it. Then there's the Plutonians, of course. They used to buzz round Earth in the fifties and sixties, taking people from country roads to experiment on. We're all friends now, though.'

'I think we've heard about them, haven't we, Vince?' said Deborah.

This was too easy. But the more Fitz 'opened up' to the mods, the more they might tell him in return. And the more likely they were to help him find the Doctor.

The Doctor. Fitz was worried about him. He knew how capable he was, he kept reminding himself of that, but he had been through so much. He seemed to be rallying – he hadn't mentioned the loss of his TARDIS in days – but of late he had been a little too eager to plunge himself into each new experience. He had become almost reckless, as if he were trying to immerse himself in other people's problems to keep him from dwelling on his own.

Fitz had managed to depress himself again. He sighed, and took a crumpled packet of cigarettes from inside his denim jacket. 'Mind if I smoke?'

Vince and Deborah stopped walking. They stared at Fitz open-mouthed, as if he had just unveiled the Holy Grail. He gave them a questioning look.

'Cigarettes,' moaned Deborah. 'I haven't had a cigarette for eighteen years.'

'Oh,' said Fitz, mentally totting up how many he had left. 'I suppose you want one?'

'You really shouldn't,' warned Vince. 'Remember how hard it was for you last time? You know, when you had to come off them?'

'I know,' said Deborah sadly. 'It's just – it's just that it's a part of our past, isn't it? A taste of home. Just one couldn't hurt.'

Motivated by an unwelcome sense of guilt, Fitz pressed the packet into Deborah's hands. She looked at it in awe. 'So,' he said, plunging his hands deep into his pockets to stop them from needing something to do, 'where are we going again?'

'We're there,' said Vince.

He motioned Fitz towards a small alcove set into the wall. It was almost filled by an object that, at first, looked like a speak-your-weight machine. Fitz stepped on to its pedestal – not without trepidation, but he felt he had already asked a suspicious number of questions. The curved, oblong bulk of the machine raised itself to his eye level. He stared at his reflection in the large, black, glass panel that took up most of its front surface.

'Is this supposed to do something?' he asked, after a few seconds.

Deborah sighed and gave the machine a swift punch. 'It's been playing up for days,' she explained. 'The servo-robots haven't got round to fixing it.'

The machine emitted an electronic buzzing sound, three light bulbs flashed red, white and blue, and suddenly Fitz itched all over. He started as, in the space of seconds, his jacket exploded into strips of denim that joined together into a huge spiral pattern and whirled around him. He would have jumped off the pedestal, but he couldn't move his feet. He felt his shirt and jeans uncoiling themselves too, and he wondered if he was about to end up naked – or worse – in front of Vince and Deborah.

Before he knew what was happening, his old clothes had gone and he was clad in a mod uniform, complete with silver moon boots. The machine released its grip and he staggered off the pedestal, dazed. 'You could have warned me,' he complained, looking at the flat, white square where one of his pockets had been. 'I left my lighter in that jacket.'

'You haven't used a dresser before?' asked Deborah.

'Not such an old-fashioned one,' said Fitz, recovering. 'On Mechta, they ask you what you want them to do first. I only meant to change my shirt.'

'Your old clothes looked very, you know, old,' said Vince.

'The 1960s are back in at home.'

'I wouldn't mind having some jeans to wear again,' said Deborah, wistfully. 'Our dressers only do space-age clothes. They can't even make new specs for Vince.'

'I broke mine ten years ago,' Vince explained, with an embarrassed half-smile. No wonder he had to squint all the time, thought Fitz.

'I expect they've cured short-sightedness in the future,' suggested Deborah.

'You need to be in mod colours anyway,' said Vince, before Fitz could even think about answering that. 'You know, since you're going to be one of us.'

'It should make a good impression when you meet our leader,' said Deborah.

'I suppose so,' said Fitz, trying to sound remotely enthusiastic about that prospect.

'Tell us some more stories about outer space,' requested Deborah, as the trio set off along the corridor again.

Fitz thought for a moment, then took a deep breath and began.

The Doctor's footsteps echoed as he walked around the underground silo, admiring the six sleek, silver rockets that pointed skyward. He opened his mouth to share an observation about their design, but remembered that he was temporarily without a companion.

He had already tripped a motion-sensor alarm – which was careless of him: he should have checked before running in here like an eager young boy – so he had to work fast.

A maintenance hatch at the base of the nearest rocket tempted him with the promise of access to its innards. A few seconds' work with his sonic screwdriver laid its secrets open to him. Next, he hauled himself up an access ladder and into a tiny cockpit, where he had to sit with his back parallel to the floor and his knees cramped against a control panel above him. The controls, like the outward design of the rocket, were childishly simple, especially for a vessel that functioned on such advanced principles of magnetic repulsion.

He couldn't have much time left. He jumped from halfway down the ladder and hurried across the room. He flicked a switch on the wall, but nothing happened. He frowned and tried again. High above him, with a throaty rumbling sound, the roof irised open and late-afternoon sunlight streamed into the musty silo.

He found another switch, and tried that too. To his delight, a hologram shimmered into existence over the roof aperture. The sky disappeared behind a three-dimensional star chart. The Doctor bounced excitedly to the centre of the room and looked up, fascinated. 'A sky like that... you could only see it from Earth. But this can't be Earth. It can't be.'

Then he noticed something else. He searched his jacket for an electronic sextant and squinted down its eyepiece. The device burbled and bleeped as the Doctor took several readings, which he then double-checked with his naked eye and a growing smile.

When Alec and six rockers burst into the silo, he was waiting for them.

'Get him away from those rocket ships!' ordered Alec, and the rockers surrounded the Doctor. He declined to struggle as they dragged him over to their leader.

'Not as clever as you thought, are you?' snarled Alec. 'We found you before you could blast off. And if you had escaped, it would have been the worse for your friend anyway.'

'I don't see why. You don't have Fitz.'

Alec's superior expression froze on his face.

'You lied to me,' said the Doctor. 'And that's not the only lie I've been told. I've been taking a look at your star charts. They show the constellations as they appear from Earth, yes – but the alignment of the planets is all wrong for 2019, all wrong. Now, I've seen England in the mid-1960s, and it doesn't look a great deal like this.'

'What are you trying to say?' asked Alec, quietly.

'Just that, if you want my help, you'd better start telling me the truth. And, believe me, Alec, you do need my help, because I've discovered something else. This city is decaying, slowly breaking down at a molecular level. Now, if I surmise correctly, it doesn't just provide shelter and food for you humans, it synthesises your oxygen as well.'

The Doctor fixed Alec with a penetrating stare. 'So, I suggest you take this situation very seriously indeed.'

Chapter Four
Collision Course

Sometimes the memory of the headlights would invade Alec's dreams and wake him. Yellow circles of light, stabbing through the darkness, boring into his mind, coming closer. Like eyes. Like the eyes of the creature on the beach.

He rarely thought back to the days before the creature now, to the days when he was young and stupid and the future was a golden age waiting to happen and he was still Alec Redshaw and in love with Sandra McBride and they were going to be young for ever.

Sometimes he felt as if his life had begun that day on the beach, as if the nineteen years before that were no more than a pleasant dream he had had in the womb. But the moment at which he had first seen the alien was seared into his memory, like a birth trauma. Or rebirth. The start of his new life. The moment at which he was forced to grow up, although he had neither recognised nor accepted the fact until later.

The broken capsule lay on the grey beach. Alec craned his neck to see inside it, steeling his nerves and bracing his cartwheeling stomach against the shock to come. When he saw the creature at last, it was almost a letdown. He had expected some multitentacled monstrosity, not something so... small. So wizened. It looked like a baby. He could have plucked it from its nest of multicoloured wiring, and tucked it beneath one arm. It wasn't even green.

He almost laughed, but the instinct to do so was overwhelmed by the enormous realisation that he was looking, actually looking, at a being from another world.

He was disappointed, amused, awe-struck, full of wonder, excited and scared. The emotions overwhelmed and paralysed him. He didn't know what to think or how to feel.

Perhaps, deep down, he felt a sense of dread too. Perhaps he knew then that his life had just changed for ever. Or perhaps he didn't, and his mind would simply overlay that detail on to his memory in retrospect. Perhaps it was only in distorted recollections of the moment that Alec would be so keenly aware of the gentle breeze, the sting of sand particles on his cheeks, the lapping of the sea against the beach, the salty scent of fresh air and the distant, lilting sound of piano music. Familiar sensations that would very soon be lost to him.

'Its skin was a sort of purply grey,' said Sandra, 'all wrinkly.'

'Its head was bigger than its body,' Alec chipped in, shifting uncomfortably in his flimsy metal-framed chair. It had been a long time since he had talked about the Maker. Doing so brought back some of the conflicting emotions, some of the uncertainty he had felt on that beach in 1965. He wondered if he had made a mistake, inviting the stranger into his quarters. He had positioned guards outside and his personal robot within to sound an alarm if necessary, but it was still a risk. He felt exposed.

'Its face was... wide,' he said. 'Like it had been stretched by the ears or something.'

'It didn't have ears,' said Sandra. 'Its head just sort of...'

'Stuck out a bit to each side.'

'It didn't have a nose, just two nostrils: slitty things at angles to each other.'

'Its eyes were huge.'

'Yeah, really big.'

'They opened sideways like...'

'Curtains.'

'And they were all bright yellow inside.'

Sandra nodded. 'Bright yellow, like headlights. And it didn't blink, not once.'

'Was it humanoid?' asked the Doctor, in a low murmur. He sat cross-legged on Alec and Sandra's bed, listening intently. His hands were clasped in front of his mouth, his head was slightly tilted and his face was still and expressionless. His eyes, however, were wide with appeal. Alec almost felt that they were teasing information from him.

'It had two arms and legs,' he responded, 'but they were dead scrawny.'

'Hands?'

'I didn't notice.'

'Yes,' said Sandra. 'Three fingers and a stumpy little thumb. And it had a tail.'

Alec frowned. 'No it didn't.'

'Yes it did. You could see it, coiled around its leg.'

'That was probably a wire or something.'

'It was too thick. Almost as thick as its arms, and quite long. It came to a point.'

Alec felt a flash of anger at this attempt to deny even the smallest aspect of his clearest memory, of the most important experience of his life. 'You're imagining things!'

'It's you – you never pay attention to details.'

'And you're always fantasising!'

'What, because I think we can do better than this?'

'You won't accept things. You won't live in the present.'

'I'm fed up with your stupid war games, if that's what you mean.'

'So you keep saying!' said Alec, scornfully. 'You've been saying it since 1965.'

'And you still haven't grown up!'

'So, what happened next?' asked a soft, clear voice, cutting across the argument. The couple turned as one to the Doctor. His position and expression hadn't changed, except that he had raised his eyebrows a little.

'On the beach, I mean,' he elaborated. 'What happened after the pilot opened his eyes?'

* * *

56

'I would never have believed it,' said Deborah in wonder. 'Dehydrated monsters.'

'It was the best way for the smugglers to get them past Mechta's customs,' said Fitz, knowledgeably. 'Then they put adverts in newspapers and on the backs of comic books and got people from all over the colony to send for them as pets.'

Deborah gasped. 'What – children?'

'Children, adults, everyone. You got a packet of dust through the door, popped it into a tank, added water and – hey presto! – instant aliens, tiny at first but growing all the time. They were all round the planet in days.'

'And no one realised they were really, you know, an invasion force?' asked Vince.

This was too easy. Much too easy.

'No one at all. Of course, they didn't succeed.'

'Why not?' asked Deborah.

'The dehydration made them weaker than they expected. If their water was too hot or too cold or not oxygenated enough, or they weren't given the right feed or enough of it, they died. In the end, only four of them survived long enough to mature and break out of their tanks, and the, ah, space army dealt with them.'

'It's amazing,' breathed Deborah.

'Worrying too, don't you think?' said Vince.

'It's exciting and terrifying all at once,' said Deborah. As Fitz watched, her eyes glazed over, her thoughts drifting away from Earth again. 'We always knew there was something out there, of course. Something coming. But, trapped in the city, we just kind of forgot. We had our boring lives to lead. Now... now, it all seems within reach again.'

'We can fly to the stars,' whispered Vince.

'The future's almost here.'

They had arrived at the guest quarters that had been allocated to Fitz. As they entered the small room with its single table, its pair of chairs, its small cupboard and its bare bed of metal, he couldn't keep a look of distaste from flickering across his face.

'We need someone to send a ship for us first,' he pointed out, as he perched uncomfortably on the edge of the bed. 'New Earth Central Government doesn't know there's anyone here.'

'There must be some way of getting an SOS to them,' said Deborah. 'You can tell us how, can't you?'

'I don't know,' said Fitz, squirming a little. 'I can try, I suppose. But I've been meaning to ask: how come you *are* here? I mean, how did you survive the war?'

'War?'

Deborah sounded horrified, and Fitz's stomach sank as he realised that he had made a mistake. Deborah and Vince looked at each other, their faces ashen.

He had no choice but to run with his story. 'You didn't know about the war?'

'The... the rockers believe there was a war,' said Deborah, shakily.

'But they can't be right,' insisted Vince. 'They can't be!'

'We, ah, we don't really know what happened, to be honest,' Fitz hedged. 'It's just that the rockers said there'd been a war and I, er, thought they were telling the truth.'

'No one ever tells the truth,' grumbled Vince.

'I thought they'd actually lived through it.'

'No one lived through anything,' said Deborah. 'How –'

Fitz interrupted, before she could question him about 'New Earth Central Government's' suspicious lack of knowledge. 'So, what did happen?'

'We were brought here,' said Deborah.

'By, you know, aliens,' said Vince.

'Back when we were teenagers.'

'You were brought here?' echoed Fitz. 'From where?'

'From our time,' said Deborah. 'From 1965.'

Deborah didn't hear the guttural roar of motorcycle engines as she fled through the foyer of the Palladium, past its ticket office and emerged on to the pavement. She didn't see the adverts for upcoming films, nor the light that streamed from the doorway behind her and shimmered off the water-doused cobbles in the road. But she heard Vince's footsteps behind her, and felt his comforting arm on her shoulders although her eyes were shrouded with tears and she could see only a vague outline of him.

'I'm sorry,' she sobbed into his shirt.

'It doesn't matter,' said Vince, his own voice close to breaking. 'You wanted to see the film.'

'I thought it might, you know, take our minds off things, that's all. Saturday night at the pictures, like we used to do.'

'It just… reminded me…' She could say no more. She clamped her mouth shut to help fight down the misery. She thought of the monochrome image of the square-jawed American hero and his wispy princess and their perfect life that had made her wish to be somewhere, anywhere, but here.

'It'll be all right.'

'How can it be all right? It's not going to go away, Vince!'

'We should tell your parents. They could help.'

'No!' She tore herself away from him and stumbled into the road.

'They'll find out sooner or later.' Vince looked so awkward, so helpless, so slender and fragile, as he stood there with his arms spread wide in appeal, his blue eyes circular and mournful behind his spectacle lenses. But it was Deborah who had to cope with this, with the knowledge that something was alive inside her, that it would grow to consume her life.

'It's not just me,' he said. 'It's what your friend said too. She's been through it, remember?'

'I know, Vince, I know. But I'm not ready yet. I just can't!'.

'Then let's talk about it.'

'I'm sick of talking! I'm sick of going round in circles and I'm sick of it not making anything better and I'm – What the hell is that noise?'

They had heard the rumours, of course. They had dismissed them. This wasn't Brighton, after all. The idea of some great gang fight taking place in their small town was almost inconceivable. A lot of small talk by little boys with big opinions of themselves. And, sure enough, the morning had brought with it only a handful of strangers. A few leather-clad rockers hanging about outside the post office; a few mods in their smart suits and hats taking over Margaret's café.

Some of the grown-ups had got worked up about it anyway. Probably still smarting from the failure of their big dance idea two nights ago, still scandalised by the very existence of youth culture. They had walked the streets with stern expressions on their faces, to show they'd brook no trouble here. Deborah's mother had forbade her to leave the house, and there had been a blazing row. She was sixteen, she had insisted, and she could do as she liked. The words had tasted bitter on her tongue when all the time the baby was growing inside her. Such anger was uncharacteristic for her, but she couldn't have stood to be cooped up inside tonight.

This morning, a few strange faces in town hadn't seemed so many.

Tonight, twenty motorbikes were an unstoppable force as they roared down the main street towards Deborah.

Transfixed by their headlights, she didn't move until Vince appeared at her side, grabbed her hand and pulled hard. And then the spell was broken. She fell into his arms, spun around.

And saw a line of scooters turning into the road at its far end.

'It was as if it couldn't see us,' said Sandra, remembering those eyes, those big yellow eyes. 'It kept staring and it didn't blink, but it didn't react at all.'

'Sandra said something to it,' said Alec, 'but it didn't answer. It never spoke.'

'But there was this... this feeling inside my head.'

'I didn't feel that,'

'All the time.'

'I didn't feel it.'

'Like something buzzing in my brain.'

'Sandra decided to pick the alien up.'

Sandra nodded, remembering how sure she had been at that moment that she was doing the right thing. Now, though, she couldn't explain why. So, she said nothing.

'Then we got some water,' said Alec.

'Fresh water,' said Sandra. 'We tried sea water at first. We collected it in Ricky's bucket and sprinkled it over the alien, but it didn't like that.'

'It struggled and thrashed its arms, but it didn't make a sound.'

'We had to get fresh water.'

'We stayed with it for, oh, it must have been about an hour.'

'It was about twenty minutes.'

'Longer than that. And then...'

'Then...'

Sandra looked at Alec. He was already looking at her. She was lost for words. She couldn't describe how the sand had risen up around the alien creature to form a solid shape. It had looked as if the alien was pulling strings of metal from inside the very grains, without touching them, allowing unused material to crumble back to the ground. She had watched, unable to take her eyes off the incredible transformation even as she had staggered backwards in fear and reached out for Ricky, wherever he was.

The creature hadn't even moved.

Sandra looked at Alec. And, as they relived the indescribable past together, she felt more connected to him than she had done in years.

'Its flying saucer... dissolved,' Alec mumbled.

'Just sort of sank into the beach,' Sandra elaborated.

'And the beach...'

'...rose up around the alien.'

'Until it had turned into a *new* flying saucer.'

'Egg-shaped, like the first one.'

'And then there was that feeling again, the one we described.'

'Where the world just sort of seemed to blink out for a second.'

'And then it was gone. The creature, the saucer. Just gone.'

Another message came over the mods' loudspeaker system: another reminder of tomorrow morning's planned attack. Deborah greeted it with a sense of weary resignation, but noted the haunted look that flashed across Fitz's eyes. He'd get used to it, she thought.

'To help us relax before the big rumble,' said the announcer, 'our leader has decided we should hear some calming music.'

Her voice was replaced by the burbling, undulating sound of whale song. Fitz frowned, and Deborah smiled at him. 'It's not the Kinks or the Who, I know,' she said.

'I still don't know what you're fighting about,' said Fitz, as if he didn't want to go down that road. Deborah wondered what music was really like in the future. Surely not that electronic junk the rockers listened to?

'Because we're mods and –'

'They're rockers, yeah, I know. But there's got to be more to it. What are you hoping to gain? What do you actually disagree on?'

Vince gave a vague shrug. 'Lots of things.'

'Lots of petty little things,' said Deborah. 'Personality clashes, old family squabbles, arguments about who did what to whom in rumbles ten or fifteen years ago.'

'Like the wedding.'

'Yes, the wedding left a scar.'

'And sometimes the rockers just, you know, disagree with us for the sake of disagreeing.'

'Like, we use the city's machines to clothe us. We embrace its technology. They'd rather make their own clothes and spout off about being independent, out of stubbornness.'

'Fighting's become a way of life to them.'

'To all of us, really.'

'I suppose you're right.'

'That's why you can't be neutral,' said Deborah. 'In 1965, we weren't part of either gang. We stayed out of it.'

'We had better things to worry about.'

'At least, until that night when we got caught up in the middle of it all.'

'That's when we got, I don't know, scooped up with the rest of them and dropped here.'

'At first, it was all right. Everyone worked together. But it didn't take long for people to get bored and frustrated, then the old divisions opened up again.'

'We could just as easily have joined the rockers as the mods,' said Vince, lowering his voice as if afraid of being overheard.

'But we had to choose one,' said Deborah. 'One side or the other.'

Sandra did her best to ignore Ricky, who was pulling at her skirt and demanding to be read to and stomping about the house and, ultimately, crying ostentatiously when he didn't get his own way. She couldn't leave the window, even though she was looking at nothing. Nothing but the scarred brick wall and draped windows of the house opposite, the mundane sight that greeted her every day. She knew that her two older brothers were out there somewhere, and Alec, and she didn't know which of them she feared for the most.

She had been relieved, this morning, when her predictions and hopes had been proved right; when so few mods and rockers had arrived in the town. But her relief had dwindled throughout the day, as it had become clear that her brothers were spoiling for a fight anyway. And, if they fought, then Alec would too.

She kept hearing bikes and scooters through the darkening night. Mods and rockers prowled the streets, each side wanting to show the other how courageous they were; neither quite courageous enough to instigate a confrontation.

Her mother barged into the room, cigarette hanging from her mouth, arms full of washing. 'For God's sake, Sandra, will you read to Ricky? I can't do everything!'

'He should have learned to read for himself by now,' she snapped, unfairly.

'Sandra!'

She gave in gracelessly, propelling Ricky upstairs and into the bedroom that, despite her objections, they shared. He had already laid out a comic book for her, one she had read to him a hundred times before. As he settled on to his bed, she folded back the cover and looked at the first page: the stark image of a white, saucer-shaped object flying through space.

And she thought about the events of two nights ago, and the creature on the beach. The creature and the egg-shaped pod that had disappeared so suddenly, so completely, that it was hard to believe it had ever existed. She thought about how strange it had felt when real life, with all its momentarily forgotten worries and complications, had crashed back into place; how there had been nothing to do then but forget the bizarre interlude, which no one would have believed in any case, and get on with things.

She hadn't spoken to Alec since then. They hadn't discussed what they had seen. And Ricky wouldn't understand what had happened. He seemed to have forgotten all about it. But, ever since that night, Sandra had felt a weighty sense of foreboding and an emptiness in her stomach that hinted at the loss of something special.

'Come on, Sandra,' bleated Ricky. 'Story. I want a story.'

Her eyes had glazed over. The words in the speech bubbles meant nothing to her. A motorbike roared down the road, passing beneath the bedroom window, and she heard the angry shout of a neighbour. She dropped the comic book, pulled open the wardrobe door and snatched out her long overcoat.

It was a cold night.

Ricky protested loudly as Sandra marched out of the bedroom and down the stairs, but she wasn't listening. Her mother, boiling cabbage in the kitchen with the wireless turned up loud, didn't notice her until it was too late, and then Sandra cut off her futile shout by slamming the front door decisively behind her.

She plunged her hands into her pockets, set her lips into a straight line of determination, and set off to find Alec.

'So,' said the Doctor, finally, thoughtfully, 'you encountered a purple-grey being, humanoid, which communicated by telepathy or empathy and had the ability to extract elements from sand and telekinetically recombine and shape them into a vessel that could shift out of the fourth dimension.'

'That's right,' said Alec, nodding, although Sandra wondered if he had understood a word.

'Can you tell us what it might have been?' she asked eagerly.

The Doctor grinned cheerfully. 'I have absolutely no idea.'

'One minute we were looking for somewhere to hide,' said Deborah. 'The next, we were here in the city.'

'Surrounded by mods and rockers,' said Vince. 'It took them a minute to see what had happened and stop fighting, but then, well...'

'We didn't know where we were,' said Deborah.

'Except that we were clearly in the future.'

'And Alec and Sandra, they told us about the alien.'

'You know, like we told you.'

'So, we guessed he must have had something to do with it. He must have brought us here. We've never been able to work out why, though.'

'The city was empty,' recalled Sandra. 'It was just us.'

'It must have been the alien that brought us here, though, mustn't it?' said Alec.

The Doctor shrugged. 'Coincidences happen all the time.'

'I think I dreamt about the alien,' said Sandra, 'just before we arrived.'

'We call it the Maker,' said Alec, 'because of what we saw it do on the beach.'

'And you think it made the city?'

Alec looked at the Doctor blankly. 'No, it brought us to the future. Isn't that obvious?'

'We didn't know what year it was,' said Deborah.

'There was no one around, you know, to tell us,' said Vince.

'In the end, we picked a year for ourselves.'

'We knew we'd come way into the future, so we decided on 2000 AD.'

'And the day we arrived, we said that should be January the first.'

'That was when we were all still working together, at the beginning.'

'It's not like that now.'

'No, it isn't like that now at all.'

The Doctor had sat still for too long. Unfurling himself, he bounced to his feet and stretched his legs. 'So, what you're telling me is that this is Earth in the year 2019?'

'About then,' asserted Alec.

'Well, sometime in our future,' mumbled Sandra.

'And the city?'

'Well... this is what our cities will be like,' said Sandra, a pleading look in her eyes as if she needed to believe what she was saying.

'Is it indeed?' asked the Doctor, rhetorically.

'I mean, obviously we're a long way past 1965.'

'Obviously.'

'The city was built by an advanced, enlightened race.'

'In what would have been your lifetime?'

'I hope so. There must have been hundreds of cities like this once.'

'I see,' said the Doctor. 'And then?'

'There was a nuclear war,' said Alec. 'It's the only thing that makes sense. The bombs wiped out mankind and created those mutant camel things that live in the wasteland, but left the city standing. Well, it's made of space-age materials, ain't it?'

'I think the Maker brought us here to start again,' said Sandra. 'To repopulate Earth. Only we're not ready.' The Doctor raised an eyebrow, and Sandra elaborated: 'When we came here, we hadn't grown up. We hadn't built the city yet. We aren't ready to live in it. We still want our tellies and our music – and these blank walls, they drive us crazy.'

'The mods are tearing the city apart,' said Alec, gloomily.

'We all are,' said Sandra. 'It didn't matter until a couple of weeks ago. Whatever we threw at the Brain, it could cope. The servo-robots kept everything shiny and new. But now... now, we're doing too much damage, too quickly.'

'The molecular decay,' said the Doctor, nodding slowly.

'Everything's breaking down,' said Alec, 'and it *is* the mods' fault. How do you think they're getting all these weapons? They're tearing the city apart for its technology. And they've got to the Brain somehow, I know they have. What if they've broken it? What then?'

'They wouldn't go near the Brain,' said Sandra. 'They're not that stupid!'

'I can think of one person mad enough,' growled Alec. His wife shot him a venomous glare.

'This "Brain" of yours is an artificial intelligence, I assume,' said the Doctor, to distract the couple from their obvious differences. 'A controlling computer. Where is it?'

'In the central building,' said Alec. 'We can't get in there, but the servo-robots have told us all about it. They go in for maintenance work. The Brain controls the whole of the city.'

'But it's the one thing we agree on,' said Sandra. 'We don't touch the Brain. If that broke down, the food machines wouldn't work, there'd be no orders transmitted to the robots –'

'And no air to breathe,' said the Doctor. He clapped his hands together and paced up and down in the confined space, occasionally putting a hand to his mouth as thoughts chased each other through his mind. 'The key to this is the alien,' he said finally. 'We need to learn who he is, why he brought you here and why he wants you to believe that this is Earth.'

'You mean it isn't?' cried Sandra.

'Fitz Kreiner said it was,' Alec pointed out, suspiciously.

'Fitz lies under pressure, I'm afraid.'

'To be honest, Doctor,' sighed Alec. 'I don't care where we are, I just want to get away!'

'Well, I might be able to arrange that too,' said the Doctor distractedly, 'in time.'

'Are you serious?'

The Doctor remembered something, and stared at the hopeful Alec with a frown. 'I thought you had your own transport.'

'The space rockets, you mean?' Alec gave a derisive snort. 'They don't work.'

'Really? That wasn't my conclusion.'

'They'll blast off all right, but their engines cut out before they reach outer space.'

'Some sort of backup system kicks in,' said Sandra, 'and they drift back to Earth. Er… to the ground, I mean.'

'Some outside force, I wonder? Perhaps to do with the planet itself? You said there have been a few crashes here.'

'Like yours,' said Alec.

The Doctor smiled, seeing no reason to correct his host this time. 'Like mine, indeed.'

'So, you got married after you came here?' asked Fitz.

'There was no point,' said Deborah.

'No, no point,' agreed Vince, thinking about the last wedding in the city and what had happened in its wake. That was when he had realised that he could never take Deborah as his wife, never have a proper family, never get back the future he had expected for himself.

'Family doesn't mean much here, anyway.'

'We don't even use our surnames now,' said Vince.

'There's no need,' said Deborah. 'No two people have the same first name.'

'There were two Phils once, weren't there?'

'Yes,' said Deborah. 'There were, once.'

'But Davey was born in the city?' asked Fitz.

'It's the only world he knows,' confirmed Vince, wistfully.

And the only world that he had known too, for too long. All this talk of the past had made him nostalgic for his home, his time. As it always did. His parents hadn't even met their grandson. And the thought of facing Deborah's parents, of telling them about Davey, had long since been placed into perspective. It didn't terrify him any more.

'Until the future arrives,' said Deborah quietly.

'I don't get you,' said Fitz.

'The future. It's almost here. It must be, mustn't it? I mean, you're here.'

Fitz still looked puzzled, so Vince tried to explain. 'Deborah thinks – well, we both think, really – we've been brought here ahead of time.'

'And time will catch up to us,' said Deborah. 'It's got to.'

'The people of the future will, you know, appear.'

'It's got to,' said Deborah, a little more insistently, more desperately, this time. 'This can't be it for the rest of our lives, for ever. There's got to be something else.'

Fitz shifted uncomfortably, and Vince felt a pang of misery for Deborah, who had clung on to her fanciful hopes when everyone else had abandoned them. He took her hand and wished he could do more than just make gestures – wished he could actually protect her for once.

It was almost a relief when a Tannoy message interrupted them.

'Our leader is ready to meet the spaceman, Fitz Kreiner. Would somebody please direct him to the den?'

Alec ached with a familiar fear as control slipped further away from him. The course of his life was changing, and much as he railed against it there was nothing he could do. He looked at the Doctor, and saw at once both a wise old man who had come to make his future a happier one and a mischievous child who was mocking Alec, lying to him, usurping his control and breathing chaos into a life that, although hardly ideal, he had become accustomed to living.

Hopelessly, he tried to wrest back control, to guide his future towards a short-term goal that was small but knowable. 'So, you see why you've got to help us, don't you? You've got to be our Technician. Give us ray guns.'

The Doctor shook his head. 'I don't think so.'

'I can make you do what I want!' said Alec, belligerently.

'Please don't threaten me,' said the Doctor, not quite looking at him, as if he were thinking about three other things at once. 'You might force me to oppose you, and you really need my help too much to risk doing that.'

Had he just compared the Doctor to a child? It was Alec who felt like a child now, screaming at a world he couldn't affect. His authority had been challenged, and there wasn't a single rational thing he could do about it. His cheeks burned with embarrassment – and then with resentment at his wife's reproachful expression.

'What Alec means', said Sandra, as if he she thought him too stupid to speak for himself, 'is that the mods won't leave us alone. Now they've got the upper hand, they'll just keep attacking.'

'Ah, of course. There's a war to stop, isn't there?' The Doctor's eyes drifted far away. 'There's always a war. And I will help you to defend yourselves.' Suddenly alert again, he fixed Alec with a piercing stare that compelled him to believe this stranger, to trust him. 'But our most important task is to find out the truth about this place.'

Alec still felt the fear. He still remembered how his life had once been overturned. He knew in the pit of his stomach that it might happen again.

And he knew that, now as then, he would be helpless if it did.

Alec Redshaw couldn't see the future.

That had never mattered to him before. He was nineteen years old and, although his days were given over to drudgery, he had the freedom of the night: of a throbbing engine beneath him and the wind in his face; of a war to fight and a prize to win. All he knew about tomorrow was that things wouldn't be the same for him as they were for his parents now. His generation was changing this world for the better, and he was content with that.

But now, when his eyes were blind and his ears couldn't hear and he couldn't smell, touch or taste, the thing that scared Alec most was not knowing what would happen next. He saw himself barrelling through time, attempting the impossible task of charting a course around obstacles that he couldn't see coming. His past stretched behind him like the road just travelled, and he could hardly believe that, as clearly as he could visualise some parts of it, he couldn't revisit them, could never quite reach them.

He drifted alone in that dark and empty place, unable to protest or even scream, as something wormed its way into his mind and unearthed thoughts he had never examined before.

What will the future be like?

Sandra always went on about the future. When would Alec buckle down, work towards a promotion, learn to be responsible? She didn't understand. He wanted to live for today. Tomorrow would take care of itself, and it wouldn't involve his wearing a suit and dying behind the desk of a stuffy office.

She had found him with the gang, outside the petrol station, drinking beer from cans. Minutes ago now, or days? Either way, it was a moment he could not get back, never change. His mates had laughed and taunted him for letting some bird tell him off; worse still, some bird from a stuck-up mod family. Flushed, angry and drunk, he had sworn at Sandra. She had stood up to him, and the laughter had grown louder.

'I might have known I was wasting my time. When are you going to grow up, Alec? When someone gets maimed or killed? Well, don't run to me when that happens!'

She didn't understand why he had to fight. She had never experienced the adrenaline high that made it all worthwhile. She couldn't know how Alec Redshaw felt as he rode down the main street at the head of a score of rockers; as their enemies appeared in front of them; as he opened his throttle and shifted up a gear and clung on to his handlebars until his knuckles turned white; as his 200cc engine of destruction surged forward beneath him and a war cry that was one-third anger and two-thirds exhilaration erupted from his chest.

She didn't know what it was like to feel invincible.

'What are you all waiting for?' he had cried outside the petrol station, bravado masking his shame, his insecurity, his sadness at having watched Sandra walk off into the night. 'Are we gonna sort out those bloody ponces or what?'

And he remembered the headlights, boring into his mind, growing larger and brighter until all else was blotted out and he could see nothing but the circles of light.

Like eyes. Like the eyes of the creature on the beach.

It was at that moment that the fear had hit him. Fear that the mods were too close, that they weren't going to chicken out after all, that Sandra had been right and that he was about to be crippled or killed for so little reason. Fear of the future.

What will the future be like? came the question again now, somewhere inside him.

And for the first time in his life, Alec thought, really thought, about the answer.

Chapter Five
Through the Long Night

Fitz had begun to feel safe – if not exactly comfortable – with the mods. The odd loudspeaker reminder of tomorrow morning's rumble had worried him, but no one else seemed too concerned. It was a game to them, a ritual. They didn't expect serious casualties. And when they left, when the complex was empty, Fitz might get the chance to do some snooping, perhaps even get out of the city and find the Doctor. Or Compassion.

The mods' leader changed all that.

Vince and Deborah had taken Fitz to a small vestibule, at one end of which a set of double doors was guarded by no fewer than six uniformed mods. Davey had also been present, and pacing impatiently. With not even a grunt of acknowledgement towards his parents, he had whisked Fitz away from them. A guard had gripped Fitz's shoulder, spun him around and frisked him, so quickly and expertly that he had had no time to object. Then Davey had taken him through the doors, with two guards in tow.

The room in which Rick greeted Fitz was as sparse and grey as the rest of the complex. Even so, it had all the discomfiting hallmarks of a war room. Rick stood behind the head chair of a long metal table; Davey had to lead Fitz the length of it to reach him. An angular pattern had been scratched into the right-hand wall, taking up most of its surface. A plan of the city, Fitz realised. Painted red and black stars presumably marked the mods' and rockers' headquarters, although he couldn't tell which was which.

Rick was younger than Fitz had expected: early twenties, no more. A few years older than Davey. He must have been a child when he was brought here. He was Fitz's height, though. He wore the same silver uniform as his followers – clean and pressed as always – except that his sported prominent red shoulder flashes. His fair hair was severely cropped. There was a sense of pent-up energy about Rick, a feeling that, although the energy was under control, it was so plentiful that some of it had to leak out. It was something about the way he could never quite stand still: he adjusted his stance, folded his arms, cocked his head and then reversed every one of those actions. Even his expression wouldn't remain static. Muscles twitched beneath his skin, forever rearranging his thin lips. Rick's eyes darted around the room, even as he shook Fitz's hand. Those same eyes burned with an intensity that made Fitz wary of the mod leader despite his relative youth.

'Our pet spaceman, eh?' said Rick, his crooked smile twisting into a lascivious leer. 'Come to join our gang? I'm not surprised. Had a taste of rocker hospitality, have you? Savages, the lot of them. Cowards and savages! We'll sort them out tomorrow, eh, Davey?'

'You bet,' said Davey, with a dark grin. He pulled back a chair and dropped into it. Fitz wondered if he should do the same, but he felt somehow safer if he remained standing.

Rick was pacing up and down, hands clasped behind his back and then gesturing in front of him and then rubbing thoughtfully at his chin. His eyes never quite met Fitz's.

'With the guns and the new packs, they won't know what hit them,' boasted Rick. His hands performed an elaborate mime, which ended with his right fist slapping into his left palm to the accompaniment of an excited 'Boom!' Then suddenly he was facing Fitz again. 'And with our spaceman fighting for us too…'

Fitz found himself smiling politely, until his mind caught up to his ears, at which point his smile froze. By then Rick had turned away, denying him the opening he needed to speak. 'It'll serve that coward Alec right. It's been months since he's agreed to a proper rumble. Too scared of us, that's what it is. He's a sad old has-been and he knows it; he knows he can't win with that rabble he's got. Well, now we've got the power to smash our way into his HQ and take the rumble to him. Power from outer space!'

'Outer space?' echoed Davey.

Rick looked at him, a calculating gleam in his eye. 'Now, now, Davey, no fishing for clues. You know I'm keeping that little secret to myself.'

'But it's nothing to do with Fitz, is it?'

'No, I'm not talking about our spaceman.' Rick turned to Fitz again, as if seeing him for the first time. 'But I'm sure he'll be useful in other ways. What are you doing here?'

The question came so suddenly, so sharply, that Fitz almost jumped. He stumbled over the first few words of his answer, although it was well prepared. 'My ship crashed in the wastelands outside the city. Only two of us survived, and we got separated.'

'Your ship?'

Fitz thought for a moment, but couldn't work out what Rick was asking.

'What happened to your spaceship?' asked the mod leader, impatiently.

'I told you, it crashed. It was destroyed.'

'There must be something we can use. Components, weapons, engines, something.' The words came out like machine-gun fire.

'All burned up,' said Fitz, lamely. Rick was shrewder than Vince or Deborah. He made Fitz feel as if his lies were too obvious.

'I heard about your friend,' said Rick, turning away and beginning to pace again.

'Oh?'

'The rockers have him.'

'Oh.' That was better than the alternative.

'But we'll get him tomorrow. I'm making him our prime objective.'

'I wanted to talk to you about tomorrow.'

'What can you do?'

'Do?' Again, Fitz was nonplussed. Rick was turning out to be as bad as the Doctor for sudden changes of subject.

'Are you an inventor? A scientist? A doctor? You can fly a rocket ship, can't you? And you must know how to use space weapons.'

'I can play the guitar,' said Fitz, heavily. Rick glowered at him, so he added quickly, 'Things have moved on since the city was built. Almost everything's computerised now. You don't need to do much more than punch a few buttons. Er… I can probably use your ray guns, though. They're pretty advanced, aren't they?'

'We'll try you on the practice targets sometime,' said Rick, seeming bored with the whole conversation now. 'Just two of you, you say?'

'Just two of us.'

'You know what I'd like, spaceman?' Fitz didn't, but he didn't have time to say so. 'A lie detector!' said Rick, pronouncing the words with relish. 'I could question our prisoners, find out about the rockers' plans. That'd be cool, wouldn't it? Can you build me one?'

Rick looked at Fitz with an expression of childish longing. It disappeared as Fitz said, bluntly, 'No.'

'But you do have lie detectors in outer space? Of course you have. Well, never mind. I'll get one sooner or later. You can fight with the troops.'

'I'm not really a fighter,' said Fitz, apologetically. 'On my world, we've, er…' Oh, what the hell, he thought, go for it. 'We've eliminated war.'

'So will we,' said Rick, 'when we win.'

'I'd be more use to you as a tactician. Or a diplomat. Let me go to Alec and talk to him. I'll say I'm just there to get my friend back, but I'm sure I can get him to agree –'

'We don't need to talk,' said Rick. 'We can cream him! Look at what happened in the trial run today. Our side were all over the rockers. They only went there to protest about Davey's kidnap,

76

but they managed to get him back! And I've made my plans already. The only thing I could do with is more men up front. The more, the better.'

'Cannon fodder,' mumbled Fitz.

Rick ignored him. 'Get your hair cut before the fight. And shave. You look like a dirty rocker!' He grinned suddenly. 'If you're fighting with us, we don't want to kill you by accident. Briefing's at 0700 tomorrow morning. Now get out. I want to talk to Davey.'

'Right,' mumbled Fitz, overwhelmed. 'OK.'

'You know where your quarters are, don't you?' said Davey.

Fitz nodded and hurried out of the room, longing to put the double doors between him and Rick. He was beginning to wish he had just stayed put with his original captors.

'What do you think?' asked Rick, after the doors had slid shut behind Fitz Kreiner.

Davey shrugged nonchalantly. 'Decent enough bloke. He helped me against the rockers.'

'He was lying about his spaceship.'

'Why do you think that?'

'They always lie,' said Rick fiercely. 'They don't want us to get our hands on what they've got; to be as good as them. But we *are* as good as them. We deserve their technology. We've got some stuff now, but it's not enough. There's got to be more. I know there's more.'

'What do you want me to do?'

'Find it.'

'He was probably right, you know. It probably was destroyed. They usually are.'

'I want you to make sure.'

'OK. I'll take a few men out after the rumble and –'

'No. Do it now! The rockers have the spaceman's friend. They'll find out about the spaceship too. What if Alec gets to it first?'

'They're still using that Gillian bird as their Technician, aren't they? I can't see her being able to do anything about it.'

'Fitz Kreiner survived the crash. His spaceship might still work. Or the other spaceman might be able to fix it. If Alec gets his hands on something like that, he'll probably pile all the rockers into it and blast off away from here.'

'Good riddance,' said Davey.

He started as Rick fairly exploded. His eyes flashed violently and he drove both fists down on to the table. 'No! I won't let it happen. I won't let them leave. They'll ruin everything we've got here, everything I've built!'

Davey enjoyed his position as Rick's favoured lieutenant, but sometimes the older man scared him. 'OK, OK, if that's how you feel,' he said, 'I'll get working on it right away.'

But Rick didn't seem to hear him. He had turned his back, and his shoulders were shaking. His fists were still clenched. 'I won't go back to that,' he swore to himself in a low, trembling voice. 'I won't go back!'

With the advent of night, the supercomputer that controlled the city activated its lights. They shone from windows that had once been dark, and from globes atop the spires that supported the elevated roadways. The metal buildings were bathed in a stark halogen glow.

The moon, though, was obscured by clouds, and as Davey left the city with three members of the First Battalion – his battalion – darkness closed in around him. He didn't like travelling out of the city at night, but he did as he was told. He felt an unreasoning fear as the fresh, air-conditioned scent of home gave way to the unpleasant peat odour of the wasteland, and he tried to draw comfort from the glow of headlights that travelled with the four scooters.

He frowned as those lights picked out the shape of a woman. What was she doing here, alone, so far from civilisation? It was dangerous, and not only because of the cannibals. Without the city's heating systems, she risked hypothermia – and, as Davey steered towards her, he became aware of the effort that was now required for him to breathe.

He didn't need to say anything to his men. They followed without question. Davey drew a quiet satisfaction from that. The three mods were each a good sixteen years or more older than he – but, with Rick as their leader, youth had become a prized commodity. As one of the few youngsters in the city, younger even than Rick himself, Davey had become an important person. He liked that. He liked that a lot.

Sometimes the grown-ups talked about the small town, the small life, from which the Maker had snatched them. Many of them longed to return to that life. They wanted to leave the city behind. But this was Davey's home. *His* life. He would never leave it.

He could see the woman clearly now. She was young – but she looked a few years older than he was, so that was all right: she was no threat. She had red hair, tied into a ponytail, and freckles. He hadn't met many girls near his own age. He found himself staring at this one, wondering what she might look like if she lost a bit of weight or swapped her jeans and baggy sweater for a tight-fitting mod uniform. He shook such thoughts from his head. There were more important things in life than girls.

He braked sharply and banked his scooter into an impressive skid, stopping at her feet. She didn't flinch. She didn't even acknowledge him, although she was looking right at him.

'You don't look like any cannibal I know,' he said brightly.

The woman didn't respond. Davey felt a flush of anger. Bad enough that she was ignoring him, but in front of the others… 'Who are you?' he asked, his tone less friendly. 'What are you doing here? Can you hear me?'

'Deaf, dumb and blind,' commented one of the mods behind him.

'Have you come down from outer space?' asked Davey, loudly

and slowly, as if trying to get through to an idiot. He waved a hand before the woman's eyes. 'Did you travel with Fitz Kreiner?' He turned to the others, hoping to make it seem like he was still in control. 'She did. She came with Fitz, she must have done. It's too much of a coincidence otherwise. He lied to us. He thinks he can make a fool out of me!'

Davey's anger grew as he spoke, as he convinced himself that he had been betrayed. He felt a familiar pressure building in his chest, spreading to his shoulders and down his arms to make his fists clench spasmodically. He rounded on the woman again, and seized her arm roughly. 'You're coming with me. We'll see what Rick's got to say about you.'

'No,' she said.

That was all. Just one word. But it took Davey by surprise, almost making him jump. The woman was looking at him properly now, and he was drawn into her eyes. He felt as if he were drifting, the hard ground receding beneath him as he hovered on the periphery of a place so vast as to defy the senses. He felt small and insignificant and frightened.

He blinked and concentrated, and felt the world settle back into place around him as the anger took over again and drove out all other concerns.

He tightened his grip and tried to drag the woman to his scooter. Instantly, what felt like an electric charge passed into him and he cried out, snatching his hand away. Reacting to the humiliation more than to the minimal pain, he snarled and tried to take hold of the woman again with both hands. To his irritation, he couldn't. It was as if an invisible shield had sprung up around her, except that it didn't feel like a physical object as such. He simply couldn't bring himself to touch her.

'Help me with her,' he ordered. Hoping to make it clear that he wouldn't need such help normally, he added, 'She's got some weird kind of Martian powers.'

The other mods closed in around the woman – and, if they were laughing at Davey as he suspected, then they soon stopped. They must have experienced the same effect as he had, for they couldn't lay their hands on her either. And what was worse, in Davey's view, was that the woman just stared into the distance as if she didn't care about him or the others at all. As if they didn't matter.

He had had enough. He had not ventured out of the city unarmed, and it was time to employ the first of his two weapons. Reaching beneath the sunken saddle of his scooter, he retrieved a lovingly carved stout club and tossed it, with deliberate casualness, to one of the others. 'Here – see if this gets her attention!' He stood back and watched as the mod first waved the club beneath the woman's nose and uttered the usual threats and then, when she failed to respond, swung the weapon to deliver a punishing blow to her side.

The club bounced off the invisible obstacle and flew out of his hands.

Furiously, Davey reached into his pocket for the second weapon: the ray gun that Rick had entrusted to him for emergencies. He aimed it at the woman's legs and fired. The gun's bright yellow beam ripped through the air, but dispersed into a harmless glow without reaching her. A feral snarl rattled in Davey's throat as he repositioned his hand on the gun butt, looking for the button that would fire it at its highest setting. He never got the chance to press it.

A terrible pain stabbed into his head, and with it a tremendous sadness. The whole of his life was rammed into his brain and he saw that he had never done, would never do, anything that mattered. He was like a puppet, going through life without ever making a decision, or having an idea, of his own. He felt small again, like when he had looked into the woman's eyes, only this time it was a million times worse and the feeling wouldn't go away.

Until, at last, Davey's mind took pity on him and switched itself off.

* * *

Compassion looked at the four bodies that lay around her. Male. Human. Three in their mid-thirties; one younger, perhaps twenty. She hadn't meant to hurt them. Sensing their attack upon her, she had simply reached out to communicate with them. She should have known better. She had shown them a fraction of what she was experiencing, and it had overloaded their brains. However, they would recover.

It took a surprising amount of effort to concentrate upon the physical plane. It was strange to recall how she had once existed entirely within the confines of these three dimensions. It felt as if she had not visited this place for a long time, although her internal chronometer told her that that wasn't true. Perhaps she simply didn't belong here any more. She longed to leave again, to reimmerse herself in the glorious cosmos. But something kept her here. A nagging memory of friendship.

And something else.

Compassion turned slowly, scanning her surroundings, reacquainting herself with the process of garnering information through five limited senses. Another memory, a stray fact retrieved from a datastream many millions of gigabytes wide, told her that the Doctor had promised not to be gone long. He and Fitz had left ten hours, forty-three minutes and twenty-seven seconds ago. An emotion swam to the surface, and Compassion was distantly alarmed at the thought that it had remained buried for so long. She was worried about them.

She regarded the shining beacons of the distant city, running the image through her memory banks but coming up with no match. She decided to take a closer look, but her Randomiser precluded accurate travel through the vortex. It took her a few seconds to remember how to walk, then she willed her legs to carry her forward and they did so, jerkily.

Slowly at first, but gathering speed and breaking into a sure-footed run as she settled back into an old habit, Compassion approached the strange city.

* * *

The Doctor stepped back from the bench and frowned as he inspected his work. A tangle of silver wires protruded from the old record player that he had found amid the assorted junk in the laboratory. It was crude, but it would have to do. Many times throughout the evening and night, he had wished for the facilities of his own lab inside the TARDIS. Or rather, he had corrected himself, inside Compassion. But he had not wanted to give away any more of his secrets, so he had resolved to make do with what he had been given.

He looked at the small pile of square, silver vinyl records that he had taken from the player's spindle. Tutting and smiling indulgently, he pushed them aside.

Gillian was still perched on her stool, the innards of the ray gun spread in front of her. Even from here, the Doctor could see she had damaged some components beyond repair. She had been no more polite to him since they had both returned to the lab. However, Alec had talked to her, and she seemed resigned to letting her new colleague get on with things, at least. Her eyes were closed and, as the Doctor watched, her body sagged and her fingers fell open, releasing the weapon's plastic casing. The Doctor was there before it hit the floor.

Gillian jerked awake to find him crouching beside her, the gutted gun in his hand.

'What are you doing with that?' she cried.

'There's nothing anyone *can* do with it now,' he retorted.

Gillian snatched the gun from his grasp and turned away from him, picking a component from the bench at random and fumbling to slot it back into position. 'Just leave me alone!'

'I didn't mean to disturb you,' said the Doctor. 'I thought you needed the rest.'

'I'm OK.'

'I don't think that's true.'

'Didn't you know? Bags under the eyes are the latest fashion.'

'Didn't *you* know? The human brain requires sleep.'

'Are you joking? The mods are miles ahead of us. They could

attack any day!'

'Well, you're in no state to do anything about that – and neither is that gun.'

Gillian rounded on him furiously. 'I'm doing the best I can!' she screamed.

The words hung between them for a long moment. Gillian controlled her breathing and avoided the Doctor's eyes.

'I didn't say you weren't,' he said finally, 'but we don't want another accident, do we?'

'I told you,' mumbled Gillian, less angry now, more embarrassed, 'I'm OK.'

'Yes, so I see,' said the Doctor, gazing at the palm of her right hand and seeing no sign of the burn she had suffered earlier. 'Your medical facilities must be quite advanced. In fact, you have some interesting technology here. Quite a mismatch.' Gillian had turned away again, but he kept on talking to her back. 'You must be finding it difficult. Alec's putting a lot of pressure on you. A war to fight, and nobody else understands the city's systems. How long have you been doing this job anyway?'

Gillian shrugged awkwardly. 'Not long. I was working with Greg, our last Technician. The mods got him about a month ago.'

'Leaving you to pick up the pieces,' said the Doctor, sympathetically.

'I'm quite capable.'

'I'm sure you are, given time. You strike me as a bright girl.'

'Don't patronise me. I'm way behind the mods!'

'So, what's wrong with accepting help? I do have some experience in this field, you know.' Gillian looked at the Doctor suspiciously, and he responded with his best pixie smile. 'Don't worry, I won't be staying long anyway. As far as I'm concerned, you're still the Technician here. Just think of me as an adviser.'

Gillian's features softened slightly. She stepped aside, indicated the components of the ray gun and spoke in a tone that was only partly conciliatory. 'OK, so advise me on that.'

'I'm afraid that's quite beyond either of our skills to repair.' Before Gillian could interject, the Doctor swept cheerfully across the room. 'Don't blame yourself, though: you don't have the materials to duplicate it anyway. No, the first rule of science is to learn to work with what you've got. For example, I found a rather useful piece of equipment over here.'

'That old record player?' said Gillian sceptically, as she joined him at the next bench.

'You can accomplish an awful lot with harmonics, you know. Allow me to demonstrate.' With a flourish, the Doctor twisted the knob that ought to have turned the device on. The power light came on, but nothing else happened.

Gillian folded her arms. 'Well, what are you planning to do? Bore the mods to death?'

'Patience, Gillian,' said the Doctor, belying his own advice by leaning over the player and plunging his hand into its exposed wiring. 'Come on, come on, come on...' he coaxed it.

'They don't appreciate decent music anyway,' said Gillian, facetiously.

Locating the problem, the Doctor twisted the bare ends of two wires together. A burst of static emerged from the player's primitive in-built speaker, followed by a low humming sound. He stepped back, satisfied. 'As I told you, you can do an awful lot with harmonics. What do you think?'

'Not much,' said Gillian, stifling a yawn. 'What's it supposed to do, anyway?'

She slurred the last word, as her eyelids fell and she crumpled into the Doctor's waiting arms. 'There's your answer,' he said softly, using his elbow to clear a space for her on the next bench and not caring where its contents landed. 'Sound asleep,' he commented, grimacing at his own pun. He laid her down gently, and smiled at her sheepishly. 'I'm sorry,' he said, 'but I really think it's for your own good. You'll thank me in the morning.'

He turned back to his humming contraption, and took a deep

breath. 'Now,' he said to it, 'I just have to find a way to increase your range a hundredfold.'

Late as it was, Davey reported to Rick's den immediately upon his return to the complex. He knew it would be expected. And, indeed, Rick was still up and waiting for him. If the mods' leader ever slept at all, then Davey had never worked out when.

He had steeled himself to face Rick's wrath. Throughout the miserable ride home, he had thought about what he could say, how he could justify his failure. He had thought of all the times he had seen his leader's icy rage, and had alternated between fear of seeing it again and the more familiar sensation of bitterness. Rick never understood, never cared that his people did their best for him. He was like a child: if he didn't get what he wanted, then he didn't ask the reason why, he just threw a tantrum. Davey would have to take it, of course, if he wanted to climb higher in the gang. The unfairness of that burned inside him.

But something was different this time.

Rick greeted Davey sitting down, which was unusual in itself. He wasn't exactly sitting still, of course – but, by his usual standards, he was positively subdued. As Davey told his unfortunate tale, Rick regarded him through hooded eyes. Those eyes flashed dangerously at Davey's confession that he and his men had woken to find the mysterious woman gone; that, though they had searched the plain and the outskirts of the city, they had not found her.

But the predicted tantrum didn't come. Rick simply gave a curt nod, as if he had just been brought a weather forecast. His uncharacteristic calmness was disconcerting. At least when Rick was hurling blame at everyone else, he was predictable. Now Davey didn't know what he was thinking, didn't know if or when the bomb would drop.

'What do you want me to do?' he prompted, hoping for a clue. 'I could go back out there.'

'No,' said Rick.

'No? But –'

'I don't want you to do anything. It'll keep for now.'

Davey longed to contradict that statement, but he thought it best just to appreciate his good fortune.

'Do you know what time it is?' asked Rick. Davey shook his head. 'The briefing's in two and a half hours. You'd better get some sleep. I'll need you.'

'You're still going ahead with the attack?'

'Of course we are!' snapped Rick, and a trace of his usual fire returned. 'So, there's some Martian bird walking round out there. So what? All the aliens in the universe can land here for all I care. It won't matter – not once we've sorted out those greasers once and for all!'

Fitz spent most of the night wandering the mods' part of the underground complex. Everyone else was asleep, so he could feel like a superspy as he sneaked into room after room – those that weren't marked as private accommodation, of course – and tried to memorise their layout. He passed a couple of servo-robots, which seemed to be buffing the corridor floors with the soles of their feet. A third was working on the unreliable dresser; Fitz watched it for a while, fascinated, as it performed its task efficiently despite the handicaps of its rigid arms and clamplike hands.

Finding himself at the foot of the antigrav tube, he inspected the wall-mounted control panel and wondered if he had the courage to try it. Could escape really be so easy? He wandered beneath the circular opening in the ceiling, looking for signs of light above, and suddenly the choice was taken from him. He almost cried out as he was snatched from his feet, but his voice was stolen. Seconds later, he landed suddenly but impossibly gently beside the hole in the room above, his momentum cancelled as it had been on his way down.

He peered out of the room to see that the opposite door,

which led into the café, was ajar. He could make out shapes through it, and hear the low mutterings of mods discussing the upcoming rumble. Somebody was playing a pinball machine, and its electronic whoops and the clacks of its flippers drowned out most of the conversation.

Fitz made a cursory search for a back door out of the building – until he heard a voice growing louder and footsteps coming towards him, at which point he raced back to the antigrav tube and threw himself into it, electing to resume his explorations below.

Having expected to find a miraculous labour-saving device behind every door, Fitz was increasingly disappointed. Most of the rooms were bare, or contained nothing beyond a few chairs. He did find what looked like a row of shower cubicles in a large rectangular area but, when he experimented with the controls of one, nothing seemed to happen. After a few more tries, he realised that a low humming sound was coming from what should, by rights, have been the shower head. He held a tentative hand beneath it, and watched curiously as a thin layer of dirt peeled away from his palm, hovered in midair and then disintegrated.

Feeling grimy and sweaty, he thought about taking full advantage of his find. But, after a few minutes, he concluded that he had no idea how to remove his mod uniform. He contented himself with letting the device do its work on his other hand, and then on his face. But the sensation was nothing compared with the refreshing feel of water for which he had hoped, and Fitz left the room disappointed.

He took another daring trip to the surface, but the café showed no signs of emptying. He returned instead to his quarters. He was deeply weary. He didn't know how long he had until Rick's briefing, but he did know he had to get some sleep at least. On the wall behind his bed, he found a dial that dimmed the ever-present light without giving any clues to its source.

However, the combination of a solid metal bed and a mind made overactive by worry conspired to keep Fitz awake. Using his arms as a pillow and studiously trying to think of nothing, he did eventually doze off, but woke again in a few minutes. So it seemed, anyway: it was impossible to know for sure in the timeless night-light of the small room. His muscles ached down one side, and his neck and shoulders were stiff.

He turned over, wondered blearily how the mods coped with such discomfort, and opened his eyes again to find the room fully lit and Davey standing over him, shaking him.

'What's wrong with you?' hissed the young man. Fitz worked his mouth, but only a confused grunt emerged from his fuzzy vocal chords. 'Didn't you hear the alarm?'

He searched his befuddled mind, and found a vague memory of a squawking noise like a cat in distress. He didn't know how it had got there. 'Sort of,' he mumbled, levering his sore body into a sitting position and rubbing his heavy eyes. His mod uniform was still clean and without creases. 'Must've gone back to sleep.'

'You look like crap,' said Davey.

'Only just got off,' mumbled Fitz. 'I couldn't get comfortable.'

'I'm not surprised. Was your gravity mattress on the fritz or what?'

Davey reached under the bed and flicked a switch. Fitz felt himself rising, as if something was inflating beneath him, until he was bobbing on a cushion of air. He concealed a rueful scowl. 'I've got a bad back,' he lied. 'I thought I'd be better off on a flat surface.'

'You're missing the briefing,' said Davey. 'Rick'll kill you!'

A jolt of fear did more to wake Fitz than any of his own efforts thus far. 'What, literally?'

Davey frowned. 'No, of course not. We're not rocker savages!'

'Oh. Right.'

'But he might break your legs if you don't get moving. Come on, will you?'

Fitz didn't know if that was a joke or not, but he chose not to find out. Instead, he followed Davey as he hurried out of the room. It wasn't easy, though. Apart from his tiredness, his legs felt like lead and his every nerve screamed at him to turn and run.

This didn't feel real. It still seemed like only minutes ago that the morning had been a long time away and Fitz had been able to comfort himself with vague plans and hopes. Now, suddenly, it was upon him and all his plans seemed threadbare and useless. He felt as if he had been robbed of time, and his empty stomach groaned with the knowledge that he could not get out of being sent into battle.

Gloomily, Fitz wondered which of the warring gangs was the more likely to kill him first.

Chapter Six
Get Ready to Rumble

A saucer-shaped aircar lay, gutted and burned out, in the street below.

Fitz looked down at it from the elevated roadway, his vertigo momentarily giving way to strange feelings of nostalgia and regret. The abandoned vehicle seemed to symbolise the plight of the city: a glorious future, deemed ultimately disappointing and left to rot. Then Davey banked his scooter to negotiate a sharp right-hand bend, and Fitz closed his eyes, held on tight and worried about his own plight instead.

He had missed the briefing. In some ways, that was probably a good thing. Rick had had a bloodthirsty gleam in his eye, and Fitz was not sorry to have been spared thirty minutes of his manic posturing. Even the few seconds he had spent with the mods' leader had made his nerves itch. 'You're late,' Rick had said, 'and you've not done as I told you. You still look like a rocker!' Fitz had run a hand over his stubbly chin, self-consciously. Already marching away, Rick had added, 'Davey will fill in you in. We'll discuss your punishment later.'

Later, Fitz had thought, you won't find me anywhere near you. But even now, his long-considered escape plan boiled down to a desperate hope that he would find the Doctor at the rockers' headquarters and that he would be able to do something.

Not that Rick's plan was any more complex, despite his pretence at military organisation and precision. The mods were going to break into the rockers' malt shop, catch them unawares as they slept and beat them up. Or shoot them. There were only a few ray guns, and they had been given to the First Battalion – Davey's battalion – with which Fitz was riding. He didn't have a gun, though. He wasn't trusted. Not that it bothered him. He didn't want to hurt anyone, and a gun would only give the rockers an excuse to hurt him. Davey had given him a stout club instead, carved from the black wood of the thin trees out on the plain.

Rick had taken four members of the Third Battalion aside, apparently to kit them out with a new piece of technology. Fitz didn't know what it was. Nor did Davey. 'I don't know where he's getting any of this stuff from,' the young mod had confessed, as he had taken Fitz into the mods' extensive ground-level garage and the pair had mounted his scooter. He had said little more than that. In fact he had been short with Fitz all morning, as if he was annoyed with him. Surely it couldn't just be because he had overslept? There was no time to find out, before Davey guided the scooter out on to the road and the rush of wind in Fitz's ears made conversation impossible.

When Davey's friend Jono had taken an injured Fitz to the mods' café yesterday, the journey had seemed to take forever. Now that Fitz made it in reverse, as part of a force of mods almost forty strong – many eager for battle, some like him just keeping their heads down and doing what Rick told them – it seemed to be over in seconds. He didn't recognise the nondescript building at first but, as it drew closer, the scorch marks left by yesterday's 'trial run' gave it away. A few of the mods let out gleeful war cries and did something to their scooters that was analogous to gunning the throttles.

Standing by the road, a green servo-robot turned its rigid body to follow their course.

For the second day in a row, Alec was woken too early by the squealing attention call of his attendant robot. He levered himself into a sitting position, the tail end of a dream receding from his mind, confusing him so that he didn't know where he was at first. Sandra groaned, rolled over and stole the blanket from him, burying herself beneath it.

'I do apologise for disturbing you, sir, but the perimeter alarm has been activated.'

Alec grunted something unintelligible as his brain struggled to process the robot's words, his senses reaching out for information that would bring some order to his world. 'What time is it?' he murmured blearily.

'The time is seven forty-three, sir.'

'What the hell's going on?'

He managed to focus upon the servo-robot's yellow eye-strip. As the only source of light in the room – the door was open, but the corridor beyond was equally dark – it seemed to hover eerily in midair. As usual, beads of brighter light darted across the strip as the robot spoke. 'As I said, sir, the perimeter alarm has been activated.'

This time, the words registered. Alec felt a stab of fear. 'Intruders?'

'I can show you if you wish, sir.'

'Yes, yes, get on with it, then.'

The robot's chest screen flared into life, casting a grey light across the bed and making Sandra flinch, even beneath her cover. 'This picture was recorded one point two minutes ago, sir,' said the robot. Alec squinted to make out the details, and felt cold prickles on his skin at the sight of literally dozens of mods descending upon the milk bar.

'What does he think he's doing?' he cried. 'Sandra, Sandra, wake up! Your idiot brother's attacking us!' Sandra stuck her head out from beneath the blanket. By this time, Alec was already on his feet, propelled by sheer terror, reaching for his clothes.

He had known this day would come. As much as he had tried to convince himself otherwise, he had known exactly what Rick would do once it became clear that his side was winning the arms race. Had their positions been reversed, Alec would have done the same. Even so, now that the day had finally come, it felt unreal, as if it couldn't possibly be happening.

'Robot, sound the red alert!' rapped Alec, appalled with himself for leaving that order so late. His mind was disorganised;

the plans he had made for just this situation had deserted him. 'And send a message up top. Tell the guards not to fight back, just to barricade the door until reinforcements get there.'

As the alarm siren started up, the lights came on, so suddenly that Alec had to blink stars out of his eyes. Sandra was fully awake now, her hand still on the light switch, a worried expression on her face. 'You think they're trying to break in?'

'Why else do you think they're attacking this early? They're not calling us out like yesterday. This is a raid! They want to catch us all asleep.'

'They won't get down here, will they?'

'Not if I have anything to say about it.'

Grimly, Alec reached for his old leather jacket.

Gillian dreamt that she had failed in her duty. She had slept instead of working, and now it was too late. A red alert had been sounded, catching her unprepared. In the dream, Alec was berating her, blaming her for the rockers' downfall, and she was crying and scared. She felt she ought to be doing something, anything, but she didn't know what. Propelled by this sense of urgency, she dragged herself to the surface of sleep, only to find her stomach turning with dread as she realised that some of the dream was true; that the persistent wailing of the alert siren, for one thing, was real.

'What did you do to me?' she cried, scrambling off the lab bench and on to her feet.

The Doctor was working on the record player at the next bench, as before. He turned and beamed at her. 'Ah, you're awake. Good, good. I took the liberty of ordering a cooked breakfast and coffee. Unfortunately, we got vitamin tablets and protein shakes instead. I'll have to do something about that.'

Gillian ignored the unappetising meal, which sat on a metal tray beside her. 'Have you got cotton wool in your ears or something? Can't you hear what's happening?'

The Doctor frowned and cocked his head, as if listening

intently. Then his face lit up with realisation. 'Oh, you mean the alarm.'

'Well, I can't hear much else. Can you?'

'That rather depends what you're listening for. What does it mean?'

'It's a red-alert siren.'

'But specifically?'

'We're probably under attack.'

'Probably?' The Doctor looked around the lab, with a thoughtful expression. 'You need a better communications system.'

His indifference annoyed Gillian; so too did the knowledge that she had always meant to fix the loudspeakers in the rockers' living quarters. Other tasks had always seemed more important. 'What we need', she said acidly, 'is weapons. The mods have got guns. They'll kill us! And you – you did something to knock me out, when I needed to work!' Frustrated, she pounded on his arm with both fists. The Doctor simply reached out and took her wrists, holding tightly until she gave up and backed off. 'It's too late!' she cried. 'We're defenceless, and it's all your fault!'

'It looks like I was wrong,' said the Doctor, contritely.

'What?' said Gillian, deflated.

'I thought you'd thank me. Never mind, I don't think a few hours would have made much difference, do you? And besides, being without weapons is not the same thing as being defenceless. Here, you can help me with this if you like.'

Gillian frowned and looked past him. 'What, that old record player?'

'I'm afraid it doesn't play records any more,' said the Doctor, almost guiltily. Then his demeanour changed in an instant, and he began to lecture her like one of her old teachers. 'However, it does still produce sound – in this case, low-frequency vibrations that have a tranquillising effect upon the human mind.'

'What are you talking about?'

'It puts people to sleep. Well, it will do.'

'That's what you used on me!' The realisation made Gillian look at her unwanted assistant in a different way. Before, this strange, irritating man with his ancient clothes and his patronising words had seemed more of a clown than a Technician. Now, as the alert siren echoed through her head, he became her only hope. A desperate hope, she told herself. He would have to be a miracle-worker. Even so, she found herself drawn to his side to inspect his night's work, towards which he directed her with an eager, childlike grin.

And she felt bitterly disappointed when she saw exactly what she had seen last night: a record player with its innards hanging out.

Her accusing glare must have said it all, because the Doctor's face fell and he said, 'Well, it isn't quite finished yet, of course.'

'Then it's useless,' retorted Gillian. 'We've run out of time!'

The Doctor sighed heavily, and a distant look crossed his face. 'Time, always time. I always seem to arrive at the last minute. Time running out, things coming to a head...' He snapped himself out of it, clapped his hands enthusiastically and threw himself back into his work. 'Still, it makes life interesting, don't you think? Now, the device worked on you, but then you were standing right next to it and you were tired anyway. I've increased the gain since then, but I seem to have blown out the capacitor. I don't suppose you could have a hunt around, see what you can come up with?' He swung round to face her again, and his eyebrows were raised in an expression of hopeless optimism.

Whether it was because he had won her over or because she simply didn't have any better ideas, she didn't know, but Gillian found herself doing as he asked.

First, some of the mods with ray guns blasted the door of the milk bar. Under a concentrated onslaught, the metal buckled and blackened, but didn't give. Rick ordered an end to the firing.

'Save your shots for the rockers!' With a curt hand signal, he brought three of his followers forward, and they set about the weakened door with boots and clubs instead. 'Come out and fight, you yellow scum!' yelled Rick at the building. This seemed to excite the other mods, and they joined in with taunts of 'Cowards!' and 'Greasers!'

Catching sight of Vince and Deborah, Fitz took a step towards them gratefully. Then he saw that they were shouting as loudly and enthusiastically as anyone. He felt horribly alone.

'I know you can hear me, Alec!' screamed Rick. 'Come on, show your face if you dare!'

Fitz stood in the middle of the crowd and waved his club half-heartedly, trying not to look as if he'd rather be anywhere else. He eyed Davey's scooter longingly, and thought he could remember which buttons to push to start it. But he was surrounded, he wasn't sure how to get back to Compassion, and the Doctor was probably inside the rockers' headquarters anyway.

The door gave way with a crash, and the mods surged towards it with a triumphant roar. Fitz tried to look like he was moving with them, when he was actually letting them pass him. But Davey gripped the shoulder of his tunic and pulled him forward. 'Come on, I'll keep an eye on you!' promised the young mod. Fitz hoped he meant that in a reassuring way. It had sounded a bit like a threat.

There must have been sentries inside the milk bar, for the mods' progress was halted. As three or four mods presumably fought inside, the rest clustered around the entrance, the nearest of them shouting encouragement to their colleagues within. The lithe Davey slipped through the crowd easily, but always stopped to make sure that Fitz was keeping up.

The mods inside must have won their battle, for suddenly everyone was moving forward again. Fitz was alarmed at just how quickly, thanks to Davey, he reached the door. Stumbling over the threshold, he found the milk bar already heaving with bodies. The rockers had fallen back to the far end of the room, but there were at least a dozen of them, and more were arriving all the time through the inner door. The room was too narrow for the attackers to use their advantage of numbers, with many mods unable even to get near a rocker. Conversely, no rockers were able to get near Fitz, which was something. But, as more mods jostled to get into the building behind him, he knew he was trapped and he began to feel claustrophobic.

Davey left him alone now, at least. He struggled towards the mods' front line, his expression twisted by fanatical hatred, which made Fitz realise that this was what the boy lived for. Rick was near the front too; he had drawn a ray gun and, like some of his followers, was firing into the mêlée whenever he could get a clear shot. In contrast to Davey's anger, he laughed with youthful exuberance. The sound brought a chill to Fitz's bones.

The rockers soon realised that too many of them were being downed by the ray guns. Joining arms, a group of four put their heads down and waded into the mods, breaking through to one of the armed men and barging him into a booth. As their victim fell backwards over the table, a rocker stole his weapon and began to fire it wildly into the mods' ranks. Some people fell, others reacted to the rockers who were suddenly in their midst and new combatants kept pouring in through both doors. The crowd shifted in all ways at once, and Fitz let out a gasp of pain as he was crushed between four people. Suddenly, he felt very hot.

And then he was face to face with a rocker. A knife swung in his direction and he brought up his club clumsily, to parry the strike. The patch on his chest still felt stiff, and he wondered how long it would take to get medical attention if he suffered a similar wound today. Attempting to back away, he tripped over a rubber tyre and fell, although the density of the crowd ensured that he didn't reach the floor. He flailed helplessly, and was fortunate that the rocker chose to pursue another target. By the time he found his feet, the crowd had shifted again and the rocker was gone.

The next few minutes were full of noise and fear. Despite their weapons, both mods and rockers were keen to fight with their fists. Even the sound of ray guns became less frequent, as they ran out of power or their wielders accepted that a clear shot was now almost impossible. Fitz kept his head down, cursed the silver uniform that identified him with one side, and concentrated on keeping away from anyone who might feel like hitting him. Failing spectacularly, he found himself wrestling with a burly, bearded, leather-jacketed man. 'Rick's making me fight with them,' he bleated into the man's ear. 'I'm on your side really.' The rocker ignored him, and bloodied his nose. However, Fitz's tactic of keeping as many mods around him as possible paid off; they tore his attacker away and set about him viciously.

Fitz found himself pressed up against the counter, and thought about taking shelter behind it again until he saw that the battle had spilled over into that area too. The attendant robot stood immobile as mods and rockers exchanged blows around it. 'Please,' it twittered, 'you must desist from this activity. I am unable to perform my duties.'

And then a new sound cut through the cacophony: a shrill, prolonged whistle. And the milk bar began to empty.

The whistle, Fitz realised, had come from Rick. It must have been a prearranged signal to the mods to withdraw. Suddenly, he wished he had been at the briefing after all. Belatedly, he fought his way to the door, desperate not to be left behind.

Mods spilled out on to the street, the last few fighting a rearguard action in the doorway of the milk bar until everyone was clear, at which point they too fell back. They taunted the rockers again, waving their clubs and daring them with hand gestures to attack. Perhaps emboldened by the mods' unexpected retreat, the rockers took the bait readily. The battle resumed, in more open surroundings this time – which in some ways was worse, because it gave Fitz less opportunity to hide.

And then he realised why Rick had wanted to draw his

enemies outdoors. From behind the milk bar came the four missing members of the mods' Third Battalion, eliciting surprised stares from both sides alike. They flew – literally flew – above the mêlée, unreachable but armed with ray guns that allowed them to pick off the rockers with ease.

'Jetpacks!' breathed someone next to Fitz. 'That's brilliant!' And indeed, the four flying mods wore Rick's latest technological advance upon their backs: shining silver boxes of machinery, exerting some force or other which caused visible ripples in the air around them.

With the rockers in disarray and the ecstatic mods renewing their attack, Fitz was momentarily left alone. He seized his chance.

He had seen no sign of the Doctor. So, he was left with Plan B.

He leapt on to the sunken saddle of a mod scooter and turned on the engine, grateful that the so-called vehicles of the future didn't need ignition keys. He thought he knew which button controlled the vehicle's acceleration, and he was pleased to be proved right. As quickly as he safely could, trying not to look behind him for fear of what he would see, Fitz steered the scooter away from the battle. It handled awkwardly, and felt unlike any bike he had ever ridden before. Not that he was an experienced rider – but what was it with these push-button controls anyway? What was wrong with good old-fashioned pedals?

As the scooter picked up speed, Fitz allowed himself a quick glance over his shoulder.

His stomach sank as he saw that he was being followed.

Despite his other concerns, Davey must have been watching Fitz as closely as he had promised. Now, he and two other mods had taken to their vehicles in pursuit of the would-be escapee. They were only a few yards behind him. And Davey's furious snarl left Fitz in no doubt that he had no intention of letting the mods' spaceman get away.

* * *

The Doctor had insisted on carrying the modified record player himself, but its weight didn't seem to burden him. He and Gillian ran side by side through the corridors of the complex, until they reached the foot of the gravity pit, where they found Alec pacing restlessly. Two guards watched on, as did Alec's wife. Sandra leaned against the wall, her arms folded, her own impatience visible only in her tense expression. Gillian shot her a scowl: it was one thing for the rockers' leader not to endanger himself by fighting, but Sandra was just flaunting her position. She probably wouldn't know which side to fight on anyway.

'You've got something!' cried Alec, hopefully. 'At last! What's in the box? Ray guns?'

'No time to explain,' mumbled the Doctor as he leapt into the pit's field and was snatched upwards. With an apologetic shrug, Gillian followed him.

The milk bar was empty but for a few injured rockers, who lay moaning or unconscious. The more badly injured ones had already been taken downstairs, along with only two or three captured mods. The battle wasn't going well. The Doctor spared its victims a sympathetic look, shaking his head sadly, but didn't break his stride as he headed for the front door.

As he reached it, he stopped suddenly and turned to Gillian. 'You weren't planning to come outside with me, were you? You can't. The machine will send you to sleep along with every other human being in its range.'

'Me?' protested Gillian. 'What about you?'

The Doctor smiled at her, winked, and then he was gone.

Fitz kept one hand on the handlebars. With the other, he pressed frenetically at the accelerator button until it ceased to have an effect. The whining of the engine drowned out all sound of pursuit, but the scooter's many wing mirrors told him that Davey and the other two mods were distressingly close behind him. Fitz's gaze lingered on Davey's determined expression, as framed by one mirror. Hatred flashed in the young mod's eyes.

The sight distracted Fitz for a second too long. Returning his attention to the road, he realised that it had bifurcated, and that his lane had begun to climb. For an instant, he panicked. If he took the chase above ground level, then he would surely give the more experienced riders an advantage. Apart from which, should the worse come to the worst, he didn't know how to activate his stolen vehicle's antigravity disc. Making a rash decision, he yanked the handlebars to the right and steered the scooter straight off the road. It soared through the air for a second, and Fitz braced himself for an impact that, when it came, felt like it would jolt his skeleton out of his flesh. He heard the squeal of rubber against metal and watched a boxlike building slide by. Then, to his relief, he wrestled the scooter back under control and guided it between the edges of the lower roadway, with little loss of speed.

The mods, of course, were still behind him. A little closer now.

Fitz's heart leapt with unexpected joy as the road opened up and he passed through a large square with a fountain at its centre. Was this where he had encountered that first servo-robot, a seeming lifetime ago? He tempered his enthusiasm, realising that there could have been many squares like this one. But as he guided his scooter down the road along which, he hoped, he had first entered the city, he found some familiar graffiti and knew he was right. All he had to do now was ride in a straight line and he should find Compassion.

That wasn't as easy as it sounded. The flat land beyond the city offered no landmarks and, as the Doctor had pointed out, the horizon was nearer than Fitz was used to. He didn't know if he was going in the right direction or veering off at an angle. He spotted a few cannibals in the distance, clustered around three of their animals, so he bore away from them to be safe.

Then one of his back wheels hit a large rock and left the ground, causing the scooter to tip dangerously before gravity reasserted itself. Fitz felt himself sweating. He looked at the rows of unlabelled controls and wished he knew how to make the vehicle fly. He didn't dare to experiment, though: what if he slowed it by accident?

Come to think of it, he would have to find the brakes sometime.

The hard, brown ground rolled on beneath him. Skeletal black trees flashed by on both sides. There was no sign of Compassion, and Fitz began to worry. He told himself to stay calm and keep going. He had probably misjudged the distance. Any second now, she would come into view, bringing with her the promise of sanctuary behind whatever shields her transformation had endowed her with.

He glanced in his mirrors again. His pursuers were still the same distance behind him as they had been all the way out of the city. The scooters must have had a uniform top speed: the three mods weren't gaining, but neither was Fitz pulling ahead of them. And they were hovering a few inches above the ground, and were therefore less prone to obstacles.

He was breathless, and only now did he realise that panic wasn't the only cause. He had been wrong to believe that the whole planet's atmosphere was rarefied; that he had simply become used to it. The earthy smell of the tree-spotted plain became noticeable only now, by its absence. The air, he realised, must grow thinner with distance from the city. His chest started to hurt, and each hard-won breath made his lungs burn.

What was more, the symptoms confirmed his fear that he had come far enough. Either he was heading in the wrong direction or Compassion simply wasn't where he had left her.

His mind racing, looking for hope, he remembered what the Doctor had said about the bike they had found. Off the city's metal roads, the scooters wouldn't be recharging themselves. He could only hope that, by applying their discs, the mods were using power faster than he was. Perhaps he could outrun them after all.

The problem was, he wasn't sure where he was running to any more.

And the air was growing thinner still. He was already beginning to feel light-headed.

If he went much further, he would be unable to breathe at all.

'So, that's the end of that, then.' It was with a small, guilty measure of satisfaction that Gillian watched the Doctor place the remains of the record player on a lab bench. He looked like a little boy who had broken his favourite toy. 'We're defenceless again!'

He had almost begun to win her over. The Doctor displayed effortless knowledge of things that Gillian had worked so hard, and so often in vain, to understand; once her jealousy had begun to subside, she had found that knowledge alluring. But, in somehow conspiring to keep her off the field of battle as he used his machine, he had made it clear to everyone that she, the rockers' Technician, had had nothing to do with its development. He had humiliated her. His assurances that he wouldn't usurp her position had been lies.

Even so, she had felt a heady mixture of relief and joy as he had left the milk bar and walked slowly through the mêlée outside, heedless of the combatants, the record player held at arm's length as people dropped all around him. A few mods had worked out what was going on; they had rushed the Doctor, but he had sidestepped them without even looking up from the machine. And then they too had slumped to the ground.

At first, Gillian had worried that as many friends as foes were being knocked out. But then, finally, incredibly, Rick had blown a shrill whistle three times and the mods had retreated, dragging as many of their fallen comrades on to their scooters as they could.

By the time the record player had exploded, with an impressive shower of sparks, the fight had ended.

'I wouldn't say "defenceless" exactly,' said the Doctor now, stroking his chin thoughtfully. 'Your enemies know we're capable of pulling a surprise or two out of the hat. I imagine they'll think twice before acting so rashly again.'

'You don't know Rick,' retorted Gillian. 'He doesn't even think once, usually. And, when he does come back, we'll have nothing to stop him. You've bought us time, but that's all.'

'Don't underestimate time, Gillian,' said the Doctor quietly.

The lab door opened and Alec entered, trailed by two guards as usual. 'How's the work coming?' he asked curtly.

'Ah, Alec,' said the Doctor, clapping his hands together and beaming as if greeting a long-lost friend. 'How are things with the rockers? Not too many casualties, I hope.'

'A few bruises, nothing we can't fix up – and we caught eleven mods, thanks mainly to you, even if you did leave it a bit late. Not bad. Not bad at all. But we need more.'

'I was just saying that,' said Gillian, letting Alec know that she had everything in hand.

'The mods had rocket packs!' said Alec, and there was a glint of fear in his eyes. 'I mean, rocket packs, for God's sake! It was only yesterday we found out about the ray guns. How are they doing it? How are they coming up with this stuff?'

Gillian turned as the door swished open again, but the new arrival was just a servo-robot. Must be cleaning day, she thought.

'That's a good question,' said the Doctor, nodding to himself. 'Here's another one: why did Rick go to the trouble of breaking into your headquarters only to withdraw when he was winning? To test out his, ah, rocket packs in the open, maybe? But then, why sacrifice his main objective for the sake of putting on a display? And what is that robot doing?'

Alec turned and jumped, startled to find the servo-robot so close behind him. 'Do you want something?' he asked with a frown, as he backed away from it.

'Guide destiny service marmalade duty,' said the servo-robot.

The Doctor sprang into action. 'Get away from it!' he warned in a throaty yell, seizing Alec by the shoulder and propelling him backwards. The guards reacted to the apparent attack; one pulled his knife and leapt at the Doctor, even as the robot trundled forward. It brushed against the guard, and Gillian shrieked and recoiled from a sudden bang, a vivid blue flash and the smell of ozone and burned flesh.

The guard's blackened corpse hit the floor with a sickening smack.

For a second, nobody moved. Even the servo-robot was still, as if its electronic mind were contemplating what it had just done. Then something whirred inside its casing and it jerked back into life. It rounded on Alec and the Doctor.

The Doctor backed away, extending a hand in front of Alec's chest to ensure that he did the same. The robot rolled after them, not quickly but relentlessly. As Gillian and the second guard watched helplessly, it backed its targets into a corner of the room.

'I think we've answered one question,' murmured the Doctor – and, if he was trying to sound unafraid, then his wide-eyed attention to the advancing automaton belied his efforts. 'The attack was a diversion, to allow Rick to get this robot into your part of the complex. It wasn't an invasion after all – it was an assassination attempt.'

Fitz felt as if he were waking from a deep sleep, but he could have closed his eyes for only a second. His scooter was still speeding away from the city and he was slumped over the handlebars, the pain in his chest having grown until it felt as if a ten-ton weight were dancing on his ribcage. He wanted nothing more than to let his eyelids fall again, but something in the recesses of his addled mind insisted that he couldn't do that. His wing mirrors told him that the mods were no longer following him. He didn't stop to ask why. Still unsure where the brakes were, he guided the scooter around in a wide arc until it was taking him back the way he had come.

Then he saw them, through the red mist that had descended

over his vision. Davey and his friends were waiting for Fitz, back where the air was thicker. They had simply stopped following him, knowing he would have to come back to them. And now they were moving across the plain to intercept him. There was no way past them, and no time anyway. Fitz's empty lungs screamed out for oxygen and he thought he was going to faint. He stabbed at the accelerator, knowing it would do no good, and gritted his teeth as his scooter roared towards the three mods. They simply waited as if playing chicken, daring him to ram them.

And all Fitz could think of was that, if he couldn't go around them, then he had to go over. As if in a dream, he tried first one button and then another, hoping to chance upon the one that would activate the antigravity generator and send him soaring to freedom. If the controls had any effect at all, then he couldn't see it.

He was almost upon the mods. He even managed to force his lungs to take one ragged breath, but it was too little, too late. In desperation, he slapped the dashboard with his palm, activating at least half of its controls at once.

The scooter took to the air.

It also ceased its forward motion, rolled to one side and unseated its rider.

Fitz sprawled face first on to the unyielding ground. He was aware of the pain for only an instant before he blacked out at last.

Chapter Seven
A Better Place

The servo-robot approached relentlessly. Alec gaped at it in horror, and felt a terrible lurching sensation in his stomach born from the fact that, faced with his own death, he could work neither his brain nor his muscles to prevent it. If it weren't for the Doctor, he would have suffered the same fate as his guard already. And even he could only delay the inevitable.

'We're cornered,' he cried, painfully aware of the wall only a couple of feet behind him, desperately hoping that the resourceful alien could pull off another miracle but desperately afraid that he couldn't. 'I order you to stop. End program, do you hear me? End program.'

'That won't do any good,' the Doctor mumbled. 'Whoever turned that robot into a killer corrupted its lexical database in the process.'

Alec tensed himself to run, praying his legs would respond, knowing he couldn't possibly get past the robot anyway. It was too close. And suddenly the Doctor was in front of him, holding out his arms to prevent Alec from passing. 'What are you doing?' he squealed.

'Keeping you alive, I hope,' said the Doctor. 'The robot's been programmed to kill you. It won't kill anyone else – well, not intentionally. Now stay behind me and move to your right.'

The Doctor's living barricade appeared to work. The robot came to a halt, as if confused. But as the Doctor and Alec edged their way along the wall, it turned slowly to follow their progress. Then it trundled after them again.

The Doctor exploded into action. 'Run, Alec, run!' he yelled hoarsely, as he sprang towards a thin-framed metal chair, scooped it up and hurled it at his pursuer. The robot brought its arms up together, and the chair fell neatly over them and over the aerial on top of its head. 'Hoopla!' cried the Doctor enthusiastically, before turning around, running straight into the dumbfounded Alec, gripping his arm and dragging him onward with a shout of 'I said, run! No, don't get up on the bench – it could send a charge right into that.'

It wasn't until they reached the door – where Gillian and the surviving guard waited nervously – that Alec dared to turn and look for the servo-robot again. To his relief, it hadn't moved. The chair had slipped partway over its head, and it was well and truly tangled. A corona of blue fire sizzled around its metal frame. The robot thrashed its arms up and down in unison, but it was too inflexible to extricate itself from the trap.

'What's happening?' asked Gillian, her eyes rooted to the gruesome spectacle.

'The robots draw power through the metal floor,' explained the Doctor. He too was fascinated, and Alec wondered if he was actually enjoying himself. 'This one's overcharging itself and draining off the excess through the upper part of its casing. The question is, how long can its circuits cope with such abuse before they overload?'

Even as he spoke, something popped and fizzed inside the robot's chest. It ceased its frantic motions, its eye-strip went dark and a thin cloud of smoke seeped out from somewhere between its head and its body, carrying a faint ozone tang towards the onlookers.

The Doctor clapped his hands together, satisfied. 'I think we have our answer.'

'No,' grumbled Alec, aware that he was shaking and trying to control himself, 'the question is, how did that bloody maniac manage to rewire and reprogram a servo-robot?'

'And why?' asked Gillian, taking a few tentative steps forward and peering glumly at the blackened corpse of the unfortunate guard. She pursed her lips and looked as if she were going to be sick. 'I mean, people have died before, by accident, in battle, but this was cold-blooded murder. Rick actually murdered Matt.'

'He's too powerful,' said Alec. 'However he's getting this technology, it's made him think he can do anything. He's out of control. And he'll keep on trying stunts like this till we're all dead.' He moved to Gillian's side, but the sight of Matt's body brought tears to his eyes. He blinked them away angrily, and turned back to the Doctor. 'Now do you see what we're up against? Do you see why we need more weapons? He'll kill us all!'

The Doctor put a hand to his mouth and adopted a thoughtful expression. 'Perhaps I should take a look at this central computer of yours, this...'

'Brain. The Brain. Yeah, Rick must have got to it. He must have! What else could it be?'

'But let's not forget our more immediate problem,' said the Doctor. 'The degeneration of the city,' he prompted, when Alec's reaction made it clear that that hadn't been uppermost in his mind. The Doctor trotted across the room, passing the deactivated robot without sparing it a glance. He rummaged through the junk on one of the lab benches, found a metal cylinder to which a length of rubber hose was connected, and turned to display it to the others.

'There's something I'd like to investigate.'

Cold contempt twisted Rick's expression as he stared into the face of a traitor. Fitz Kreiner had been brought into his reception room by Davey and two members of his battalion, along with a sorry tale of a failed escape attempt. The spaceman still looked pale and weak from his ordeal; when Davey had kicked his legs from under him, he had collapsed easily. He was on his knees now, although the other two mods held him up by his arms. Davey stood behind him, clenching and unclenching his fists.

Fitz looked scared. Which was how Rick liked it.

'You lied your way into my gang, then stabbed me in the back!' he accused Fitz. 'You're a disgrace to that uniform. You even look like a scummy rocker!' He leaned in closer to his prisoner, allowing his teeth to show. 'What other secrets did you give Alec?'

Fitz's only response was a puzzled frown, so Rick slapped him across the face. 'I asked you a question! I know you gave him the machine. Thanks to you, I've lost nearly a dozen men!'

'I don't know what machine you're talking about,' said Fitz, sullenly.

'So, how else do you think a bunch of brainless rockers got that sort of technology?'

'I don't know,' said Fitz. 'Same way you get yours, I suppose.'

'That's not possible,' said Rick, tight-lipped.

'Well… the Doctor, then. They've probably made him help them.'

'Your spaceman friend.'

'My… friend, yes. Look, he's good with all that sort of stuff.'

'So, you've both decided to work for the rockers!'

'I'm not working for anyone!'

'Oh yes? You told me you were taking our side.'

Fitz found a fresh seam of defiance. 'I didn't say that,' he snapped angrily. '*You* told me I had to fight with you. Ever since I came to this world, I've been held prisoner and threatened, first by the rockers and then by you. I don't want to join either of your gangs. I don't care who wins your war. You're as bad as each other!'

Rick let those words hang in the air between them for a moment. Then he stepped forward and dealt Fitz a swift, precise kick to the stomach. The spaceman gasped and tried to double up, but his arms were still held. Breathing heavily, he glared at Rick reproachfully.

'Don't you ever compare us to the rockers!' said Rick, in a low growl.

Fitz was wise enough to say nothing. Rick let him sweat for a while longer, as he clasped his hands behind his back and paced from one side of the narrow room to the other. Then he pulled back a chair at the head of the long table and sat down.

'I've got some more questions for you,' he said, 'and this time I want the truth.' He waited another few seconds before leaning forward, resting his chin on his hands and regarding his prisoner coolly. 'You told me there were only two of you.'

Rick watched Fitz Kreiner's reaction carefully, and grinned to himself. The spaceman was worried and suspicious. He didn't know what Rick knew.

'That's right,' he answered, uncertainly.

'Liar!' exploded Davey. 'He's lying, Rick.' The young mod jabbed Fitz in the small of his back, with his foot. 'Rick said he wanted the truth.'

'I'm telling you the truth!'

'So, what about the woman then? What about her?'

Rick silenced Davey with a glare. His subordinate, overeager and undisciplined as ever, had revealed too much. But it was said now. He would have to make the best of it. He would speak to Davey later. 'Go on then, spaceman. Tell us about the woman.'

Fitz must have known the game was up. He sighed and closed his eyes wearily, until he was prompted by another jab from Davey. 'The woman is...' he began, before tailing off as if he couldn't find the right words. 'I mean, she's... what I'm saying is...' He sighed again, and gave the closest approximation to a shrug that he could manage in his current circumstances. 'Look, this might sound a little bit unbelievable, but...'

'You can't go!' said Alec.

Sandra glowered at him, now more than ever seeing him as a symbol of the life she yearned to leave behind. 'I'm going, Alec,' she said wearily, 'whether you like it or not.' She pushed past him and searched in the cupboard for her coat. It was right at the back, neglected.

'You should be telling him to stay here, not encouraging him.'

'The Doctor's trying to help.'

'Then why won't he do as I say?' cried Alec.

'Because you only want him to play your war games!' Sandra returned, with equal force.

Alec recoiled as if struck. He had probably forgotten how forceful she could be. She had not stood up to him, not properly, for so long. She had made her token protests and surrendered. But now, for the first time in too many years, she had something important to fight for.

'The Doctor's given us two oxygen tanks; put straps on them and everything, so we can carry them on our backs. We can go further than we've been before, find out what happens after the air runs out. I want to see what's out there, Alec – and it's not so long ago that you did too. That's why we had Greg start work on the tanks in the first place.'

'I've got better things to worry about now.'

'I don't believe you! The number of times we've talked about this – about how there had to be something else, perhaps other cities, if we could only look. Now we've got the chance to do that, to get away from here, to find out a bit about our world.'

'Fine! Great! So, you and the Doctor go out and explore, why don't you? I'll just wait here for your lunatic brother to kill me!'

Sandra clicked her tongue in exasperation. 'Don't you see? If we could find somewhere else, we could take the others and settle there. We could leave Rick and the rest of the mods here. We could start a new life, without all the fighting.'

'They'd come looking for us,' said Alec. 'So long as Rick's in charge, he's not going to leave us alone. He'd have the Brain to himself. He'd get it to make even more weapons, and oxygen tanks, and he'd come after us. You know he would.'

Sandra had an answer to that, but she had used it so many times already. She looked at her husband instead, and felt her anger draining away at the sight of this pathetic figure, grown up but still playing at being a teenager, unable to imagine a life without his gang and his bike and his knife. She felt sorry for him. But he wouldn't keep her here. Not any more.

'Goodbye, Alec,' said Sandra, sadly.

She swept out of the room without looking back once.

Rick had sent Fitz Kreiner away, to be confined until he could decide what to do with him. His reception room was empty now, and the mods' leader stood alone, leaning against the chair at the head of the table and thinking about the events of the day.

Fitz had probably told the truth this time. The rockers' sudden advance was probably the work of the mysterious Doctor. That same Doctor had been responsible for saving Alec's life; Rick had watched that sorry business through the video-camera eyes of his reprogrammed servo-robot. He felt disconcerted. His new Technician had given him an edge over his foes, and he had enjoyed that. Now that advantage was eroded, and a shadow of doubt was cast over his view of the future.

He hated not being in control. It reminded him of his early life, in that miserable house in that miserable town in that miserable decade. He didn't know how he had survived: always being told what he could and couldn't do, knowing things would never get better. He would only have exchanged parents for teachers for employers as he grew. There would always have been someone to restrict him, to control him, to take away his freedom.

He remembered how all that had changed, how he had made it change.

Sandra had never cared for her little brother. She had resented him, although he hadn't realised it until later. That day on the beach, she had forgotten him altogether, caught up in the breathless excitement of discovery. Nor had she talked to him later about what they had seen, probably thinking, even hoping, that he hadn't understood.

But three-year-old Ricky McBride had seen aliens and monsters in his comics – and, since his parents had gone upmarket and bought a television set, in black and white on a flickering screen as well. He had always known that they would exist in real life.

Sandra probably wasn't aware of just how much Ricky had

seen – and understood – that day. But when the Maker had returned, he had felt its presence as she had. He had recognised the strange sensation, which felt as if the world had been remade. And he had realised then that his older sister had tricked him, abandoned him, gone to find the future without him.

He had felt the Maker leaving, with Sandra and Alec and his older brothers and all the other youths, and a few older fools who had got caught up in its net. And he had burst into tears at the unfairness of it all, because Sandra's plan had worked and the alien had left him behind.

Rick remembered how he had dived out of his bed and run to the window, hammering on the glass and screaming with all the power in his three-year-old lungs, 'Come back, come back! You've missed me, I'm still here! Come back!' He remembered hearing his parents as they stirred downstairs; hot tears on his cheeks; and the beginnings of despair because he had missed his chance to escape. Because he was still here and the alien had gone.

And he remembered the indescribable joy that had filled him when he had sensed its return, when he had known that it had recognised him and come back for him. When, for the first time in his life, somebody – something – had confirmed that he was important.

For most people, the trip from the Earth of 1965 to the city in the year 2000 AD had been instantaneous. For Ricky, as for Sandra and Alec but for nobody else, there had been a transitional phrase, a long period of drifting in a dark void. Unable to see, hear, smell, touch or taste, he had listened and spoken with his mind as the Maker had told him just how special he was and asked him over and over again what he wanted from the future.

And Ricky McBride had told it.

Now, thanks to the Maker, Rick lived in this wonderful place, this magical city, where nobody told him what to do and, just like when the Maker had come for him, he only had to shout loud enough and he could have whatever he wanted.

The Doctor's interference was a minor setback, Rick knew that now. It didn't change anything. He still had his Technician and he still had his spaceman – more or less – and he still had one other, whose talents he hadn't yet explored. He would still get his own way.

Feeling consoled, he stood up and marched towards the door that led into his personal suite of rooms. He opened it – and jumped, startled, to find somebody standing behind it.

'What the hell are you doing there?' he demanded, covering his embarrassment with anger. 'I thought I told you to stay in your room. Do I have to lock you in?'

The woman looked bemused. 'I was looking', she said, in a halting, uncertain voice, 'for the Doctor.'

'So, you can talk after all.'

'Have you seen the Doctor?'

'He can't see you now, Compassion.'

The woman didn't react to Rick's use of her name at all. If anything, she had forgotten he was there again. 'Part of me, part of him…' she murmured softly.

Rick put his arm around her shoulders and guided her back along the corridor. 'I'm doing my best to bring the Doctor here for you. The best thing you can do is stay put and wait for him. You'll do that, won't you?'

'The one I sensed,' said Compassion. 'Why won't he talk to me?' She stopped suddenly, and looked around as if seeing her surroundings for the first time. 'How did I get here?'

This was beginning to irritate Rick. He wasn't used to dealing with people he couldn't intimidate. Still, now that he knew what this woman – this creature – was, he knew he couldn't let her go. He had to be polite. 'Don't you remember?' he asked.

'I remember… so many things. So many sensations. It's difficult to separate them, hard to remember how time flows from one point to another. I can see yesterday and tomorrow and they look the same. I can see the whole of the tapestry, but I'm lost when I step inside it.'

Something about her words, her voice, transported Rick away from this world. He saw universes in her eyes, and they sparked a flame of desire within him. Then Compassion blinked, snapped out of her reverie and shrugged Rick away with a disgusted frown.

'Who are you?'

'I'm Rick. I'm in charge of this world.'

'What, you?'

Rick bristled at her look of contempt. He almost slapped the woman to teach her a lesson, but that would have been counterproductive. He reined in his anger. The key to controlling others lay in first being able to control yourself.

'You didn't answer me,' the woman said. 'How did I get here?'

'You came looking for me,' said Rick, grandly.

'I doubt it.' It was a statement of fact, not an insult.

'We're going to be friends. You're going to show me time and space and other dimensions. You're going to help me sort out the rockers.'

Rick was irritated to see that Compassion was ignoring him. She had spaced out again. 'There was somebody,' she murmured distantly. 'I felt... another mind. Not the Doctor, somebody else... somebody who understood. But he won't talk to me.'

And suddenly Rick understood too. He understood why Compassion had wandered into the mods' café in the early hours of the morning, surprising the few remaining revellers who, for some reason, had not been warned by the usually vigilant servo-robots. His men had brought the intruder to him, of course, and he had ordered them to say nothing about her to anyone. Even Davey hadn't known, when he had reported his encounter with the woman on the plain, that she had been sitting on the other side of a wall, just a few yards away from him. Compassion was another of Rick's little secrets. And he had enjoyed the idea that, like his Technician before her, she had chosen to come to him because he was important. But his new theory, though somewhat less flattering, made more sense.

Compassion hadn't come in search of him. She had come looking for his other guest. They had something in common. And that in itself was an exciting thought. It suggested to Rick that yet more power lay within his reach.

He took Compassion by the shoulders again, and she didn't object as he guided her towards a locked door in the left-hand wall of the corridor. 'I think it's time I introduced you to another new friend of mine,' he said.

Sandra had never cared much for motorbikes. To her, they had always been a symbol of the lunacy that had gripped her friends and family. So, in preference to a jetcycle, she chose a rarely used aircar from one corner of the rockers' capacious garage. She probably wouldn't be able to bring it back anyway, and it would be missed less by the others.

The car was shaped like a flying saucer although, like the cycles, it was powered by a single antigravity disc and couldn't lift itself more than a few inches off the ground. The Doctor's face lit up when he saw it; he clambered eagerly over its sleek bodywork, somehow managing to hold an oxygen tank beneath each arm, to join Sandra in the front of its four-seater cockpit. She brought the transparent, permeable, bubble-shaped lid down over their heads and operated the childishly simple controls to guide the car out on to the road. She kept its wheels down as she drove through the city, ensuring that the vehicle would be carrying a maximum charge when it eventually had to leave the metal surface.

She felt a thrill of excitement as she finally retracted the chassis and let the aircar soar over the hard, brown earth. The angular lines of the city gave way to the stunted vegetation of the plain and, while her new surroundings could hardly be described as picturesque, Sandra felt as if she were casting off chains. She didn't get out of the hateful city enough, nor even out of the underground complex in which she lived her monotonous life.

Nor away from Alec.

Sandra made sure she kept ahead of her escorts. She didn't look in the rear-view mirror lest she should spot the rockers behind her on their bikes: two tangible reminders that her illusion of freedom was no more than that. Even so, she could almost feel their mutinous glares burning into the back of her head. The rockers were Alec's gang. They hated it when they had to take orders from Sandra. She thought about what might lie ahead instead, what the Doctor might show her. His confirmation that this wasn't Earth at all had opened up a whole new range of possibilities. A new set of dreams.

'What are you hoping to find?' asked the Doctor gently, as if he could read her mind. He didn't interrupt her train of thought; somehow he managed to ease himself into it instead.

'I don't know,' said Sandra, wistfully. 'A better place than this one, I suppose.'

'Better how?'

'A place where we don't have to fight all the time.'

'A widely held ambition – and yet sometimes I wonder if it's possible. I'm not sure a change of scenery would solve your problems. It's not the city that's choosing to fight.'

'I know that. But it doesn't help, does it? We've got nothing to do except stare at blank walls and drink protein shakes that taste like glue. We've got no books, no tellies, hardly even any colour – and I can't stand space-age music!'

'I see your point, but there are other ways of making entertainment.'

'Not for someone like Alec. This mod/rocker business is all he knows, all he's got left.'

The Doctor nodded briskly. 'And I imagine it's self-perpetuating. A closed environment like the city...'

'You can't get away from it,' confirmed Sandra.

'Except by leaving the city altogether and becoming a – what do you call them? – a dropout. But even they're not entirely free.' The Doctor stared into the distance, his hands working frenetically but absently in front of him. Sandra could almost see thought bubbles being pumped out by his brain. 'That's what the plain-dwellers meant when they said the city wouldn't let them go. Not just that the land isn't fertile enough to sustain them without its technology, but the city produces oxygen, keeps its charges close to it. You must love your husband very much.'

He caught Sandra by surprise with his sudden direct question. He had turned to look at her, and his eyes bored into her soul. She shifted awkwardly in her seat and renewed her concentration on the ground ahead.

'You don't like what he does, but you stay with him,' the Doctor prompted.

'I don't have a choice.'

'I think you do – even if it's only between mods and rockers.'

Sandra laughed bitterly. 'Neither of them would have me.'

'Why is that?'

She looked at the Doctor sharply. His expression was wide-eyed and hopeful, as if he knew he had asked an intensely personal question but was confident he could charm her into answering. He probably could, too. She felt herself wanting to open up to him, no matter how painful it might be. She had not had anyone to talk to, really talk to, for over a decade. Not since her relationship with Alec had deteriorated into grunted acknowledgements and occasional routine exchanges. Unfortunately, this made it difficult to articulate what she was feeling, to compress nineteen years of misery into a succinct explanation.

'I did the worst thing anyone can do,' she mumbled, avoiding the Doctor's appealing gaze. 'I changed sides.'

'You were a mod?'

'My family were mods. Rick still is.'

'Your brother. Of course. The mods' leader. That must

complicate things. But you joined the rockers for Alec's sake?'

'It was different back then. When we first came to the city, we all worked together. Mods, rockers – and a few people who didn't belong to either. Like me. I mean, the old gangs weren't forgotten, but it wasn't like it is now. After a while, I thought… well, I loved Alec then, and the others kind of respected us because we saw the Maker. I thought if we got married it would bring everyone together. I thought it would help. Stupid, eh?'

'It's never stupid to hope,' said the Doctor, 'nor to act with noble intentions.'

'Mr Bennett performed the ceremony, what with him having connections to the church and all that. That was before he dropped out.'

'And then what happened?'

Sandra didn't want to answer that. She could sense the Doctor's silent encouragement, but the events that had followed her wedding were still too hard to talk about. She felt as if her heart were full of tears; that she had trapped them inside a cocoon for all these years, and that the slightest prick on its surface would unleash a dreadful torrent.

'The fighting started again,' she said simply, trying to keep her voice steady, to not think about the details. 'I ended up on this side.'

The Doctor must have seen her discomfort, because he changed the subject. 'So, now Alec and Rick are in charge of the rockers and the mods respectively. I imagine that's because they saw the Maker. They're his chosen ones, if you like?'

'Something like that.'

'And you?'

'I'd get out of the city altogether, if I had the nerve. I'd drop out.'

'No. You had the answer earlier. You can't just hide away, not when you can work towards changing things.'

'And how am I supposed to do that?'

'Everybody can do something. It's only a matter of finding out what.'

'It's different for me,' said Sandra. 'Nobody trusts me. The mods think I'm a turncoat, the rockers think I'm a spy. It doesn't matter that I was on that beach too, that I saw the Maker. They only leave me alone for Alec's sake, and for Rick's. If it wasn't for them, I think one side or the other would have killed me long ago.'

'Is that the only reason you stay with Alec?' asked the Doctor.

Sandra couldn't answer that either, and her travelling companion didn't force the issue.

She spent the next few minutes of the journey in silent, moody contemplation.

Alec liked to interrogate his prisoners in the milk bar. With the space-age music of the jukebox thudding through his veins, and its ever-changing light spilling upon the frightened faces of his victims, he felt he could do anything. He remembered those long-gone days of 1965, looking up to the leaders of his gang, and he appreciated how far he had come. He was somebody now, just as they had been then.

But now, although the music beat on behind him, it seemed distant. It didn't beat through him as it had before. He looked down at the pale, staring face of the man he had just killed, washed in light blue, and his skin felt cold and he trembled involuntarily.

It was an accident, he told himself. It wasn't my fault.

But perhaps it was. Perhaps he had treated this prisoner more roughly than usual. Perhaps he had let his irritation – at Sandra's defiance, at Rick's increasing brazenness, at the Doctor's empty promises – push him too far. He had meant to hurt the mod, to punch him harder and harder until he had given in and told him how Rick was getting hold of all his futuristic technology. He had certainly meant to throw him to the ground. He had hoped to assert his superiority, make his captive scared of him.

But he hadn't meant for him to crack his head on the edge of one of the booths. He hadn't meant for him to die. It was an accident.

Joey. That was the dead man's name. Alec had known Joey all his life – Joey Roberts, as he had once been – although he had hardly spoken to him since they had been in the same class at primary school. Joey had turned into a mod, after all.

Alec looked at the faces of the rockers around him, finding stunned expressions and glazed eyes. 'It was an accident,' he insisted out loud, but he sounded unconvincing. 'But so what? So, some prissy little mod has died. They killed one of ours, and Rick tried to kill me! They escalated this war, not us. They asked for it, didn't they?'

The words were meant as a statement, but they came out as a plea and Alec turned away, ashamed. He took a few steps towards the internal door and his private room below, where he could curl up and catch up on his sleep and not think about what he had done. But his people looked to him for leadership, and he couldn't risk losing their faith. So, he faltered.

'It was an accident,' he said again, without turning back. He swallowed, willed himself to sound more authoritative and ordered: 'But let's make use of it. I want Tiger Group to take his body and dump it outside the mods' café. We'll show them what happens when they take on the rockers. They kill one of ours, they lose one of theirs. Tit for tat!'

He didn't dare look to see how his pronouncement had been received. He strode out of the room with as much confidence as he could muster. But, once he was out in the corridor and he had closed the door behind him, he sagged against the cool metal wall, breathing heavily and sweating. The frantic hammering of his heart merged with the beat of the music and formed a new, unfamiliar and frightening rhythm.

When their vehicles were at half power, they came to a stop. The air was beginning to thin out and there was no sign of either mods or plain-dwellers, so the guards agreed to stay behind with their jetcycles as the Doctor and Sandra donned their oxygen tanks and drove on in the aircar. When the car's power was exhausted, they stepped out on to the dry ground and continued their journey on foot. The Doctor urged Sandra onward with encouraging hand movements. Privately, though, he was worried. The plain stretched ahead of them, seemingly without end, and he knew they could not go far. The oxygen tanks had a limited capacity and it would be a long, airless trek back to the cycles.

Then he walked straight into something unexpected: an invisible barrier. And, once his initial bemusement had worn off and he had taken the time to rub his bruised nose ruefully, he felt a triumphant grin spreading across his face.

The Doctor watched as Sandra felt her way along the barrier in each direction, including upwards, finding it was slightly curved. With a demand valve in his mouth and no air for sound to carry anyway, he missed the opportunity to explain to her what she was seeing. But that was more than made up for by the growing light of comprehension in her eyes as she worked out the details for herself.

The horizon still stretched out before them, but like the sky itself, it was an illusion. The city and its environs – and, of course, the inhabitants of both – were contained within a huge, impassable globe of energy.

Or, as the Doctor was coming to think of it, a giant goldfish bowl.

Chapter Eight
Prisoners (In All Sorts of Ways)

Fitz was hungry and tired. He had been left for hours in a tiny, unfurnished room, cursing his luck and fretting about how he could have done things differently. He couldn't see any lock on the door, but it wouldn't open for him: the sensors on this side must have been disabled or removed. He had relieved his boredom for half an hour by trying to prise the door open manually, without success. He had also tried knocking on each wall, in the hope that someone might hear him: perhaps there were other prisoners in the next room. All he could hear was the background noise of the complex, of which his enforced solitude had made him acutely aware: a constant faint rhythm of clashes and clangs, reverberating through the metal walls until it was impossible to tell where any one sound had originated.

He gave up, lowered himself to the floor and slouched against the wall in one corner of the room. His ribs ached all down his left side. He could only imagine that Davey or one of his friends had laid into him while he was unconscious on the plain. He probably had an impressive bruise, if only he could get through his indestructible mod uniform to inspect it.

The worst part of his captivity was not knowing what would happen next. When the door slid open, then, Fitz was as much hopeful as fearful. But hope turned to disappointment, just as fear became relief, at the sight of the sombre-faced Vince and Deborah. 'Visiting time already, is it?' he asked dryly. As the door closed behind his visitors, he caught a brief glimpse of a silver-uniformed guard out in the corridor.

'We heard what had happened,' said Deborah.

'You know, that you ran away from the fight and all that.'

'It's not true, is it? You're not really a traitor?'

Fitz didn't bother to stand. He buried his head in his hands and groaned loudly.

'You said you could get us away from here,' said Deborah, accusingly. 'You said you could show us the future.'

'No I didn't,' Fitz mumbled into his hands.

'Were you lying to us?'

He wanted to say no, but then he remembered some of what he had told them. 'I might have exaggerated a bit,' he confessed. He looked up, to be met by the distressing sight of Deborah's pixie face contorted into an expression of horrified betrayal. 'Well, I didn't know who I could trust!' he protested. 'I don't want to take sides here, but I'm not getting anywhere with Rick and I thought –'

'You thought you'd throw in with Alec,' said Deborah, disapprovingly.

'My friend – another spaceman – is with the rockers. I want to talk to him.'

'I think we should go, Deborah,' said Vince, quietly. 'There's nothing we can do here.'

Fitz scowled. 'No, I'll bet there isn't – because you were never interested in helping me, were you? You just wanted to know what I could do for you.'

'You promised,' said Deborah, sulkily. 'You said the future was here.'

'And suppose I thought you didn't deserve my help. I saw you outside the rockers' headquarters – you threw yourself into that fight like all the other mods!'

'What choice did we have?'

Fitz opened his mouth, but couldn't think of an answer that wasn't belied by his current predicament. 'You didn't have to enjoy it so much,' he said lamely.

'We told you before,' said Vince, 'we don't have a choice. This is our life now.' He put an arm around his distraught partner and guided her towards the door. Fitz thought he should say something, but he didn't know what. He climbed to his feet, but didn't approach the couple. Then Vince hesitated, ran a nervous hand through his sparse hair, and turned back.

'Look,' he said in a low, conspiratorial tone, blinking rapidly and not quite looking at Fitz, 'if you do get to the rockers' place, you should talk to Sandra.'

Fitz frowned. 'She's Rick's sister, isn't she? The one who found the Maker. You mentioned her before.' And so, he remembered, had an anonymous graffiti-writer – someone who had thought her a traitor. And more. 'Is she a spy or something?'

'Oh no,' said Deborah, as if shocked by the idea. 'She's just nice, that's all.'

'Sensible,' said Vince, 'and practical.'

'She was our best friend here for a while.'

'Our only friend, really, when we first came here. It's a shame, her ending up on the other side like that.'

'Yes, such a shame. But Vince is right: she'll help you.'

'She helped us once,' said Vince, 'back home.' He and Deborah exchanged a wistful look.

'OK,' said Fitz, forcing a smile, 'I'll do that, thanks. But my real problem is, how do I get to the rockers' headquarters in the first place?'

His visitors looked at each other awkwardly, and Fitz knew he would have to give them his most persuasive spiel. But a loudspeaker announcement pre-empted him. 'We regret to inform you,' said the usual female voice, 'that there has been a death in our ranks. You all know that Joey was captured during the rumble, after putting up a brave fight against our enemies. The rockers have now shown again how cruel and cowardly they are, by murdering him in cold blood.' Despite the nature of her news, the speaker maintained her usual clipped, businesslike tone. But Fitz could see that her words were having an effect upon Vince and Deborah. It was as if shutters had slid down behind their eyes; as if such tragedies could no longer hurt them, just make them withdraw further into themselves. Instinctively, he knew that they would now be dead to his pleas.

There was more about Joey, about how courageous and noble and full of joy he had been. But no more words were spoken in the tiny cell. By the time Fitz thought of something to say, the loudspeaker woman had announced a two-minute silence in Joey's memory, and he felt he couldn't break it.

He watched mournfully as Vince rapped on the metal door, and the guard outside opened it to allow the visitors out. Deborah turned in the doorway to look at Fitz, but all he could see in her eyes was disappointment.

And then he was alone in the tiny room again.

The Doctor had seen too much death in his time. Sometimes, when it surrounded him on a grand scale, when he had to ignore the carnage and get down to the job at hand, he feared he would become inured to it. But the sight of one corpse could still affect him, still make him desperately miserable at the loss of so much potential.

It had taken the Doctor and Sandra a long time to walk back from the invisible barrier to where the other two rockers waited to return them to the city. Their oxygen had barely held out. They had unearthed a vital piece of information, but the Doctor had still worried that he had been gone too long. He had been relieved, upon arriving back at the rockers' headquarters, to find that war hadn't broken out in his absence.

Then Alec had met him in the milk bar, concerned about something and barely listening to what the Doctor and Sandra had to say. Taking them down to the complex via a dusty and rarely used flight of stairs, he had shown them to the bottom of the gravity pit.

The Doctor didn't recognise the dead man, but Sandra did. She turned from the grisly sight with tears in her eyes. The Doctor watched sadly as she shambled away, her shoulders stooped as they had been when he had first met her. On the way back from the barrier, she had walked with her shoulders back and her head up.

The position and condition of the corpse confirmed that it had fallen from a great height. Two rockers hovered nearby with a blanket; when the Doctor had seen enough, Alec motioned to them and they covered their dead comrade, then carried him away.

Gillian was present too. She had prised open a control panel in the wall and was poking about inside it with a screwdriver. She looked startled when Alec asked her what she had learned so far. 'I can't find anything wrong with it,' she said helplessly.

'It was outside interference, wasn't it?' said Alec.

'It could have been.'

'You see?' He turned to the Doctor. 'Do you believe me now? That maniac mod's killed another of ours. You said you'd help – well, give me something I can use!'

'I can see why you're agitated,' the Doctor murmured, clapping Alec on the shoulder in a fatherly way as he hurried past him and peered into the exposed circuitry behind the panel. 'But I *am* trying to help, if you'd only see it. I doubt if Rick is responsible for this particular misfortune.' He straightened and, seeing that Alec was about to protest, interrupted him. 'No, I think this is just another symptom of the continuing degradation of the city.'

'You can't know that!' said Gillian.

'Oh, don't you agree?' asked the Doctor in all innocence.

'It's not that,' she spluttered. 'It's just that you've hardly looked!'

'An educated guess. I'm sure further analysis will confirm it.'

'We don't have time for that!' cried Alec in frustration.

'My thoughts exactly.'

The rockers' leader had turned a shade of red. 'Look Doctor,' he snapped angrily, 'I've had enough of this! You keep playing things your way and people keep dying. The mods are slaughtering us, and all you can do is go out on day trips and play with record players and air tanks. Well, no more. From now on, you do as I tell you, all right?'

The Doctor stuck out his lower lip, sulkily. 'If you insist.'

'And the first thing you can do is see what's happening to the Brain.'

The Doctor brightened immediately. 'That's exactly what I was about to suggest,' he said, clicking his fingers. 'Yes, yes, yes, I think this "Brain" of yours could tell us a great deal about what's happening in the city. Well done. Now, how do I find it?'

'I'll show you,' said Gillian. She turned to Alec. 'I want to go with him.'

'No,' said Alec quickly.

'I think you should let her,' said the Doctor. He beamed at Gillian and put a hand on her shoulder, ignoring her answering scowl. 'She could learn a great deal.'

'More to the point,' said Gillian, 'you need someone to keep an eye on him.'

'You sure you want to do this, Gillian?' asked Alec.

'I'm sure.'

The Doctor clapped his hands together. 'Excellent, excellent. Well, let's get started, shall we? Not a moment to waste. Does anyone mind if I drive?'

Fitz had almost managed to doze off in the corner when the door next opened. This time, he knew straight away that he was in for trouble. There was no sign of the guard he had seen before, but Davey had brought two colleagues with him; they remained in the doorway and kept the automatic door from closing.

Davey wielded a long club, and his face was twisted with rage.

Fitz scrambled to his feet, only just making it in time to duck as Davey swung the club in his direction. 'What do you think you're –' he spluttered, but the question was cut short as the club whistled towards him again. This time, it connected with his stomach. Fitz doubled up in pain, and stumbled blindly towards Davey in the hope of denying him the space he needed to use his weapon effectively. They grappled for a few seconds:

Fitz got an arm around Davey's neck, until Davey tripped him and he needed that arm for balance. Davey used his momentary advantage to barge Fitz into the wall. He held the club lengthways with both hands and pushed it towards his victim's throat. Fitz caught it in time and strained to hold it back. With his back against the wall, he had leverage on his side – but Davey was strong, despite his slight stature.

'One of my friends is dead!' the young mod spat, his face inches away from Fitz's own.

'So, you thought you'd come and take it out on me,' Fitz snarled in return.

'You betrayed us!' yelled Davey.

'I haven't hurt anyone!'

Somehow, Fitz managed to raise his leg far enough to plant a foot in Davey's stomach and push. His attacker fell backwards, and the club ended up in Fitz's hands. At first, he didn't know what to do with it. Then Davey rushed him again, and he swung it wildly to keep him away. It worked. Davey's eyes still burned furiously, but he kept his distance. But then the other two mods abandoned their guard posts and came towards Fitz. Typical gang, he thought, with a bitterness born of experience. They had been content to leave things to Davey, so long as he had been winning. But they had never intended this to be a fair fight. He wondered how long he could keep all three of them at bay.

Then he saw that, with no one in range of its sensors, the door was closing. He was about to be trapped in here with the mods. And that realisation spurred him into action.

Fitz leapt across the room, spinning his arms – and, by extension, the club – like an insane whirlwind. He reached the door in a second, but it felt like a minute, as if the world were moving in slow motion and yet too quickly to think. His only plan was that, if he didn't know what he was doing, then no one else could anticipate it. Davey tried to intercept him, but he wasn't close enough. One of the other mods shied away; the third was braver but, by luck more than skill, Fitz landed a blow to his jaw and sent him reeling. He was just in time to squeeze himself between the door and the frame. He emerged into the corridor, thinking for a heady instant that he had trapped his attackers in the cell behind them. Then the external sensors detected him, and the door slid open for them.

Fitz ran.

Gillian had rarely ridden a jetcycle herself – it was still the custom for women to ride behind men – but she still felt resentful as the Doctor monopolised the controls. She sat in the saddle behind him, her arms folded, determined not to cling to him for support.

At Alec's insistence, they had a six-strong escort: the mods would be on the alert for anyone approaching the Brain. Indeed, as they neared the towering central building – at the bottom of which the supercomputer was located – Gillian heard the familiar high-pitched whine of scooters, and suddenly they were under attack.

The Doctor kicked the bike into high gear as yellow beams of energy crackled around them. The vehicle described a sharp curve, leaning dangerously so that the road surface scraped sparks off the panels on its left-hand side and Gillian almost toppled out of her seat. 'Hold on!' the Doctor shouted to her, belatedly. 'This could be a rough ride.'

Mod scooters flashed by, too quickly to count. One second, the bike was heading for two oncoming vehicles; the next, it veered off and joined an elevated roadway at its base. As the ground receded behind and beneath her, Gillian abandoned her pride and threw her arms around the Doctor. Even as she did, he steered off the edge of the road. She would have screamed, but she was breathless. By the time she fully realised she was upside down, the bike had completed its barrel roll, the Doctor had engaged the antigravity generator and they had flown beneath the road they had just left. As they hit the ground, Gillian's stomach lurched, although the kinetic dampers had supposedly cushioned the shock, and all she could hear was the Doctor's rich, joyous laughter.

She risked a look behind her. The other rockers had drawn off some of the attackers, but two still followed them. They had probably recognised their enemies' Technician and their alien helper, and made them the primary target.

'Will you stop showing off and just get us away from here?' she shouted.

'That won't achieve anything.'

'Just keep going in a straight line. They won't catch us on those hairdryers!'

'Their vehicles seem to have the same top speed as ours.'

'The hell they do!' Suddenly, Gillian realised what the Doctor had done. His uncanny control of the jetcycle had outstripped that of the mods on their scooters, such that they no longer stood between their foes and the Brain. But she knew something he didn't.

'It's not going to work!' she screamed in his ear.

'What isn't?'

'The Brain. We can't get into it.'

They had almost reached the central building by now. The featureless tower loomed above them, looped by most of the city's roads at various heights, and Gillian would have had to strain her neck to see its top. The building stood alone in the centre of a large open square, into which the cycle now roared. The Doctor steered the vehicle around three sides of it before remarking, 'I see what you mean. No doors.'

'There's a hatch,' said Gillian, pointing. 'You can just about see the seam. It opens for the servo-robots; they go in there for maintenance. We have to wait for one and follow it in.'

'There's no time for that.'

'I know. That's why I said this wasn't going to work. Thanks for listening!'

They left the square on the road by which they had entered it, even as the two mods rounded the nearest corner of the central building behind them. Gillian was so preoccupied with staring over her shoulder that she was taken by surprise when the cycle suddenly left the ground and banked right. An instant later, she saw why. Another scooter was diving at them from an elevated roadway. The Doctor had seen it just in time. Its rider was armed: he let off three bursts of energy from his ray gun, but the first two went awry and the third hit a spire that the Doctor had now put between them.

They continued to rise. This close to the city's centre, the roadways crossed each other frequently. The Doctor used that, keeping off the roads themselves but twisting between them, forever denying his pursuer a clear shot. He glanced back at Gillian, and she was astonished to see that he was grinning like a lunatic. 'You know how they say you shouldn't look down?' She nodded dumbly. 'Well, just this once...' She followed his pointed finger, but all she could see was a robot trundling along a ground-level road below them. And then the motorbike banked again, and she could no longer see even that.

They were on the topmost road now, heading for the central building itself. Another blast sizzled past Gillian's ear, and she turned to see that all three mods were back on their tail. She tightened her grip on the Doctor, realising unhappily that she was his human shield. Then he swerved around the building itself, sped along another road for a moment, then hurtled off it and hit the kinetic dampers.

The jetcycle hung in midair for an instant.

Then it dropped straight down, leaving Gillian's stomach behind again.

The Doctor hit the antigravity control at the last second. The cycle landed softly in one of the roads just off the central square. He wrenched the handlebars around to the right; the dampers strained but held as the cycle turned one hundred and twenty degrees in less than its own length, its tyres protesting at the seeming impossibility of the manoeuvre. The Doctor set off on a new course, gathering speed, as his pursuers hurtled over his head. It took the mods seconds to react to the sudden change of course. They lost ground, but not enough for Gillian's liking.

'This is the way back to the Brain!' Her words were whipped away as the bike continued its acceleration and wind whistled in her ears. Somehow, the Doctor heard them anyway.

'That's where we want to go.'

'Have you got a problem with your short-term memory or something?'

'Remember that robot? It was coming this way. Now, assuming a constant rate of movement along the shortest path to its destination...'

He made another turn, and suddenly they were racing towards the Brain's maintenance hatch and Gillian knew what he was planning to do. 'You're mad!' she yelled.

The hatch was open. The back of a servo-robot was disappearing through it.

'I miscalculated,' shouted the Doctor hoarsely. 'Only by a second. We might still make it.'

'Might?'

'Hold tight. And duck!'

The hatch was closing. The cycle screamed towards it. Gillian shrank down as far as she could into the saddle, burying her head in the Doctor's back and bracing herself for the inevitable impact. Her primal scream merged with the rending of metal, as the cycle proved too wide for the aperture. She smelled burning as the metal edges of the hatchway tore at its bulky panelling, but the Doctor refused to be slowed.

And then, miraculously, they were through. The Doctor applied the brakes, and suddenly the world was silent and empty and safe.

Several seconds passed before Gillian dared to look up.

Fitz raced through the underground complex, grateful for the time he had spent exploring it. Davey was at his heels, and his two comrades weren't far behind him. At one point, Fitz turned a corner to find another two mods in front of him. He had no option but to put his head down and keep running and, thankfully, although Davey shouted to the mods, they didn't react in time. As Fitz sprinted past them, however, they did join the chase.

He took the only chance he had. If he was lucky, then the café upstairs would be empty – or perhaps, if he just barrelled through it, he would be able to reach the street before anyone thought to stop him. He hurtled into the chamber that held the antigrav tube, and took a flying leap into its area of effect. It plucked him from midair, and he felt a sense of exhilaration as he shot up towards freedom.

Then his stomach lurched towards his chest and he was standing beneath the tube, reeling with disorientation. Slowly, he took in the scene. Davey stood by the control panel on the wall: he must have used it to reverse Fitz's direction. Now he clenched his fists and moved towards Fitz menacingly, even as the other four mods arrived.

He was cornered. Experience had taught him that, at times like this, it was probably best not to fight back at all: just throw down the weapon, curl into a ball and take the beating, without provoking your attackers further. But he was too much of a coward to let the club go. He brandished it in a warning gesture, intending to land at least a few good blows against whoever came at him first.

'Rick would like Davey to bring the spaceman, Fitz Kreiner, to him,' interrupted the measured tones of the loudspeaker woman. 'In one piece,' she added meaningfully. Somebody must have seen and reported what was happening. Either that or there were hidden cameras, as well as lights, in the walls somewhere.

Davey faltered, his expression so thunderous that Fitz could almost have laughed, had he not thought that it might push the young mod over the edge. He wanted to smile anyway, to toss the club to Davey and to say, ever so casually, 'Well? You heard your orders.'

Instead, he felt the weapon falling out of his numbed fingers. He closed his eyes, took a deep, shuddering breath and let it out in a heartfelt sigh of relief.

Sandra sat on the edge of her bed, cradling her head in her hands and wishing the world would just leave her alone. 'You killed Joey,' she repeated, her tone hardly less disbelieving than when she had first said it.

'It was an accident,' said Alec, and Sandra couldn't tell if that bothered him or not.

'You killed Joey.'

Alec scowled at her. He had actually seemed contrite at first, afraid even, but now his arrogant mask was back in place. How typical. 'He shouldn't have attacked us in the first place, should he? Then we wouldn't have caught him.'

'He used to come to our house all the time. He was one of Jack and Phil's best friends.'

'So?'

Alec put so much disdain into that one word. Did he care so little? Did he think that, even after so many years, the pain of a loss such as Sandra had suffered could lessen? Could he not see that he had severed one more link to her past, to a family long gone?

'You didn't get so upset when your precious Ricky killed one of ours,' he sneered, 'when he tried to kill me.'

'You just don't understand, do you?'

'I understand that you think more of some sad mod than you do of your own husband.'

Shock gave way to anger, and Sandra jumped to her feet. 'That's not true! I hate it when *anyone* dies. It's so pointless. And we don't need you making things worse!'

'It was an accident,' repeated Alec, through clenched teeth this time.

'And you having the body dumped on Rick's doorstep – that was an accident too, was it?'

'I didn't start this. It was your crazy brother who messed with the Brain, not me.'

'You don't know that.'

'I'll soon find out.'

'What does that mean?' Alec turned away, but Sandra wasn't ready to give up. She had done that too many times already. 'I said, what does that mean?'

'I've sent someone there.'

'To the Brain?'

'It's about time we found out what's happening.'

Sandra felt queasy. 'You've sent the Doctor, haven't you?'

'I might have.'

'Haven't you?' The question came out as a shriek, and Alec turned back to Sandra, visibly startled. 'Who else, Alec? Who else?'

'Gillian. I didn't want her to go with him, but she insisted.'

'And did you warn her?'

'How could I, without making the Doctor suspicious?'

Sandra surprised herself then by slapping Alec hard across the face. 'Do you know what you've done?' she screamed.

'Get off me, you mad cow!' he spat, pushing her away before she could hit him again.

'You know what happened last time,' she raged impotently, 'and you didn't tell them! You sent them into that place to die!'

'Do you think that's what I want?'

'You tell me.'

'Of course I don't. I don't want to lose the Doctor – he's the best Technician we've had – but he's no good to me if he won't make weapons.'

'So you thought you'd teach him a lesson.'

'No, that's not it. I thought… I thought if his own life was in danger, he'd be forced to do something useful – like knock out the Brain's defences and get us in there.'

'Or he might just die – like Gillian might die!'

'I had to take that risk. You know how things have been. It's our last hope.'

As always when his decisions were challenged, Alec's façade had slipped. He was weak, vulnerable, unsure of himself. Usually, that was enough to make Sandra remember why she had fallen in love with him. Today she just despised him all the more for continuing to play the tough guy, the leader, when all he could lead his people to was disaster.

'What's up with you, Sandra?' he pleaded. 'Why do you keep arguing with me? You haven't been like this since we were kids.'

'Well, maybe I should have been,' she muttered, just loud enough for him to hear. She sank back down on to the bed, buried her face in her hands despairingly and ignored him until she heard him sigh heavily and march out of the room.

Sandra had suffered many disappointments over the past nineteen years, but this time it was different. She felt all the worse because the Doctor had given her hope, made her believe things could change. Even the barrier at the end of the world had felt like a minor obstacle. The revelation that this wasn't Earth had made everything possible.

But then she had returned to the city, this damned city, and her hopes had been destroyed one by one. That was why she had lost her temper, she realised: because of the stark reminder that she was helpless after all.

No, she couldn't accept that. She couldn't go back to just putting up with the way things were. Her wish for something better had been rekindled, and she refused to let that fire die out a second time. She had to do something.

So Sandra did something. She made a decision that she knew she ought to have made many years ago. And she forced herself to go through with it, before she could change her mind; before she could decide that it was better not to take risks, to leave things well alone.

She found a metal suitcase at the bottom of her cupboard and began to fill it with clothes.

* * *

'Compassion's here?'

Fitz surprised himself by being more relieved than worried. At least he knew where his ticket off this world was now, and he was fairly sure that Rick couldn't harm Compassion in her current state. 'Where is she?' he asked. 'Can I see her?'

Rick, still overflowing with energy, beamed broadly and nodded. 'I insist on it. I've got a job for you. You can communicate with her?'

'As much as anyone can, I suppose.'

'You'll have to do better than that.'

Now we're getting to it, thought Fitz. He had been suspicious of Rick's motives ever since he had been dragged back to his reception room. Rick had dismissed his prisoner's escorts, despite Davey's attempt to object. 'Our spaceman knows better than to cross me now,' he had said, 'and there's only one way out of here if he does.'

When Rick, his lips twisted into a superior sneer, had boasted of his latest 'acquisition', Fitz had begun to understand. The mods' leader clung to his privacy; he didn't want even his own men to know the secrets of his power. He was probably afraid they'd take it from him. So why was he opening up to a relative stranger, and a potential enemy at that? He was hiding more than the presence of Compassion, Fitz was sure of it.

'What's wrong?' he asked, the absence of guards making him feel brave enough to taunt his captor. 'Won't she talk to you? You can't have made a very good impression.'

With exaggerated politeness, Rick opened the room's inner door and motioned his prisoner through it. 'She'll talk,' he vowed as Fitz passed him, 'if she knows what's good for you.'

'Yeah, right,' muttered Fitz under his breath.

'You're privileged,' said Rick, as if he believed it. 'Not many people get to see inside my suite. There are some things here I don't want anyone knowing about. Remember that.'

They were at the end of a short corridor, from which six doors led, three to each side. In contrast to the bare floors elsewhere in the complex, Fitz found himself walking on a thick fur rug. He smiled inwardly. The mods' leader may have been happy to fight with his troops, but he still insisted on the perks that came with his position.

Rick led the way to the second door on the left, and stopped in front of it. 'She's in here,' he said. Fitz stepped forward, but the door didn't respond to him – not until Rick triggered what must have been a voice-activated lock with the words 'Rick here. Open sesame.'

The room into which Fitz stepped was furnished like all the other living rooms: metal bed, metal table, metal cupboard, metal chairs. Compassion was sitting on the floor beside the bed, her back to the wall, her knees against her chest. She didn't react to Fitz's presence at all. Her eyes were open but staring through the ceiling. That, he supposed, was pretty normal for her now. She was all right.

His attention was taken by the room's other occupant. The creature lay on the bed – or, rather, it bobbed a fraction of an inch above it, presumably resting on a gravity mattress. It was humanoid, but its arms and legs looked wasted and its head was disproportionately large. Its skin was scaly and grey, tinged with purple. It lay on its side, a long tail curled beneath it and, although it didn't move, its eyelids opened sideways and bright yellow eyes rolled like balls in their sockets to regard the new arrivals. The creature's wrists were bound with knotted chains, which in turn were connected by numerous small padlocks and threaded through a ring that was set into the wall above the bed head. On closer inspection, Fitz suspected that the awkward angles at which the creature's legs were bent were not natural. It had been crippled, presumably for the sake of keeping it here. His stomach turned at that notion, and he couldn't help but wonder if Rick might do something similar to him.

He turned to Rick, to see that he was wearing a manic grin. 'What is it?' he asked, but even before the words were out he knew the answer. He had heard this creature described before.

'It isn't… I mean you haven't…?'

'I have,' said Rick, with inordinate satisfaction. 'Do you see now why the rockers can't beat me? Do you see why I'm going to rule this world? I've captured the Maker!'

Chapter Nine
Reel to Real

They were folded up at the very back of the cupboard: the black skirt, the white blouse and the long overcoat. The clothes that Sandra had worn that night, when she had gone out into the dark to find Alec; the night on which she had been brought here to the city. She had almost forgotten about them. They were probably too small now, of course – like Alec's stupid leather jacket – but that wasn't why she had stopped wearing them.

She had last worn the clothes on the day of the funeral. Not that she had attended it, although that had been her plan when she had put the clothes on. The mods had been burying their own, and rockers weren't welcome. And she, apparently, was a rocker now. Sandra would have gone anyway, except that her new husband wouldn't let her out on her own. He talked about accompanying her, taking some of the other rockers and doing whatever it took to allow her to pay her respects in safety. But that would have led to a fight, and Sandra didn't want that. Not on the day that her two older brothers were laid to rest.

Instead, she had a servo-robot relay pictures to another in her quarters. She sent Alec away, knowing that he only wished to comfort her but needing to be alone. And she watched as the mods lined up at the edge of the city, resplendent in the silver uniforms that they wore as a mark of respect, and Jack and Phil were lowered into the ground in metal caskets.

At one point, the robots showed her Ricky's face. Nearly five years old, and he had lost so much already. But he wasn't crying. He looked almost impassive, but Sandra could see through his mask. Beneath it, she knew, boiled the same turbulent mix of emotions that she was feeling. One of the mods – Joey, an old friend of her brothers – drew the boy protectively to his side, and Sandra knew then that she had lost him too.

'You made your choice.' The last words that Jack had ever said to her.

She had worn the skirt and the blouse and the overcoat that evening, when she slipped out of the complex and visited her brothers' grave alone. Alec was furious about that, and perhaps Sandra had been unwise. But she had needed to say goodbye. After that, the clothes were folded away carefully and hidden. She needed no more reminders of the life she had lost.

Now, though, the clothes brought all those memories back. Sandra didn't know how long she had knelt there on the metal floor, crying into the fabric of the skirt and replaying old sorrows in her mind. But as she stood up and wiped her eyes on her sleeve, she was surer than ever that she was making the right decision.

She had lost so much. It was time she got some of it back.

There were five corpses in all. Gillian hadn't meant to count them, didn't want to even look at them. Three rockers and two mods; ten eyes staring sightlessly out of dead faces. Blood had trickled from one rocker's ears to harden on his cheek. There was so much else to see, so much to take in, and yet she kept finding her eyes drawn back to them.

The Brain's chamber must have taken up the whole of the inside of the central tower. It was probably the biggest room she had seen in the city, and certainly the highest. All the way up to the distant ceiling, the walls were festooned with buttons, levers, dials and multicoloured lights which blinked and flickered in an almost hypnotic pattern. The floor was crisscrossed with cables, each with a thick rubber coating of red or green. It was impossible to walk without stepping on them. The hatch had fully closed now, and the damaged jetcycle lay a short way inside it. One of its side panels had been ripped free altogether. There was no sign of the robot that the Doctor had followed in here.

In the middle of the room was a freestanding machine that could only have been the Brain itself. It looked just as Gillian had imagined: like an oversized tape recorder, smooth and silver like the walls of the city. On the nearest of its four vertical surfaces – the one that faced them – was a square panel with curved edges, into which three reels were set in a triangular pattern, two at the top. Gillian wondered how that could possibly work. Beneath the reels was a rectangular glass monitor screen with a green light behind it. The red and green cables all seemed to terminate at the machine. There were various slots in its sides, which Gillian guessed would take programming cards.

'You are the inhabitant designated Gillian,' said the Brain, in a voice not dissimilar to those of the servo-robots but richer and more booming. As it spoke, a visual representation of the sound it made flickered across its screen and its reels turned first one way and then the other. Gillian couldn't help but think of the top two reels as impassive eyes, and the bottom one as a gaping mouth. 'And you are not an inhabitant. Your form does not appear in my databanks.'

'No,' mumbled the Doctor. He had plunged his hands into the pockets of his green velvet jacket, and he regarded the machine through hooded eyes. 'I don't expect I do. That worries you, doesn't it?'

'You are intruders. You cannot be allowed to harm me. I must effect countermeasures.' The Brain's words were underscored by a persistent chattering sound, and only now did Gillian see that a length of tickertape was being extruded from one of the slots on its side.

The Doctor pouted. 'Oh dear, that would be dreadfully boring. Can't we talk instead?'

'Countermeasures?' repeated Gillian in a small voice. She was just beginning to connect the Brain's pronouncement with the presence of the dead bodies.

'I'm afraid so, Gillian,' said the Doctor, not sounding apologetic at all. 'You see, Alec lied to us again. The rockers and the mods didn't leave the Brain alone for fear of damaging it. They left it alone only because the Brain made sure of it.'

Gillian became aware of another sound then: it started as a low hum, but it was already building to a piercing shriek. 'I do apologise for any inconvenience,' said the Brain. 'I am programmed to protect the city's inhabitants. I do not wish to harm them.'

'Then what's this supposed to be?' cried Gillian, clapping her hands over her ears, which were beginning to hurt. 'A soothing ballad?'

She barely heard the supercomputer's response, but it sounded like, 'Your presence here jeopardises the city itself. For the sake of the majority of its inhabitants, you must die.'

Then the sound grew louder, and the pain grew much greater.

'Look,' said Fitz, trying to control his impatience, 'my life's on the line here. Will you listen to me please?' At least Compassion was looking at him now, but she didn't react at all. 'You can communicate with the Maker, can't you? Mind to mind. Please tell me you can.' Still no response. 'Rick thinks you can, and he thinks I can talk to you. He wants to use us both. Do you understand? The Maker's given him ray guns and jetpacks, but he thinks he can get more if he can only get through to him properly.'

Slowly, Compassion turned away from him, back to the Maker.

Fitz leapt to his feet, fighting down the urge to scream. 'Christ, what does it take to get you to say something?' he bellowed, but that did no good either. 'It's all right for you,' he said bitterly. 'He can't hurt you. But what about me?'

He could hear Rick pacing in the corridor outside. He would be back soon. It had been hard enough to get rid of him in the first place. He had been all but ready to haul Fitz back to his cell, to leave him at Davey's mercy. He couldn't invent anything like the Doctor could, he couldn't communicate with the Maker as Compassion could, and now he couldn't even talk to his one-time companion. So, what use was he at all?

He had tried reminding her of all they had been through together, all they had meant to each other. It hadn't taken long. 'OK,' he had concluded, 'so you've always been a frosty cow and you've never liked me much, but do you want me to die here?'

He crouched beside her again, seized her by the shoulders and shook her. He remembered what the Doctor had said about her senses extruding into other dimensions. 'Can you hear me?' he shouted. 'It's Fitz. I'm down here in the real world. For God's sake, the least you can do is let me in there where it's safe. Talk to me, can't you?' Still nothing.

He stood again, turned away from her and buried his head in his hands in frustration.

'There's no need to shout,' said a familiar haughty voice behind him.

'Compassion!' He whirled around, hardly daring to believe it. She hadn't moved, but there was something about her eyes, something that told him she was seeing him, really seeing him now. He fairly leapt across the room towards her. 'I've never been so... you don't know how...' He frowned. 'Were you winding me up?'

'You were right,' she said. 'I am in communion with the alien.'

'Well, good for you. And what's he thinking?'

'It is hard to explain. The Maker, as you call it, exists in many dimensions. You see only one aspect of it. The truth is... distracting. Overwhelming, even.'

'You're kidding. Is that why you zoned out on us? The Doctor thought –'

'Even I can't process everything at once. I'm seeing – learning – so much. It's an effort to concentrate on the physical plane at all.'

'Don't you dare go drifting off on me again,' warned Fitz.

'I'll show you,' said Compassion, her eyes already misting over. 'Show you...'

She took his hand, and suddenly he was somewhere else entirely.

* * *

'People underestimate how effective a tool sound waves can be,' said the Doctor, as he rummaged through his pockets. He glanced at Gillian, who was on her knees now, her arms wrapped around her head in a futile attempt to block out the ever-increasing noise. 'Or a weapon. Even as it turns the brain to jelly, it disrupts the victim's thoughts and prevents him from fighting back.' He grinned as he found his sonic screwdriver. He held it up and activated it. Its familiar whine was lost in the cacophony but, undaunted, he began to adjust the device's frequency. He continued to talk: Gillian certainly couldn't hear him, but perhaps the Brain could. In any case, the words were more for his own benefit, something for him to focus upon. 'Of course, two can play at that game, as they say. Especially if one has a Time Lord brain and knowledge of concentration techniques.'

For all his bravado, the sonic attack was beginning to affect him. His knees felt weak and his eyes closed involuntarily as he stumbled around in a clumsy circle, continually adjusting the screwdriver's output and trying to find the cancellation wave. Then something popped on the far side of the room, and the noise halved in volume. As the Doctor congratulated himself inwardly, there was another explosion behind him. He started as he was showered in sparks.

The silence that followed rang in his numbed ears. He flew towards Gillian and yanked her unceremoniously to her feet. She fell against him, dazed, and he supported her. A deep, muffled voice was saying something, but he couldn't make out what. He turned to the Brain. 'So, your voice circuits still work. Or do they? You'll have to excuse me, I'm a trifle deaf. No, Gillian, don't step on the floor. Keep on the cables; that's right. I must learn how to read sound waves – I could be missing a good rant. Now, I don't suppose I can get to those controls?' He reached out gingerly and tapped a switch on the wall with the sonic screwdriver. The severity of the ensuing blue flash took him by surprise. He recoiled, and almost put his foot down on the metal floor. He caught himself in time and pivoted back to face the Brain. 'Nice try. What other surprises do you have in store, I wonder?' The Brain spoke again, and spat more tickertape at the Doctor. He reached out, tore off a length and read the printout expectantly. 'The usual dull threats,' he said with a despairing sigh.

A seamless panel in the wall slid upwards, revealing the missing servo-robot. It trundled out of its alcove, shaking unsteadily as it forced itself over the ubiquitous cables. Gillian must have been feeling better because she looked up and saw it, and squirmed out of the Doctor's embrace to stare at the automaton in horror. The Doctor pushed her behind him, protectively. 'Run!' he yelled, as loudly as he could, backing up the instruction by gesticulating wildly. Whether Gillian heard or not he didn't know, but she got the message. 'And keep off the floor! Don't touch anything!' he added, as he stooped and gathered up two thick red cables.

'Doctor!' screamed Gillian – and, at that moment, the robot bumped into him.

He flinched, almost expecting to be electrocuted. To his relief, his deduction proved correct. 'Don't worry,' he called to Gillian, 'it's not as dangerous as the other one. The servo-robots don't tend to be wired up that way.' Even so, the robot kept coming, forcing him to skip backwards away from it and to snatch his arm clear from its grasping pincers. Its intent was clearly to barge him into a wall or into the Brain, or to force a misstep on to the floor, so that its controlling computer could fry him. He recovered and dived forward instead, ducking beneath his attacker's rigid arms, still holding the cable. The robot turned to face him, and it began to close in again.

'There's really no need for this, you know,' the Doctor shouted to the Brain. 'You could try talking instead. I'm ready to listen – well, almost.'

He dived past the robot again, but this time it was ready for him. Its arms snapped down in unison and a pincer clamped around the Doctor's neck. He gave a grunt of pain and resisted the urge to fall to his knees, but dropped one of the cables. 'It always amazes me what you artificial life forms can achieve with such ungainly appendages,' he remarked through gritted teeth, as he completed the task of threading the other cable around the robot's base section and knotting it to itself. He braced himself with his foot – he couldn't see where he was putting it, but luck allowed it to find another cable – and pushed hard with his shoulder. The robot toppled, lost its grip on him and crashed to the floor face first.

He bounced back to his feet, grinned broadly and rubbed his hands together with satisfaction. The robot thrashed about, unable to right itself. The computer's reels spun frantically and, perplexingly, in different directions. 'Any more defence programs you'd like to run?' the Doctor asked gleefully.

'Don't engage it in conversation,' cried Gillian from across the room. 'Just shut the damn thing down before it kills us.'

'Yes, yes, yes, of course.' The Doctor scampered towards the Brain, balancing on one green cable with his arms stretched out like a tightrope walker. He stooped down, placed his hands on his knees and examined his electronic foe closely. 'Now, let me think…' He buried his face in his hands. 'Mab, Macra, Macsellians, Mad Computers… ah!'

Something exploded, Gillian shrieked and the Doctor leapt up. The rockers' Technician was scrambling away from a panel on the wall, from which smoke billowed. 'Don't let it rattle you,' he advised. 'Keep off the floor. Now, let me see…'

'You only delay the inevitable,' said the Brain.

'Yes, yes, yes, of course, but first: if all elephants are pink and Nelly is an elephant, what colour is Nelly?' The Doctor's voice was speeding up, as it often did when he became excited. 'Everything I say is a lie, and I'm lying now. No flashing lights? No "does not compute"? Tell me: which came first, the chicken or the egg? How long is a piece of string?'

'Your statements are illogical,' said the Brain. 'Therefore I shall disregard them.'

'Oh,' said the Doctor, disappointed. 'That never seems to work any more.' Then he brightened. 'Well, it's nice to know you lot have come on a bit, anyway.' He hopped back towards the fallen servo-robot and brandished his sonic screwdriver again.

'I am removing all oxygen from this chamber,' said the Brain – and, as if to confirm its words, the Doctor heard a sinister hissing sound. He crouched beside the robot and adjusted the screwdriver. 'In precisely three point four four minutes, you will be unable to –'

'Yes, yes, I heard you. But what do you hope to gain?'

'You are intruders. You cannot be allowed to harm me.'

'Why not?'

'I control the city's systems. Without them, the inhabitants will die.'

'But they'll die anyway, won't they?' The Doctor kept his back towards the Brain, but he heard its reels spinning back and forth in confusion. 'They'll die, because both you and the city are decaying. So, what if your intruders are here to help and not harm you?'

It took the Brain several seconds to process that problem, but then it responded with its familiar phrase: 'You are intruders. You cannot be allowed to harm me.'

By that time, the sonic screwdriver had vibrated one of the robot's hands free at the wrist. The Doctor snatched it up, delighted. He turned to the Brain, even as he pulled off his jacket and wrapped it around the metal appendage. 'Three point four four minutes, you say? But I resisted your sonic attack for longer than you predicted, didn't I? What if I can survive longer without oxygen too? Can you even be sure I need it at all?' He whirled around and, with a manic grin, hit one of the wall-mounted control panels with his makeshift weapon. 'How much damage do you think I can do in three point four four minutes? Or five? Or twenty?' He danced across the room, aiming blow after blow at the controls, sometimes causing explosions of light. When he reached the corner, he pivoted back towards the Brain and brandished the artificial hand in triumph. 'Kill me and I'll take you with me. Talk to me and I'll help you. You've got nothing to lose.'

Another few steps took him to Gillian, who was watching, pale and frightened. He put a comforting arm around her, and she didn't resist. He crossed his fingers behind his back.

The computer's reels still spun. The hissing sound of departing air continued.

'Come on,' urged the Doctor. 'That's logical, isn't it? Don't disappoint me now.'

Fitz felt a cool breeze on his cheek, tasted salt in the air and heard an upbeat tune played on a distant piano. He couldn't move. He was lying on his back, held immobile by wires and rods. The pungent smell of burning chased away the fresh, bracing scent of days at the seaside. He opened his eyes, although the effort was immense, to find his vision blurred. He stared at a grey sky, and tried to bring two pink blobs into focus. Faces. The pink blobs were faces, but he couldn't make out whose they were.

He reached out with other senses instead, senses that he hadn't known he possessed. The sudden inrush of information threatened to wrench his mind out of place. His stomach pitched and rolled and his head spun dizzily.

Alec. One of the faces belonged to Alec. He had travelled only nineteen years along his own timeline, but he was unmistakably Alec. Fitz could see him as the thirty-eight-year-old man with whom he was familiar, and as a baby and a pensioner. The faces blurred together, became as one, and Fitz could see the life of Alec Redshaw from start to finish; could see the day he gave up his leathers and sold his bike, his bust-up with Sandra, his marriage to Michelle Watkins, his resignation from a dead-end job to set up on his own as a motor mechanic, his eventual death from cancer. He could see all that, but none of it with clarity. He felt as if he were too close to the picture, as though, if he could step back, it would all become clear. The images collided with each other, piling up until Fitz could hardly stand it, could hardly cope with their relentless assault, and only in some distant recess of his subconscious mind did he think to ask why Alec's years in the city weren't among them.

In the here and now – inasmuch as Fitz understood that concept any more – Alec reached for Fitz uncertainly. The woman beside him – Sandra, her name was Sandra – clutched his arm in concern, and he withdrew. She said something, but Fitz couldn't hear what it was. He tried to ignore her; he could feel the images ghosting around her too and he was afraid of seeing them, afraid of overloading his brain.

The images were changing. Fitz realised, with a stab of fear, that *he* was changing them. Alec stayed with Sandra, fought her brothers for her, married her, gave up smoking for her, was divorced by her four years later, stayed in the dead-end job because he had a child to support, died peacefully in his sleep at the age of seventy-two. Fitz saw the changes, rippling across time, and he knew that his presence here was a fire in the course of Alec Redshaw's life. The fire consumed the old pattern and ensured that the tapestry could never be knitted back quite the way it had been before.

Fitz saw all this in an instant, and much more besides, and it was too much. He opened his mouth and lungs and screamed. And, once he had started screaming, he couldn't stop.

The coat was far too small, as Sandra had feared – but she wore it anyway because it felt right. It felt as if she were reclaiming some of her old life. Not that a few clothes were much to show for that. But then, neither were the contents of a small metal case much to show for her new one. Anyway, the coat hid some of her rocker clothing, and that seemed appropriate.

Her journey up to the surface was a long one: Alec had closed the gravity pit, so Sandra had to use the stairs. Each step took forever. The inconvenience worked in her favour, though. The milk bar held fewer rockers than usual. Their conversations were stilled as she appeared in the doorway, but she didn't let herself falter. They watched her as she crossed the room, and she thought she might get past them unchallenged. Then one of them stepped into her path. She recognised the lean-faced Kenny, the leader of Eagle Group.

'Going somewhere?'

She made an effort to straighten her shoulders and look him in the eyes. 'Yes, I am.'

Kenny glanced down at her case. 'Looks like you're planning on staying a while.'

'That's none of your business.'

'Depends where you're going, dunnit?'

'On an important mission. Alec knows all about it.'

'Oh, really?' Kenny raised an eyebrow and sneered in disbelief.

'Get out of my way,' said Sandra, trying to remain calm although she was trembling inside. When Kenny didn't move, she repeated the instruction more forcefully.

'I don't take orders from you,' he said bluntly.

'That's where you're wrong,' snapped Sandra. 'I'm Alec's wife.'

'You're a traitor!'

'Think what you like. But I'm walking out of that door now, and the only way you'll stop me is physically. Do you think you can do that? Lay a hand on the boss's wife?'

Doubt flickered in Kenny's eyes, and gave Sandra her single chance. She set off towards the door again, resisting the urge to even look back at him. She expected to feel his hand on her shoulder, expected him to wrestle her to the ground and hold her there until somebody could fetch Alec. She didn't know what Alec would do then. She couldn't even guess any more.

To her surprise, she reached the front door unmolested. Her new-found determination failed her then, and she faltered on the threshold and looked back. The sight of her former comrades glaring at her with such hatred in their eyes was all she needed to tell her that her decision was now irrevocable.

'Good riddance,' said Kenny in a spiteful growl, as Sandra left the rockers' milk bar. A few seconds later, the pavement whirred into action and carried her away for the final time.

Compassion and Fitz had joined hands, and Fitz was screaming as if he had been subjected to all the pain in the world. 'What are you doing to him?' cried Rick, hurling himself into the room but faltering, not knowing what to do, not wanting to even touch Compassion if she could do that to a man. She took her hand away from her companion's.

'I showed him what he wanted to see,' she said dispassionately. 'I was wrong. His mind could not cope with so much information, such an alien viewpoint.' Her face softened, and a note of pity entered her voice. 'Poor Fitz.'

Rick's first impulse was to send for assistance, but he didn't want his people to see what he had here. He approached Fitz instead, skirting around Compassion warily. She didn't move. She had turned away from her supposed friend and had lapsed into a trance again. Rick took the gangly spaceman's arm and hauled him to his feet. Fitz was a dead weight, his eyes blank, his face still locked into a scream that had now petered out into silence. As Rick dragged him towards the door, he regained some control of his muscles, but his attempts to walk were unco-ordinated and only made him more of a burden.

Rick took a few steps into the corridor, and gave up as the door of the Maker's room slid shut behind him. Fitz crumpled, like a puppet with its strings cut. Rick wondered if he was hurt, but then the spaceman rolled on to his back, pushed himself up with his arms until he was sitting against the wall, and laughed hysterically.

'What is it?' demanded Rick. 'What's funny? What's wrong with you?'

'Like dolphins,' stammered Fitz between outbursts of laughter, wiping tears from his eyes. 'That's how the Maker sees you. Me. Us. Dolphins.'

Rick wasn't sure whether to take that as an insult or not. 'What did she do to you?'

'She showed me,' Fitz babbled, 'showed me so much. So many images.' His eyes were unfocused, as if he were looking for those images still. 'Too much to remember. Too much to take in. Too much at once. Just pictures, sensations, ideas...'

Rick crouched in front of him and placed steadying hands on his shoulders, as if he could impart some of his energy, some of his control, to the spaceman. His heart was beating so hard and so fast that it was painful. For weeks now, he had felt close, so close, to the greatest secret in the world. He hadn't been able to get it from the Maker. He hadn't been able to get it from Compassion. Now it was in Fitz Kreiner's head. It was attainable.

This was going to change everything.

'Tell me what the Maker told you,' he insisted. 'Quickly, while you still can.'

'Don't know where to begin,' Fitz mumbled.

'Anywhere,' said Rick, his voice rising to a squeak. He made himself calm down. 'Anything. Just latch on to something. Tell me something!'

'Like dolphins,' Fitz said, lapsing into giggles again. 'Oh, it knows you have intelligence. Some intelligence, anyway. But you – we – we're nothing like it. Sad, limited creatures, crawling along without seeing. Like dolphins. We can't leave the water, can't see the world beyond it. Can't look up.' Something seemed to occur to him. He reached out blindly, and Rick offered his hand. Fitz took it, and clasped his own hands around it urgently. Rick leaned in closer, tense with anticipation, aware of the sound of his own breathing.

'We can't see where we're going,' said Fitz, in hushed, reverential tones.

Rick snatched his hand away angrily. 'Give me something useful! I want to know how to make things. Did it tell you how to make a lie detector? A mind probe? An atom bomb?'

Fitz's head lolled back against the wall and he was laughing again, and talking as if to himself. 'It can't communicate with us, can't understand us. When it found you on the beach, when you rescued it…'

Rick stood up, disgusted. Perhaps Fitz would make more sense, tell him something worth knowing, when he had calmed down and recovered his senses. If not – if his spaceman was no use to him after all – well, then he would have to dispose of him somehow. After all, Fitz Kreiner knew his secrets. He couldn't be allowed to share them.

'Like dolphins,' said Fitz again, as Rick abandoned him and marched back to his reception room. 'Like a school that pushes a drowning swimmer ashore. It wanted to reward you. It took pity on the little blind animals. It gave you… gave you…'

An unnatural chill came over Rick. Despite himself, he stopped in his tracks, and turned to find that Fitz was staring right at him, unnerving him further. Suddenly, he felt as if he were on the verge of learning his momentous secret after all. Only it wasn't at all what he had expected, and he was afraid of it.

'It gave you the future,' said Fitz, in a deathly cold whisper.

Gillian needed to sit down, or at least to lean against something. She could hardly believe that the Brain – the Brain of all things, the supercomputer that controlled everything she knew – had tried to kill her. The Doctor seemed to have persuaded it to rein in its homicidal impulses, but she still couldn't bring herself to touch anything. She took deep breaths instead, wrapped herself in her arms and tried to take in what was being said without thinking, really thinking, about what it meant for her life and for her world.

'The humans could not see what lay before them,' said the Brain. 'They dreamed of the paths they wished to take, but they knew not how to navigate the fourth dimension. They would wander off course, lose sight of their ambitions and find only disappointment.'

'I think I'm beginning to see,' said the Doctor, distractedly. For the past few minutes, even as the Brain had recounted its tale, he had hopped around the walls of the room, flicking switches here, pulling levers there, reading dials and collecting printouts.

'The Maker, in its gratitude, chose to assist these poor, blind creatures. It planned to guide them through the fourth dimension, picking out a path for them. But no path existed that would lead them to the world they had dreamed of building. So, the Maker created that world for them. Here on this planetoid, it built them a future.'

'So, none of this is real,' said Gillian, her voice sounding faint in her ears.

'Oh, it's real all right,' said the Doctor, 'but it's dying.'

'What you said about molecular decay...' To Gillian, the deterioration of the city had been one more problem among many. It may have been the most serious, but it had also been the least imminent. Not any more. The Brain had tried to kill her. Suddenly, the idea that the city had been corrupted, that it was breaking down, even rotting away, was chillingly plausible.

'I had thought for a while that the Brain might be responsible,' said the Doctor.

'But it isn't?'

'I'm afraid not. It's being affected like everything else.'

'But... But Alec thinks...'

'He thinks I'll shut down the Brain's defences so he can use it against the mods.'

'And he can't?'

'He'd only make things worse, as usual.' The Doctor sighed, buried his face in his hands, paced out a small circle and then leapt back into action. He had put his coat back on, and its tails flapped as he whirled around to face the Brain again. 'How long have we got?'

'The rate of decay is increasing exponentially,' said the Brain. 'Current projections indicate that I will be unable to sustain the inhabitants after one point three nine days.'

'Less than two days?' gasped Gillian.

'What if you turn yourself off?'

'I do not understand.'

'Oh, *now* I confuse you!' said the Doctor ruefully. 'Conserve power. Shut down everything except the oxygen generators and, oh, say emergency lights in the underground complex?'

'Two point zero three days,' calculated the Brain, 'but my programming will not permit –'

'Oh, please let's not argue again. Human beings can survive without food and water for that length of time, yes? So, do you have an option that will keep them alive any longer?'

'You can't do this,' said Gillian, as the Brain spun its reels in contemplation.

'Not you as well,' he groaned. 'Why do I always have to explain myself?'

'Alec won't let you shut the Brain down.'

'Alec isn't here.'

'He's our leader.'

'He's *your* leader.'

'How are we going to live without it?'

'For the next two days, you'll be more concerned with trying to escape this world.' The Doctor raised his voice to address the Brain again. 'You say your function is to protect the inhabitants, yes? Then prove it. Give them a chance to live!' He turned back to Gillian and nodded grimly. 'It'll do it.'

'How can you be so sure?'

'Because it's logical. Do I have to convince you of that too?' She shook her head. 'Good. Because we're running out of time. Help me stand this robot up.'

Gillian was wary of touching the fallen servo-robot at first, but she was swept along by the Doctor's urgency. They righted the automaton between them, and the Doctor asked it how it was. 'I am functional, sir,' it said, 'although the loss of my hand will impede –'

'Yes yes yes,' he said impatiently, 'I want you to do something for me: record a message.'

'Certainly, sir,' said the robot. Something whirred inside its casing, and its chest screen turned a faint shade of red. 'Recording now, sir.'

The Doctor cleared his throat, straightened his jacket, clasped his hands behind his back and drew himself up to his full height so that he was looking down his nose at the screen. 'Ladies and gentlemen of the city,' he intoned. He paused for a second before adding: 'Mods and rockers. I have an announcement to make: one of extreme importance to all your futures.'

Chapter Ten
When the Lights Went Out

'I'm asking the Brain to send this message to as many of you as the servo-robots can find in the next ten minutes. After that, the robots and the Brain itself will go off line, along with all other nonessential systems.'

Fitz should have felt comforted. This was the first he had seen of the Doctor since arriving in the city. It may only have been a low-resolution image of his head and shoulders on a tiny screen in a robot's chest, but at least it proved that his companion was alive and well and taking charge. But the Doctor's earnest expression and grim tone gave Fitz a feeling of impending doom, which Rick's increasing agitation did nothing to ameliorate.

'For the next couple of days,' said the Doctor's recorded message, 'you're going to have to make do without your vehicles and your weapons and, I'm afraid, your food machines. We can get those things back, but only if we're prepared to work together.'

'What's he doing?' whispered Fitz.

'He's killing us!' said Rick.

The mods' young leader had helped Fitz to a seat in his reception room, as soon as Fitz could walk again. He had even had a servo-robot fetch him a drink – although, to Fitz's dismay, it had of course turned out to be the usual tasteless paste. Rick was being quite pleasant, which was worrying in its own way. He wanted something – probably for Fitz to open his mind to the Maker again, to learn more at the cost of his own sanity.

Fitz felt much better now, although he was still shaky. The images that the Maker had shown him, via Compassion, had blazed a trail of fire through his mind, disrupting every thought in their path. But they had gone now, leaving only a few traces of debris behind. A few random pictures. A few vague ideas. A small measure of knowledge.

He was ashamed of the way he had lost control. He was terrified of its happening again.

The Doctor was offering to mediate between mods and rockers. That was just like him, thought Fitz. He stressed over and over how the gangs couldn't face their common problems until they had settled their differences.

'I suggest you think about what I've said. Then we should all meet. The leaders of both sides. Outside the Brain. Two hours from now. Without your weapons, please.'

And then the message ended, and the servo-robot that had brought it to Rick apologised for the fact that its program was about to terminate and that it could be of no further assistance.

For the next minute and a half, Fitz watched, not daring to speak, as Rick paced up and down, playing with his hands, his head bowed in thought. Then the light faded from behind the robot's eye-strip, and simultaneously from the room itself. Left in complete darkness, Fitz entertained a moment's panic at the thought of being trapped in the underground complex, of perhaps never finding the surface again. Without power, the antigrav tube wouldn't work. Then the room's lights returned, albeit to a lower level than before and tinted with red: the seemingly universal sign of emergency lighting. The robot remained inactive.

The doors that led out of the room in both directions had slid quietly open. Several guards stood in the main doorway, not knowing what to do, looking to Rick for guidance.

The silence was overwhelming. Even the clatter of everyday life in the complex had stopped as, it seemed to Fitz, every inhabitant of the city stopped to consider his or her future.

To those who were outside, the power cut was heralded by a more spectacular sight.

Sandra hadn't heard the Doctor's message – she didn't know what he had done – but she knew immediately that something momentous was occurring. Evening had drawn in even as she had crossed the city on foot. The buildings and the spires had counteracted the twilight gloom with their usual harsh light. Now, without warning, that light was extinguished. The windows became dark again. And the metal walls of the city were bathed in a softer, more natural, blue glow.

Sandra looked for the source of that glow, and caught her breath. A moment ago, the dull grey sky had been filled with clouds. Now she was staring up at a breathtaking panorama of stars, so much clearer and brighter and bigger than those she was used to seeing. She was looking up at space, but parts of it had been painted in broad strokes of orange and purple. There were three moons, and one of them was so close that she almost felt she could touch it. It hung above the city, wreathed in mist, and even the pockmarks on its dusty surface appeared to have been arranged into the most striking patterns.

Sandra wasn't on Earth. The Doctor had told her that, of course, and she had believed him – or wanted to, at least. But only now did she really feel that she was far away from home, on another world altogether. She didn't know whether to be excited or frightened. But she did know that it seemed like the most beautiful world in the cosmos.

So caught up was she in her miraculous discovery that she failed to notice at first that the pavement beneath her had ceased its motion. When she did eventually look back at the ground, it took her a moment to remember where she was, to work out how far it had brought her. Then she realised that she was just around the corner from her destination.

Sandra set off towards the mods' café on foot, unable to keep herself from stopping to look up at the wonderful new sky again before she had taken even half a dozen steps.

She had never believed in omens before. But just this once it felt as if the heavens were really sending her a message. They were telling her that she was doing the right thing; reminding her of what the Doctor had taught her.

It wasn't stupid to hope. She could change things. Everybody could do something.

Alec could hardly take in the Doctor's message. For so long, his position had been a heavy weight upon his shoulders. For so long, things had been sliding inexorably away from him. For so long, he had been telling himself that things would get better but not really believing it. Now he had lost Sandra and he had lost the city and it had all happened so quickly. He couldn't think, couldn't act, couldn't answer the people who clamoured for his attention. They expected him to take charge, to save them, but he didn't have the spirit any more.

By the time the lights had dimmed, he had trudged back to the quarters that he had once shared with his wife. He greeted the darkness sitting on their bed, with his elbows on his knees and his head in his hands, remembering better times and wishing he knew what he had done that had made everything go so wrong.

His other problems meant nothing beside Sandra's departure. She hadn't even talked to him. Sure, they may not have been getting along that well, but she was part of him. She had been part of him since their early days in the city, when a temporary truce had allowed them to grow closer without fear. He remembered their wedding, how happy they had been before her brothers had disrupted the ceremony. She had begged Alec not to retaliate, but he couldn't let some stuck-up mods get away with making her miserable.

Within days, the biggest of all rumbles had broken out. For the first time there had been no mounted police, no threats of the law to stop the mods and the rockers from tearing into each other. The fighting had raged throughout the night and well into the morning. It had left some of its more enthusiastic participants dead.

The clashes since then had never been quite so violent.

164

Nobody wanted a repeat of what had happened, not even Rick. Even so, the scars from that first rumble had never healed. It had been the first of many.

Keeping Sandra had been difficult after that. She had talked about Ricky a lot, and even tried to see him a few times. Alec had always been secretly thankful that the other mods had prevented her. She had wanted so much to be with her only surviving brother that he had feared what might happen should she ever get the chance to choose between them.

But he had thought those problems long past. He had thought that Sandra had accepted things the way they were, become used to her new family and stopped pining for what she had lost. Had he paid her so little attention, had he really been so caught up in leading the rockers to victory, that he had missed the return of all those signs?

Had he made the wrong decisions all along?

Alec looked back over his nineteen years in the city, and he saw that all the arguing and the fighting and the posturing had accomplished nothing at all. For the first time his head acknowledged what his weary heart had concluded long ago: that things really wouldn't get better; that, since the Maker had brought him here, his life had been on a steady downward spiral that never seemed to end. And he was too far down to ever climb out of it.

'A rocker trick,' concluded Rick.

It wouldn't have been smart to contradict him, so Fitz settled for groaning inwardly.

'A rocker trick,' the mods' leader repeated, 'that's what it is. This Doctor friend of yours is working with them. He thinks I'll believe all his drivel about the city decaying. He just wants to get me to this rendezvous point. It'll be some sort of an ambush.'

'I don't think the Doctor would do that,' ventured Fitz.

But Rick wasn't listening. He was pacing again, becoming more animated as he made sense of his new situation and his confidence returned. 'I didn't think they'd dare tamper with the Brain, but they have. They're scared of me, that's why.'

'The Doctor wouldn't do that. He wouldn't take sides.'

'They want to bring me down to their level, that's what it is. They're scared of our new weapons. They'll be waiting to attack us with their knives and sticks and chains, and they think we'll only have the same now. Ha! As if we couldn't beat them anyway. But Alec doesn't know my secrets.' He cast a glance towards the main doorway, probably to check that no one was listening. He had dismissed his guards. Lowering his voice, he concluded: 'Alec doesn't know about the Maker, or about Compassion.'

'I think he's telling the truth,' said Fitz.

Rick snatched his gun from his pocket, and Fitz flinched as he fired it. But he had aimed for the wall, on which he left a minor scorch mark. 'The guns still work,' he said with satisfaction. 'I suppose we can't recharge them, but they're good for a few shots each. Same goes for the jetpacks, I bet. But how many ray guns did Alec's mob capture?'

'I've no idea.'

'We need something else, something better.' Rick swung around to face Fitz and, in that moment, the fanatical gleam in the eyes of the mods' leader seemed the brightest light in the room. 'I need you to communicate with the Maker again.'

'You've got to be joking!'

'Only this time *you're* going to talk to *him*, not the other way round. Yes, yes, this is going to work. He can make things in seconds, you see? The problem has been making him understand what I want. Now I can tell you, and you can pass the message on.'

'I said, you must be joking!' protested Fitz. 'I'm not going through that again.'

'You don't have to touch the Maker's mind. Compassion can be your interpreter.'

'I suppose...'

'We can be ready for the rockers when they attack. They think they can beat us by turning off the power, do they? Wait till they see what I've got planned. And you, spaceman, you can tell the Maker that he's got to do as I say.'

'Why would he?'

Rick's eyes narrowed and a dangerous grin spread across his face. 'Because he knows you now. You're his friend – and I'm sure he'll want to do whatever it takes to save your life.'

'Do you think it's the end of the world?' asked Deborah in a trembling voice.

'It's the end of the city,' said Vince. He trailed a hand along the wall, and watched mournfully as silver flakes cascaded to the floor. 'It depends what else is out there, I guess.'

'Do you think we should find Davey?'

'Do you think he'd want us to?'

Deborah sighed heavily and slumped forward in her chair. She was nonplussed to see that even this was beginning to decay, cracks spreading across its surface. The couple didn't speak for a few minutes, adding to the preternatural silence that filled the recreation hall. The mods had reacted in different ways to the Doctor's announcement. Some had shouted and sworn and marched off to find a way of settling their problems with violence. Others had remained, shell-shocked, speaking in hushed tones when they spoke at all. The dimming of the lights had been met not with fear or with anger but with a tangible despair.

As Deborah watched, a group of six mods – the largest in the room – rose and left, their heads bowed, shuffling their feet. They must have concluded that anything was better than sitting here and doing nothing. They were probably right, but Deborah wasn't ready for that yet. She wasn't ready to see what had happened to the rest of her world, and she didn't see what could be done about it anyway, no matter where she went.

'Do you think we've failed him?' she asked.

Vince would normally have reassured her – but Deborah could see from his expression and from the look in his watery eyes that, this time, he couldn't. 'I don't know,' he said simply.

'Sometimes, when I see how he's turned out...' she began falteringly, still looking for that reassurance. 'He's so angry all the time. So ready to hurt others.'

'It's the city,' said Vince. 'It does that to people.'

'But we're his parents.'

'In name only. Not even in that any more. Family doesn't matter here, Deborah, you know that. The gangs are everything. Davey has never listened to us and he never will.'

'Then perhaps we should have made him listen, taught him a better way.'

'There is no other way,' said Vince, despondently. 'Not in the city.'

'But we don't have the city any more,' insisted Deborah. 'Is it too late to try?'

The Doctor stood beneath the central tower and looked up at the new sky. He recognised the constellations, of course, and knew that the city's occupants had come a long way. Now they stood poised on the threshold of another giant leap. He didn't yet know if that leap would take them into an abyss.

For beings who lived such brief lives, humans could sometimes be infuriatingly slow about their business. For now, all he could do was wait for them to adjust to their new situation. Then, one way or another, they would come to him. He concentrated on suppressing his pent-up energy. He licked his dry lips and didn't quite know what to do with his hands.

'It's no use,' Gillian called through the open hatchway behind him. 'The cycle's kaput!'

'I suspected it might be,' said the Doctor. 'The Brain will have drained the power packs of all the vehicles. It's probably a good thing.'

'Yeah, right. Only this morning I was thinking what a "good

thing" it would be if we had no food or light or transport.'

'Were you? Anyway, it should force Alec and Rick to confront their problems.'

'You really think they're going to turn up to this meeting, don't you?'

'They'll meet eventually. When they have no choice. The survival instinct is strong in most animals. I only hope I can trigger theirs in time.'

'And convince them that survival doesn't mean bashing the hell out of each other.'

Gillian had abandoned the useless jetcycle to join the Doctor outside. He turned to her with a smile. 'I've convinced you, haven't I?'

'I've seen what's happening to the city.'

'And it'll get worse,' he said grave The Brain isn't holding back the decay any more.'

'What are we going to do?' pleaded Gillian. The Doctor knew that tone of voice. The woman was losing her home – worse still, her future.

'I don't know,' he said, 'but there are better places than the city. Why fear when you can hope instead?' He put an arm around her shoulders and pointed enthusiastically upwards. 'Look at that sky! Isn't it the most beautiful thing you've ever seen?'

'It's very nice,' said Gillian primly. 'I can see something else too.'

'Tell me,' said the Doctor, still grinning at the heavens.

'I can see a big bunch of rockers coming towards us.'

The grin drained from the Doctor's face. He frowned, then thought to lower his sights to ground level. A large contingent of rockers had indeed entered the road that faced the open hatchway into the central building. Alec was marching at their head. The Doctor shrugged and grinned again, determined to be optimistic. 'Excellent! I knew they'd come.'

'They're not here to talk,' Gillian pointed out, pursing her lips.

'Oh? What makes you say that?'

'They're carrying knives and clubs – and, in case you hadn't noticed, there are about a hundred of them.'

'About twenty, I think,' said the Doctor, 'but I do see your point.'

'So,' said Gillian, 'you fancy turning the Brain back on again or what?'

'Do we have to go through this again?'

Fitz sighed and perched on the bed beside the Maker. The alien opened its huge yellow eyes to look at him, but showed no other reaction. 'Can't you do something?' asked Fitz, rhetorically. 'Make her talk to me. Or perhaps *you* could talk to me – cut out the middle man.'

'That would be difficult,' said Compassion, from her position on the floor. 'The Makers don't fully understand human perceptions.'

'Oh, you're back, are you?' said Fitz.

'I never left. I was aware of you. I just thought it best not to say anything until Rick had left the room.'

'Yeah, he took his time, didn't he?'

'He had no choice in the end. His people are frightened. He has to lead them.'

'I don't know how long we've got,' said Fitz.

'The Maker does. Rick will return in twenty-three and a half minutes.'

'I forgot. It can see into the future, can't it? Can it see if we get out of this?'

'The timelines are in flux,' said Compassion. 'Our presence is causing an anomaly. There are too many possible futures surrounding the city. The Maker is confused. That's what keeps it here, as much as the chains and its injuries. It's half blind.'

'Rick wants it to –'

'The Maker knows what Rick wants.'

'Makers. Before, you said Makers. But when I... I mean, when you showed me…' Fitz tailed off, unable to put his experience into words. 'I thought it was alone,' he concluded.

'The Maker is both one and many.'

'A group being? Is that what you're saying?'

'Their minds are linked. They are not tied to their bodies, so they don't think of themselves as discrete entities. They don't define individuality in terms of their bodies as you do.'

'Can they – I mean, it – can it see a way out of here?'

'The door is not locked.'

'I know that. But there are still a few dozen mods down here with us. With you, I might actually stand a chance of getting past them.'

'I don't want to leave the Maker. You can take shelter inside me if you wish.'

'Well, since you mention it –'

'That is, if you don't have the courage to help the Doctor.'

'You really are back to your old self, aren't you?'

'No. I don't like being distracted by physical concerns, Fitz, not when there is so much more to see. But you made it clear that the alternative is to let you die – and I don't want that.'

Compassion delivered the words without a hint of emotion. Even so, Fitz was taken aback. 'Oh. Well, thanks for that. That's sweet.'

'Your death would affect the Doctor, and therefore me in turn.'

'I don't care,' he said doggedly. 'That's sweet anyway. Er… if you want to help the Doctor, then how about we stop the city from wasting away? Any ideas on that score?'

'The Maker could halt the decay with a thought.'

'Great!'

'But it won't.'

'Why not?'

'It is responsible for it.'

'OK. Fine. Let's talk about that, shall we?'

'The Maker thought the humans were friendly. It felt grateful. It gave them the city, their future. But when it returned, they attacked this body, hurt it and imprisoned it.'

'Not all of them,' said Fitz. 'Just Rick!'

'I made that point,' said Compassion, 'but the Maker doesn't understand. It has —'

'No concept of individuality,' said Fitz. 'Right.'

'The Maker has decided to take away its gift.'

'And kill everybody in the process!'

'That isn't the Maker's objective — but it will happen, yes.'

'And let me guess: the Maker's not too bothered about that side effect, yeah? Well, I can't say I blame it, but where does that leave us?'

'The Maker finds it harder to destroy than to create. Elements combine easily, but cannot so easily be separated. There may be time to change its mind.'

'Do you think you can?'

'I don't know. The Maker feels betrayed and disillusioned. However, we do have certain perspectives in common. I can ease its pain. It considers me a friend. It has agreed to do one thing for me already.'

'What's that?' asked Fitz.

'It will provide the machine that Rick has asked for.'

'It will?' Fitz had been so concerned with the city's long-term problems that he had almost forgotten Rick's ultimatum. 'I mean, that's good. Thanks. It'd do that just for me?'

'It doesn't matter to the Maker whether the humans kill each other or not. That's why it provided weapons for Rick in the past. It won't change the future.'

'No,' said Fitz, 'I don't suppose it will. Not for the Maker, anyway.' He had a disturbing thought. 'But what about the Doctor? He's trying to get the mods and rockers talking. If Rick gets his weapon —'

'There are no possible futures in which the mods and rockers make peace. But it is possible for you to escape and find the Doctor.'

'Now you're talking.'

'I hope to guide events towards that point.'

'And if we can take the Maker with us, then Rick will have lost his advantage.'

'The Maker will have its freedom soon enough.'

'You mean when everybody else is dead.'

Fitz was surprised to see Compassion smile. He had rarely seen that, even before her transformation. 'Before then,' she said confidently.

Rick had not seen his sister for three years, not since he had become the mods' leader. He had often wondered how he would feel when they met again, whether he would be able to control the bitterness that festered within him. That bitterness had been born when Sandra had gone to the Maker without him. It had grown when she had betrayed him and destroyed his family.

She had changed, in a way that he couldn't quite define in the dim light. Her hair was a little darker, a good deal longer. The lines on her face had deepened. But that wasn't it.

She was in a cell, but her guards hadn't been able to lock the electronic door. They surrounded her instead, five mods in all, Davey among them as he always was. The kid was commendably keen to impress Rick. He almost certainly had his eye on the leader's job. Rick indulged him because he knew he was no threat. Davey had no control.

It occurred to Rick that the mods might have hurt Sandra, but he saw no sign of it. Even Davey wouldn't dare to lay a hand on the leader's sister. That realisation came as a relief to him, although he wasn't sure why that should be.

'You wanted to see me?' he asked, trying to sound casual even though the bitterness was stirring within him. It was tempered, at least, by satisfaction. She had come back here, back to him. Rick had won. Now he had a choice. He could punish Sandra or he could welcome her back, show her off as a trophy and prove that the rockers were abandoning their own sinking ship.

She was in his power. He was in control, and that in itself almost made up for the suffering of the past.

'I've left Alec,' she said.

'About time too.'

'I suppose you're right.'

'What did you think you were doing, playing around with that grease monkey?'

'I didn't leave him because he's a rocker.'

'It's disgusting, the two of you shacking up like that.'

'Don't start, Rick. I'm not in the mood.'

'Especially after what it did to our brothers.'

Sandra would have hit him then, but her guards restrained her. She looked more angry than Rick had seen her before, and suddenly he knew what was different about her. She had an energy, an air of determination, that she had not possessed for almost two decades. Her eyes gleamed with purpose where once they had been dulled by defeat.

'Don't you think I feel guilty about what happened to them?' she cried. 'But it wasn't my fault. It wasn't anybody's fault except their own, because they couldn't think of anything but fighting. They couldn't let it end.'

'Why should they?'

'Yeah, that's right,' said Davey. 'Why should they have to kiss up to your boyfriend just because you couldn't see him for what he was?'

'Won't you at least listen to me?' pleaded Sandra, ignoring Davey altogether. 'I put my life on the line coming here, Rick. Doesn't that mean anything to you?'

'You probably just realised which side was going to win this war.'

'You've been saying that for years. So has Alec.'

'It's different now. We've got weapons.'

'There's been a power cut.'

'You haven't seen my new weapon. My Technician's making it now.' At least, it better had be, thought Rick. 'It's bigger and better than anything you've seen before, and it's got a self-contained, everlasting power source. I asked for that specifically.'

'You're making the same mistake that Jack and Phil did.'

'You want this war ended, don't you? I'm ending it!'

'Perhaps you should go and talk to Alec,' said Sandra sourly. 'You already sound like him.'

'That's a filthy lie!'

Rick's control was slipping. But he couldn't let that happen. Not in front of so many of his people. He might destroy the illusion, remind them that he was just a child inside.

'Do you know why I came here, Rick?' said Sandra. 'Really?'

'Sick of the smell of rockers, I bet,' spat Davey.

'Because I can't get through to Alec. He won't listen to common sense. So, I thought I'd try you instead. You keep saying you're so much better than him; here's your chance to prove it.'

Rick meant to dismiss her with a sneer, but it froze on his face as he saw the new look that came into his sister's eyes. Contempt. *She* was showing contempt for *him*.

'It looks like I was wasting my time,' said Sandra.

For years, Alec had dreamed of what the Brain would look like. In the end, it was surprisingly unimpressive. A big computer, just as he had expected. Of course, its mystique was diminished by the fact that its lights were dead and its three reels still. The Doctor had destroyed his dream.

He had allowed only two rockers into the Brain's chamber, plus Gillian and himself. They had dragged the Doctor in, protesting all the way. The others formed a barricade outside: without power the hatch could not be closed, and Alec didn't want to expose the Brain to a possible mod attack.

'You aren't listening to me,' the Doctor complained. 'If you turn the Brain back on, you'll shorten the life span of the city.'

'The city's dying anyway.'

The Doctor seized on Alec's admission. 'Right, right, and the longer it takes the better, or don't you think so? We need time to make plans.'

'I already know what to do.'

'Do you?' asked the Doctor, looking genuinely surprised.

'This is the mods' fault. They're causing it somehow. If I can –'

'No no no no no no *no*!' The Doctor hobbled around in a small circle, tearing at his hair in dismay. 'Why can't you see that there's more to this situation than your petty concerns?'

'I'm not arguing, Doctor.' Alec motioned to his two men.

The Doctor fixed him with a fierce glare. 'Having me beaten up would be a very boring and futile thing to do.' As the rockers marched past him, he added, 'And I doubt very much that they can find a way to reactivate the Brain.'

The rockers halted before the controls and displays in the far wall, and raised their clubs. To Alec's satisfaction, the Doctor's jaw dropped open and his voice rose an octave. 'And vandalising it would be very foolish.' Gillian shot him a look that could have meant anything, and in a weaker tone he added, 'That is, if you don't know what you're doing.'

Two clubs thudded into the wall, glass breaking beneath them. 'Do you want to shut down the oxygen generators?' cried the Doctor angrily. 'Gillian, tell them. Gillian!'

Gillian looked helplessly from the Doctor to Alec, then down at her feet.

'I don't care,' hissed Alec, as the rockers struck their second blows in unison. 'We're all dead anyway unless I can use the Brain to sort out the mods once and for all.'

'You don't understand!'

'No, *you* don't understand, Doctor. It's gone too far now. This is the only way. The only way to put an end to all our problems. The only way to make things better.' He was talking about saving the city, Alec assured himself of that. But he was thinking about Sandra.

'It's too late to do anything else,' he said plaintively.

* * *

'Why don't you go back to your greaser friends?' said Rick, coldly. 'You will sooner or later, anyway. You always betray me in the end.'

'That's not true,' protested Sandra. She glared at him for a moment, then sighed. 'But OK, you're probably right. I should never have gone with Alec in the first place.'

'Ha! You admit it then?' cried Rick, feeling a surge of satisfaction at his small triumph.

'I thought it would help. I thought I could bring the gangs together. We needed to work together, Rick. We needed to make something of this world. Instead, look at what we've done to it. We've torn it apart!'

'But you shouldn't have gone off with that greaser! You said that, didn't you?'

'I shouldn't have left my family. I shouldn't have abandoned you.'

'You never cared about me.'

'Don't say that!'

'It's true, isn't it?'

'I tried to come back, but I couldn't get near you.'

'You made your choice.'

'I never stopped thinking about you.'

'Why?' As Sandra had raised her voice, so too had Rick raised his. They were shouting at each other now, but he didn't care any more. 'I'm just your stupid little brother.'

'No you're not!'

'You never wanted to be with me. You went to the Maker without me.'

'You think I planned any of that?' cried Sandra, incredulously. 'You think I chose to come and live here? To be torn away from everything I knew? To lose my family? To lose you?'

Rick found he didn't have an answer for that. He and Sandra glared at each other for a long moment, before he remembered that the other mods were still present. Four of them were inspecting the walls, looking as if they'd rather be anywhere else but here. Davey's arms were folded and he watched on with the merest suggestion of a smile on his face.

Suddenly, Rick's cheeks felt very hot. He had allowed the bitterness to control him.

He turned to Davey. 'Well?' he rapped, covering up his hurt. 'You have a rocker prisoner. You know what to do. Interrogate her. Find out what you can about Alec's plans.'

'Rick!'

'And what if she won't talk?' asked Davey, guardedly.

Rick shrugged as if he didn't care. 'Do what you like.'

'You can't do this,' cried Sandra. 'We're family, Rick!'

'You're no family of mine.'

Rick made to walk away. The mods were already closing in around Sandra. Davey slapped his club into his palm, and his smile grew and twisted into something evil and hateful.

'I'm your mother, Rick!' screamed Sandra.

And everything came to a stop.

The anger drained from Sandra's face as she realised what she had said, and even Davey was pale and open-mouthed.

'I'm your bloody mother,' spluttered Sandra, almost crying, 'OK?'

And the bitterness within Rick welled up and overflowed.

Later, he would remember little about it, except that a red mist had seemed to engulf him and he had felt Sandra's throat beneath his hands and heard himself screaming incoherently. The other mods did nothing. Sandra struggled, and she was stronger than Rick had expected, but he forced her to her knees anyway before the reality of what he was doing struck like a dagger through his heart and he tore himself away, holding back tears.

He didn't dare look at the others after that. He would only have seen his shame reflected in their eyes. Sandra was on her hands and knees, her face red, gasping for air. 'Just leave her,' he ordered, subdued now and hoarse. 'She's not my –' He almost choked on the word, and started again. 'She's nothing to us. Just let her go. And send word around the complex. I want every mod to assemble in the briefing room. Tell them to bring ray guns, clubs, knives, anything they can find.'

There was only one way to restore their faith in him. One way to regain control.

'So, Alec says he wants to talk, does he? Well, we'll make his rendezvous all right. But we won't just walk into his trap. He'd better be prepared for the biggest rumble there's even been around here – because, by the end of it, there'll only be one side left standing!'

Chapter Eleven
The Ultimate Weapon

'Yes, that's it, that's it!' Rick shook his fists in the air and fairly squeaked with excitement. The Maker lay on its bed, its eyes wide and bright but showing no other sign of what must have been an intense mental effort. Compassion had picked herself off the floor to sit beside it and hold its hand. She showed no interest in what was happening otherwise.

And Fitz just stood in the doorway and gaped as the walls, ceiling and floor of the corridor outside twisted and tore and streamed like living ribbons of steel. The hard earth beneath the city was revealed, and a tidal wave of dirt rose up to join the maelstrom. The dancing elements recombined and slowly created a new structure, a machine from Rick's imagination.

By the time the machine was finished, Rick's suite of rooms was devastated. The Maker's room, like most of the others, had lost its front wall altogether. Rick didn't seem to care about the damage, though. He ran around the Maker's creation, his apparent delight increasing as he inspected it from all sides. It was exactly as he had described it, although Fitz was still surprised by the scale of it. It completely filled the area that the corridor had once taken up.

Sleek, metallic and basically tubular, it resembled nothing more than a rocket, albeit one that had been turned on its side and fitted with thick caterpillar tracks. Its back end was also bulked out by the presence of a passenger compartment into which a sliding door in its side gave access. It would hold about fifteen people, Fitz reckoned. Sitting in front of and above this compartment was a smaller cabin, into which Rick clambered now by means of rungs set into the machine's side. He dropped into its single seat and rubbed his hands together gleefully as he inspected the controls. The cabin overlooked the machine's most crucial feature: the enormous drill bit that made up its nose cone. As Fitz watched with a feeling of dread, Rick found the lever that set the drill bit spinning. Then, jerkily at first and with its gears squealing in protest, the vehicle began to advance.

Immediately, it bumped into the intact wall at the end of the corridor. Finding that the doorway wasn't nearly large enough for it, the drill went to work with terrifying efficiency. Sparks flew, and Fitz recoiled from the smell of burning and winced at the tortured shriek of metal. Within seconds, only slivers of the wall remained at the edges of a gaping hole, and the machine rolled steadily forward again and into Rick's reception room. Fitz followed it slowly, still awe-struck, and found himself coughing as his throat was tickled by drifting smoke and metal dust.

The drill destroyed one end of the long conference table and several chairs, before Rick brought it to a stop and leapt out, his face shining with happiness. 'I've done it!' he crowed. 'In the nick of time, I've done it!'

'I'm very pleased for you,' said Fitz, tight-lipped.

'Go and fetch the Third Battalion,' said Rick.

'What?'

'They're waiting in the briefing room. Go and get them.'

Surprised, Fitz looked over his shoulder and confirmed that the Maker and Compassion were perfectly visible through the remains of two walls, bathed in fresh blue moonlight. A cold breeze drifted in through the ruptured ceiling, ruffling Fitz's hair and making him aware that the power cut must have affected an invisible heating system.

'Never mind them,' said Rick, following Fitz's gaze and waving his hand dismissively. 'It doesn't matter who sees them now. I've won, don't you see? I've won!' He regarded his ultimate weapon with something akin to love. 'I've got four battalions on the way to give Alec and his greasers a good pasting. They'll still be trying to work out what's hit them when the rest of us drill straight into their part of the complex and demolish it. They've had it!'

'They've had it!' bragged Alec, standing over the Doctor as he knelt to operate the controls on one wall of the computer chamber. 'Rick and all his snooty mods. I've got control of the Brain at last. I can do what I like. So, he thought he could see me off with his ray guns and his killer robots, did he? Well, wait till he sees what I've got in mind!'

'I hate to interrupt your gloating,' said the Doctor, looking up with a sheepish grin, 'but it's not going to work.'

'What?' said Alec, blankly.

'You've damaged the Brain too much. I can't get its higher functions back on line.'

'You're lying! I'll have my men do more damage, you know I will.'

The Doctor leapt to his feet, seized Alec by his shoulders and stared urgently into his eyes. 'Listen to me, Alec. We don't have time to play games.'

Alec was about to bellow a response, when he heard shouting outside. He swung around to face the hatchway, and was alarmed to see that a fight had broken out in the central square. He had brought three groups to the Brain – twenty men in all. Now they were under attack from an equal number of mods. It suddenly struck Alec that he had nowhere to run to this time, no way to even shut himself inside this room. He was more exposed than he had ever been since his rise to leadership had made him his enemies' primary target.

His hopes of victory were slipping through his grasp again.

He broke the Doctor's hold with a sweep of his arms, and grabbed his cravat as if to strangle him with it. 'You're right,' he snarled, 'there's no time for this. Give me the Brain!'

'I can't do that!' the Doctor yelled in his face, falling back and trying to push Alec away.

'There's no other way. They're right on top of us. They'll kill us!

Are you blind or what?'

'I'm not lying to you.' Somehow, the Doctor had contrived to pull Alec over to the Brain itself, and to turn him around until he was facing it. 'Look!'

Alec hadn't meant to take his eyes off the Doctor, but the urgency in his voice and the extravagance of his gesture propelled the rocker into following his pointed finger. And once he had done that, his attention was taken by the most dreadful sight of all.

The Brain was melting, its surface bubbling and scarring.

And for the first time, Alec forgot about Sandra and Rick, about the mods and the battle outside, and began to realise just what the Doctor had been trying to tell him.

The lights had gone out, the sky was different and the city was dead, but Davey didn't care. None of this was his fault. Rick had lost it. He was no longer fit to lead the mods. That was good news for somebody who was young and fit and smart and dedicated. And when this rumble was over, when the mods defeated the rockers as they surely would, then Davey would emerge as the hero of the hour.

Because he knew something Rick didn't.

Rick had chosen the Third Battalion to follow him into the rockers' headquarters. He had tried to sideline Davey, putting his battalion with the cannon fodder instead of letting him participate in the important part of the exercise. No doubt, he was scared. Scared of giving Davey the chance to prove that he had the potential to lead more than just a few men. Scared of showing the rest of the mods that they could replace their figurehead so easily.

But Rick had miscalculated. Alec hadn't retreated underground, as he usually did when trouble loomed. Davey had seen him – only a brief glimpse, but it was enough – on the ground floor of the central building, in the chamber that housed the Brain itself. And with the city's power off and the maintenance hatch standing open, only a few weak-kneed greasers stood between him and his most hated enemy, between him and everlasting fame.

So, Davey fought as he had never fought before. He shouted to his nearest three men to follow him as he thrashed out a path for himself through the mêlée. He didn't care where or how hard his club hit, so long as it hit rocker scum and kept them out of his way. They tried to stop him, of course, but he parried every one of their attacks with ease, even when the cowards tried to jump him from behind. He had never felt like this before. His anger fuelled him, as it always did, but it wasn't just pouring out of him this time: it was channelling itself through him, energising him. He was unstoppable.

Sandra didn't know where she was. The corridors in the mods' part of the complex looked identical to those beneath the milk bar, but their layout was very different. She was getting used to rounding corners and having her expectations of what might lie beyond confounded. She didn't care. She didn't know where she wanted to be either. She stumbled on, navigating randomly, as if she could leave her feelings and her memories behind – until, through her tears and through the crimson half-light, she discerned a pair of familiar faces.

'Sandra!' gasped Deborah.

'Does Rick know you're here?' asked Vince.

'What are you doing here?'

'You haven't come to, you know –'

'You've left the rockers, haven't you?'

Sandra nodded. She couldn't speak for crying. But she didn't need to. She hadn't seen Deborah for years, but it didn't matter. They rushed towards each other and embraced, sharing their misery, as Vince looked on and shuffled his feet awkwardly.

'I didn't know if you were still speaking to me,' sobbed Sandra into Deborah's shoulder.

'Of course I am,' wept Deborah in return. 'After all you did for me, how could I not?'

'I told him,' said Sandra, stepping back and wiping her ears on her sleeve. 'I told Rick.'

Deborah's mouth dropped open in astonishment. 'You didn't!'

'I did.'

'After all this time. How…? Why…? I mean, how did he take it?'

Sandra couldn't answer that either, but her expression and her half-hearted shrug must have told Deborah all she needed to know. They embraced again.

It was funny how hardship could bring people together. Sandra had hardly known Deborah at all in 1965. She was two years younger after all, and had only just left school. But she had known her sister, and through her she had learned about Deborah's strange behaviour. Even without proof, she had known straightaway what was wrong. It had been none of her business. She had told herself that throughout several sleepless nights, before she had given in. Then she had waited until Deborah's parents were out before calling upon her to offer support and to tell her the secret that nobody outside her own family knew. The secret that her parents had done everything in their power to keep. It had felt good to tell someone.

She had forged a bond between the two women that the reality of life in the city could stretch but never break.

'Oh, Deborah, I thought I could do something. I thought I could stop the fighting.'

'I know.'

They parted again, and an expression of determination came over Deborah's face. 'You're right, though. It doesn't matter how hopeless it is: we've got to do something. Even if all we can do is get a few of us away from this planet and leave the rest to it.'

Sandra shook her head. 'We can't. I thought I could do something, but I was wrong. I was so stupid. I've just made things worse. I always make things worse.'

'You could try talking to Rick again. It must have been a shock.'

'No, he won't listen. I know him, Deborah. He's like Alec. He's just like Alec.'

'You don't mean Alec...?' interrupted Vince.

'No. No, he's not Rick's father.'

'Then we forget them,' said Deborah. 'Forget both of them.'

'What can we do on our own?' asked Vince.

'We're not alone,' said Deborah. 'There's still one person who can help us.'

The last member of the mods' Third Battalion climbed into the back of the giant drill. Fitz slid the door shut behind him, banged on the window with his palm and gave the machine's occupants a grin and a thumbs-up sign. Rick had probably expected him to join them, but they didn't know that. And Rick himself was up in the cockpit, oblivious to what was going on behind him. Fitz scurried behind the machine, out of sight of the mods' leader. A minute later, he felt a thrill of elation as Rick started up the engine and the drill lurched forward. He watched as it cut through the opposite wall, crossed the corridor beyond and went to work again. He shivered at the thought of how much damage Rick was prepared to do even to his own home, and was glad he wasn't with the rockers now. He remembered that the Doctor was, and felt guilty about his part in bringing Rick's dream to life.

Beyond the far wall, the drill encountered solid earth. Its progress was slowed, and the remaining walls of the reception room vibrated in sympathy, but it was already clear that the obstacle wouldn't endure. Fitz remembered what Davey had said about parts of the complex being collapsed to separate mods from rockers. It couldn't be too long before Rick broke through to his enemies' living space.

He couldn't think about that. He was free, at least until Rick thought to wonder where he was. The majority of mods were up on the surface, at the Brain, where the supposedly final battle would have started by now. The complex was almost empty. He could probably walk straight through the café and out on to the street.

But where would he go then?

'Looks like you were right,' he called to Compassion. 'Getting the drill made has given me a chance to escape. Are you coming?'

'I will stay with the Maker,' she said.

'OK. Your choice.' No guards remained outside the reception room. Its double doors stood open in the only wall that hadn't been breached. Fitz was halfway to them before he stopped and added, awkwardly, 'Thanks.'

'You might wish to rethink your plan,' said Compassion.

'What plan? I'm just making a run for it.'

'The city's inhabitants are fighting above ground. You will find it much easier to reach the rockers' headquarters from below.'

'You mean wait for Rick to cut a path through and then follow him?'

The drill had already bored a tunnel of its own length into the rock. Its caterpillar tracks hauled it out of the corridor and over the tunnel's lip, until all Fitz could see was its back end, receding slowly. Compassion had a point, he supposed. But he itched at the prospect of having to wait longer before he could make his move.

Looking for something to occupy his mind, he scrambled over the wreckage towards her. 'You and the Maker are big pals now, I take it?'

'I told you, we share certain perspectives.'

'Yeah, I was thinking about that. I bet it reminds you of the Remote, doesn't it?'

'That isn't it.'

'Of course it is,' said Fitz. 'Telepathy, group minds and all that. It's not the same with us mere mortals, is it? I bet you were dead lonely before the Maker turned up.'

'I did not wish to converse with you,' said Compassion, icily. 'It is not the same thing.'

'Of course it's not,' said Fitz, with a broad grin.

'Your attempts at psychoanalysis were always pathetic,' said Compassion. 'But now you literally have no concept of what you're talking about. And', she added before Fitz could issue a rejoinder, 'you might like to know that you are about to receive guests.'

'What?'

'Three people will enter the reception room in eight seconds' time. Good luck, Fitz.'

The drill cut a swathe through the rockers' quarters. Rick guided it through wall after wall, demolishing furniture and labour-saving devices in the process. There were few rockers about, but the frozen look of fear on the face of one as he saw the mods' ultimate weapon was more than enough. Sometimes the drill hit a structural wall, and Rick exulted in the sound of earth crashing into the complex behind him.

He had never been more in control than this. He laughed giddily but, without his even realising it at first, the laughter turned to tears. His mind's eye flashed up pictures of Sandra, of Jack, of Phil, of the family he had once lost and had now lost again; of the life that had always been a lie. Having travelled the length of the complex, he brought the drill around in a wide, graceless U-turn. His tears became tears of anger. He would wreak as much havoc in the rockers' lives as Sandra had wreaked in his. He would destroy them.

The drill burst into a new corridor, and Rick brought it to a shuddering halt. There were people fighting to each side of him: about a dozen mods and as many rockers. He recognised some of his people. They were the ones who had been captured in the last rumble. With their prison shaking and crumbling around them, they must have taken the opportunity to fight back against their guards. Welcoming the distraction, he drew his knife and leapt from the cabin of the drill. He didn't even look to see if the mods in the back of the vehicle had followed his lead. He knew they would. He was still in control.

With a bloodthirsty scream, Rick put the past out of his mind and raced into battle.

More rockers had arrived in the central square, dividing the forces of the attacking mods. On the heaving battlefield, people were yelling and falling and screaming. Alec had not seen such a brutal conflict for nineteen years. Or perhaps it was just that he hadn't fought for so long himself that he had forgotten what it was like. All he could think of was the rumble that had broken out in the wake of his marriage to Sandra. And the people who had died in it.

Part of him felt responsible, as if he should go out there and use his authority to stop the hostilities. But it was too late. He couldn't step out of the building now, not without being cut to pieces. The mods were kill-crazy, and desperate to get hold of him above all others. Some had already reached the open hatchway and were being held off by a number of rockers, including the two guards whom Alec had brought into the Brain's chamber with him. The rockers formed an effective barricade, but they couldn't push the mods back. Alec wasn't surprised to hear Davey among them, hurling insults and threats.

His legs couldn't support him any more. He fell back against the wall, and slid down it until he landed in a crumpled heap on the floor. He felt switches giving beneath his weight, but what did it matter? It almost felt good to let go, to surrender, to realise at last that he didn't have to do anything, simply because there was nothing he could do. But the moment of relief was outweighed by the gnawing dread in his stomach: his fear of an uncertain future.

He closed his eyes and let the darkness comfort him, but knew that he would have to open them again. When he did, he was startled to find the Doctor's face inches away from his own.

'Are you feeling all right?' asked the Doctor.

'Y-yes,' stammered Alec.

'Splendid.' The Doctor took his hand and hoisted him to his

feet. 'Because there's a lot to do.' He lowered his head and peered more closely at Alec. 'Are you sure you're all right?'

'Feeling a bit sick, that's all.'

'Yes, I wondered when you'd notice that.'

'What?'

'The gravity!' cried the Doctor, as if it were obvious. He loped across to the Brain, and Alec saw that he had somehow prised open a panel in its side and removed four circuit boards. They lay atop the supercomputer's casing, connected by silver wires; Gillian was inspecting them, but the Doctor snatched them away as if he hadn't noticed. 'It's close to Earth normal, but there is a slight difference. The Brain used to compensate for you. Hold these, will you?' He thrust the circuit boards into Alec's hands, reached into his pockets and paused as a thoughtful look came over him. He bounced a few times on the spot, then grinned. 'Yes, yes, just fractionally less than Earth normal.' He produced a silver tubular device, held it up and began to adjust its bulbous head. 'Gillian, I need your help.'

'That'd make a change,' said Gillian.

The Doctor plunged a hand into his jacket again and came up with what looked like a stopwatch with two wires trailing from its dial. He tossed it back to Gillian, without even looking at her. 'It measures electrical current. I want you to find a live power cable inside the Brain and unplug it.'

Gillian looked surprised and pleased to have been given such a responsibility. But even as the Doctor rushed back to Alec and began to rummage through the circuit boards as if they were playing cards, she frowned. 'Won't that mean shutting off the oxygen generators?'

'For a minute, yes. I know it's selfish, but it shouldn't do too much harm – and it's our only way out of this building.'

Gillian nodded and went to work. The Doctor took two of the circuit boards, balanced a third on his arm and somehow managed to slot the tubular device into his mouth. It emitted a high-pitched whining sound, and Alec jumped as something popped and fizzed on one of the boards. 'What's this? Another weapon?' he guessed.

'You could say that,' the Doctor murmured indistinctly.

'And what do we do once we're out of here?'

'First things first. Friend of yours?' He stepped back, yanking on his boards so that the wires between them and the fourth board snapped taut. It flew out of Alec's grasp, and the Doctor caught it awkwardly on his free arm even as he turned away and shuffled back to the Brain.

Only then did Alec realise what he had meant. A mod had broken through the cordon, and he ran at Alec with fire in his eyes, a club in his hands and two rockers at his heels. Alec fell back, reaching for the knife that he kept in his leather jacket but hadn't used for years. It felt strange in his hand; his mind was screaming at him that he had forgotten how to fight. But one well-aimed swing of the blade was enough to give his attacker pause, and the other rockers a chance to catch up to him. Alec stepped forward to join in the suddenly uneven struggle, but an image of Joey's corpse flashed before his eyes. He faltered, his anger turning into something cold and unpleasant, as the insolent mod was wrestled to the ground.

With the realisation that he didn't want to fight any more, the last hard certainty evaporated from Alec's life.

A sharp pain brought Davey back into contact with the real world. He had hit his head against the metal road surface. He lay there, stunned, waiting for his vision to clear and trying to remember where he was and what was happening to him.

The energising anger, he recalled, had been tempered by fear. One of the other mods, Mike, had seen a gap and gone for it. He had reached the Brain's chamber even as a curtain of rockers had closed between Davey and that longed-for goal. He had seen his hopes, his future, being torn from his grasp, and he had been unable to see more than that. Time had been stolen from him. Nothing else had mattered. Nothing but that hatchway. So he had made a bad choice, taken a slim chance, lunged in the wrong direction. It had happened so quickly.

And now he lay amid a forest of legs, and he couldn't stand because they were moving around him, stamping down, pinning him, booted feet dealing him blow after blow if he got in their way. His stomach ached, and he thought he must have been kicked there too. He doubled up, wrapping himself around the tender area to protect it. But his hand felt sticky, and Davey realised with a horror that was more distant than it ought to have been that it was tacky with blood. And he remembered what had made him fall in the first place.

The rocker's ugly face, twisted with hatred, sneering in triumph. The knife plunging into Davey's guts, destroying him as it twisted inside.

Davey's forehead was soaked with sweat although he was suddenly very cold. The battle continued around him, but it didn't seem important now because his life was ebbing away from him and he couldn't move anyway.

The red haze of anger festered and began to fade to black.

Fitz picked his way cautiously along the tunnel that Rick had drilled, his three allies behind him. Except that 'allies' was too strong a word. They had come to him – Vince, Deborah and Alec's wife Sandra – because they thought he could save them; because they thought he was a spaceman from the future with all sorts of technology at his disposal. And they were wrong. He couldn't even answer their questions about the Maker. All he could do was let them follow him into the rockers' living quarters and pray that the Doctor had returned there, that he wasn't still with the Brain. Because the Doctor was his only hope.

Which meant, he supposed, that he was doing exactly the same thing they were.

'Do you know where we are?' he asked Sandra, as they stepped through a jagged hole and into a metal-walled corridor.

She nodded. 'What about the Doctor? Where will he be?'

'The lab, probably,' said Sandra. If he's here at all, thought Fitz. 'It's this way.'

Fitz crossed his fingers as Sandra led them away from Rick's path of destruction. He tried to ignore the instincts that told him he was wasting his time. The Doctor would be at the heart of the rumble. He had always had a penchant for finding trouble, and recently he had made an extra-special effort to do so.

'The Doctor can find Davey for us, can't he?' Deborah had asked that question six times before, and Fitz couldn't summon up the energy to lie to her again. As far as he could see, there would be no getting near Davey until the mods and the rockers had stopped tearing chunks out of each other – and what state he would be in by then, Fitz couldn't imagine.

'We can't leave without him,' said Vince. 'Not if this is, you know, the end of the world.'

'We've got to be with him,' agreed Deborah.

Compassion had offered the couple sanctuary, but they had refused it. They were driven by the need to find their son. Sandra, on the other hand, didn't seem to care what she did, so long as she did something. Fitz had tried to sound encouraging, to make them all believe that the Doctor could pull a rabbit out of the hat, but they needed more reassurance than he could give. The only way he could see out of this was for him and the Doctor and the select few people on this world who weren't obsessed with violence to pile into Compassion and do a bunk. Even then, her Randomiser ensured that they could end up literally anywhere.

And, of course, they still had to find the Doctor first.

The Doctor bundled his collection of circuit boards on to the top of the Brain. 'Power cable!' he rapped, clicking his fingers at Gillian. She obliged him, trying not to think about the fact that she had just shut down the oxygen generators. She remained stooped in front of the open panel, not daring to look away in case she forgot which socket she had taken the cable from. She heard the Doctor muttering something under his breath, then the whine of his sonic tool. She crossed the fingers of both hands, realising that she was pinning all her hopes, risking everyone's lives, on someone she hadn't trusted at all this morning.

Then there was an explosion and, without thinking, Gillian leapt back in shock.

The circuit boards were emitting thin wisps of smoke and the Doctor's face was a picture of dismay. 'What happened?' she cried.

He blew on his fingers ruefully. 'The decay is too far advanced.'

'You mean you can't get us out of here?'

The Doctor passed her the power cable. 'You'd better put this back where you found it.'

Gillian slotted the cable back into position inside the Brain, but she couldn't help feeling that it was a waste of time. If the mods didn't get her, then she would asphyxiate two days from now. Perhaps it was better to die quickly. But then she stood up and saw the Doctor again, and he looked more thoughtful than worried.

'*Can* you get us out of here?' she asked.

'There's always a way,' he said, but he dashed Gillian's hopes with his next words. 'I just haven't found it yet. The first thing, of course, is to stop the fighting.'

'Turn the oxygen generators off again.'

'I said stop the fighting, not kill everybody.'

Gillian bristled. Why did he always have to make her feel so inferior? 'Just until the air thins out a bit, I mean. They couldn't fight then, could they?'

The Doctor shook his head. 'It's too risky. It would take a good deal longer to reoxygenate the air than it would to deplete it. People could die.'

'Like we're not dying already?'

'I think it's worth a try.' The interjection came from Alec, who had walked over to rejoin his Technicians as they conversed. 'Unless you've got a better idea.'

A second earlier, Gillian would have been glad of his support. She had wanted to impress the Doctor, to show him that she had a brain too, to win one over him at last. Now, though, getting her own way in the face of his objections seemed like the worst possible outcome. It worried her that her hasty plan was the best they had, and that it would be her responsibility should it fail – should it kill, even – as the Doctor was sure it would.

She looked to him to save the situation, to come up with an alternative. But all he could manage was 'Something will turn up,' and he didn't seem at all confident about that.

'We can't wait for a miracle, Doctor,' said Alec.

And then, as if the fates were conspiring to undermine him, the universe blinked.

Gillian didn't know how else to describe it. It was as if the lights had gone out for an instant, but it wasn't just the lights. It was everything. The building, the city, the planet, the sky. Everything had gone. Then everything had come back. Gillian fell against the Brain, feeling as if she had been punched in the stomach. Her every sense insisted that the world around her was different but, disappointingly perhaps, not a thing had changed.

Except that the sound of fighting had stopped outside, and Alec's face was pale and his eyes were wide and he was shaking, and Gillian knew that everybody else had shared her traumatic experience. 'What was it?' she whispered, not daring to speak up in case the very sound of her voice damaged the suddenly fragile world.

'I think you should ask your friend Alec,' said the Doctor quietly.

The sensation was like nothing Davey had felt before. He screwed his eyes shut and accepted that he had died, so it came as a surprise to him when he was lifted to his feet. He didn't want to look at first, didn't want to see what kind of afterlife he had earned. Then the helping hands let him stand alone, and he teetered and had to open his eyes to correct his balance.

He was in a new world, and it was exactly the same as the old one.

In the city's central square, an uneasy peace had settled. Mods and rockers relinquished their grips on each other, lowered their weapons and stared at each other, stunned into inaction and united by a fear that nobody put into words. It was as if they could see, for the first time, that their differences meant nothing next to the unknowable forces that played with all their lives.

It *was* a new world.

All Davey had ever fought for, lived for, meant nothing.

And, with that revelation, the fire in his stomach spread to engulf his body, and his legs felt weak and his eyelids felt heavy and something clicked inside his head and the floor rushed up to meet him for a second time.

Rick was on the stairs when the world turned inside out. The knife fell from his numbed fingers and clattered away from him. It wasn't fair. He had been winning. The arrival of reinforcements had tipped the scales: for every mod who had fallen in the partially demolished complex, two rockers had joined them. Rick had given in to his wild side, relishing it, assured of his victory. He had left the drill behind – it would respond only to his voiceprint anyway – and rushed to join his comrades on the surface, knowing that his enemies had nowhere to run now, knowing that at last this was the battle for which he had lived, the one that would change everything. But now it didn't matter. Nothing mattered. Everything had changed already.

Rick fell to his knees, feeling sick and giddy, recognising the sensation but terrified of it. He had felt it four times in 1965, and once more almost a month ago. But never this strongly.

He was laughing, though he didn't know why, and crying at the same time. His eyes and his thoughts were equally unfocused. His remaining followers must have been perplexed by his behaviour, and he wanted to explain. But all he could manage to say, in a high-pitched, distant voice, was the same phrase over and over again: 'They're here!

'They're here!

'They're here they're here they're here they're here they're here they're here they're

Chapter Twelve
Meltdown

'That's what it was like,' said Sandra, her hand still clutched to her head. 'When the Maker appeared on the beach, and when it left.'

'And when it came for us in 1965,' breathed Deborah.

'Only this time it was worse. Much worse.'

'I'd forgotten,' Vince whispered.

Sandra had been affected more than the others by the passing sensation. She had been squeezing herself through a narrow gap left between a rock fall caused by Rick's drill and a metal wall at the time. She had panicked, and Fitz had feared she would end up stuck there. He had helped to push her through, and she had promptly collapsed into a heap against the debris on the far side of the passage.

Fitz had felt it too, of course, but already the memory of what it had been like was fading. Like the memory of his telepathic joining with the Maker. It was simply too big, too incomprehensible, for his mind to hold on to. But this was – what? – the fourth time for Sandra, and he wondered if her wild-eyed shock was caused by the fact that she was beginning to remember, perhaps to understand too much.

'Is the Maker here?' asked Vince urgently. 'Is that what it is? Has it followed us?'

'Or has it left us altogether?' asked Deborah.

Sandra banged a fist against her head, as if trying to knock loose nuggets of information. 'It's too big for that. I don't know what… I can almost see…'

She closed her eyes and lapsed into a pained silence. Fitz was almost aching with worry. Sandra's mention of the Maker reminded him that the creature had somehow arrived in the city without Alec or Sandra knowing about it. That must have been how Rick, of all people, had found it. He had felt its arrival. But the effect must have been localised, and weak enough that nobody else felt it at all, or recognised it if they did.

He wondered how close the source of the effect was this time, for it to have been so strong.

Or – oh, Christ – how many sources there were.

'There's something ahead of us,' announced Sandra with sudden new-found clarity. 'Around the next corner, just outside Kenny's quarters.'

Fitz was coldly aware that they were cornered. If something attacked them now, their only escape would be back down the passageway past the rock fall, and they could negotiate that only one person at a time. They were easy targets.

'We'd better get out of here,' he whispered nervously. 'Deborah, help me get Sandra to her feet – and for God's sake, everybody, keep your voices down.'

That was when the screaming started.

Somebody around the next corner was very frightened indeed. Fitz's first impulse was to run, but, as he had already noted, there was nowhere to run to. Part of his mind was screaming: *What if the Doctor's there? What if he needs help?* while another part insisted: *There's nothing you can do. You'll only get yourself killed!* In the end, it was only because the screams seemed relatively distant that Fitz was able to overrule that second voice.

'Get through the passage, all of you,' he instructed. Then, hardly believing that the words were coming out of his mouth, he added, 'I'm going to see what's happening.'

He took a few steps forward, then looked back to see that Vince, Deborah and Sandra were all paralysed, staring at him with frightened expressions. Irritated, he gestured to them to get on with it. The last thing he wanted, if he came back along this corridor in a tearing hurry, was for his exit to be blocked.

The screaming had stopped now, to be replaced by a rending of metal that was, if anything, more dreadful. But as he drew closer to the corner, Fitz heard grunting and panting and a scuffling sound that suggested that a fight was in progress. Signs of life, anyway. He didn't know how long he stood there, plucking up the will to look, to expose himself to whatever unknown peril lurked in the gloomy catacombs; probably less time than it seemed. A final glance over his shoulder confirmed that Deborah had made her escape and that Sandra, standing unaided again, was ushering a mildly protesting Vince into the passageway.

Fitz peered around the corner.

He had meant to snatch his head back immediately, to minimise the risk, but the sight that greeted him dissolved such concerns as it seized his attention.

Vince had been right. The Maker had followed them into the rockers' living quarters.

No, Fitz corrected himself. The creature may have looked identical to the one that lay in Rick's suite of rooms, but it wasn't crippled. Its legs may have seemed too spindly, too weak to support its body and its oversized head – it may even have found it difficult to stand, as its three-fingered hand pawed at the wall as if to aid its balance – but standing it was. Which was more than could be said for the other occupants of the corridor.

The floor was littered with mods and rockers alike. Fitz recognised some of the former as those he had chivvied into the back of Rick's drill; in fact, the machine itself stood idle and unmanned, partly embedded in the corridor wall behind the Maker. Many of the humans were unconscious – or worse; Fitz wasn't close enough to tell. Those who weren't – four in all – were struggling and crying out as the walls themselves erupted, reaching for them with fluid arms. Three were already held immobile, and clearly in pain as their bonds of metal contracted. As Fitz watched in horror, one mod passed out.

One mod had avoided being entangled. He rushed at the Maker, his knife at the ready, but the floor undulated beneath him like a wave and knocked him over. He recovered quickly, but not quickly enough. As he scrambled to his feet, the floor conspired to trip him so that he fell into the wall's embrace. A sheet of metal bulged outwards, became molten, cascaded over the mod's face and solidified again. Visible only from the chest down now, and almost certainly unable to breathe, he clawed at it in desperation but uselessly.

Fitz longed to do something – but, so long as his altruistic side couldn't think of a single thing to do, his natural cowardice was arguing from the better position.

Even so, he was transfixed. He couldn't leave the spot. So it was only natural that the Maker should see him eventually.

The creature didn't even look directly at him – although, with its huge, bulging eyes, Fitz thought, it probably had great peripheral vision. He felt somehow, rather than saw, that it was aware of his presence. He didn't have time to react before it waved a hand vaguely in his direction, in what – under other circumstances – could hardly have been construed as a threatening gesture. The composition of the air around him changed. A green haze hung in front of his eyes, and acrid fingers prised their way into his mouth and clawed at his throat. He coughed and spluttered and felt as if he was going to be sick, then realised that he couldn't draw breath again. His eyes were tearing, and he stumbled blindly back down the corridor, but felt his legs give way beneath him.

Fitz took a headlong dive towards the floor, but never reached it. He was righted by an amorphous blob, which then used its reassuringly strong arms to propel him forward. His head was spinning and he felt, for a ludicrous moment, as if he was floating on a breeze, with the blob – a person, of course – pulling him along on a string like a balloon.

He could breathe again, although the air still had a bitter taste to it. He was back at the rock fall, he realised. Even his rescuer was coming into focus. 'D-Doctor…?' he panted.

'It's me,' said Sandra. 'Sandra.' She was breathing heavily too, and wheezing a little.

'You should have…'

'I couldn't leave you on your own. It's the Maker, isn't it?'

'Makers. More than one.'

Sandra nodded gravely. 'I thought so. Come on, let's get you out of here.'

'We've got to find them,' insisted Alec. 'The Makers. We've got to find them before Rick can. He'll lie to them, and what if they believe him? What if they side with him?'

'I don't think it's a question of siding with anyone,' mumbled the Doctor. He crouched beside the mod who had attacked Alec. He was unconscious now. The Doctor checked his pulse, nodded in quiet satisfaction and gently eased the club from his fingers. Then he produced a white handkerchief from his pocket and began to knot it to the wood. 'Come on Alec, haven't you worked it out yet? The Maker – or *a* Maker, whatever – has been in the city for weeks.'

'Rick's Technician!' gasped Gillian.

'No. No, it can't be.' Alec refused to believe it; refused to believe that even now, even after all that had happened, his luck could still take yet another turn for the worse. But the Doctor's expression told him Gillian was right. A knot formed in his stomach as he voiced the unthinkable. 'So, the Makers are already working with Rick.'

'No, no, not by choice anyway.' The Doctor's voice tailed off as if he had forgotten about Alec and Gillian and was just talking to himself. 'Trapped within three dimensions. It must have been intolerable, especially for a group mind. And by dwellers in time, no less. Like having your hand caught in a dog's mouth.'

'Rick forced the Maker to build things for him.'

'That is a logical conclusion, yes?'

Alec seized the glimmer of hope. 'So they'll side with us, won't they?'

The Doctor's expression was pained. 'I've told you, Alec, it's not a question of siding with anyone. It's about time you realised how trivial and pointless your gang divisions look from the outside. The Makers haven't been hurt by mods or rockers. As far as they're concerned, they've been hurt by human beings.'

'What will they do?' asked Gillian.

'What would you do to a dog that bit you?'

'That's not fair!' protested Alec.

'That', said the Doctor, 'is why I'm trying to stop them.' He hefted his makeshift white flag experimentally, and beamed with satisfaction. 'Are you coming with me?'

'You're not going out there!'

'The fighting has stopped, I believe.'

'For now.' Already, Alec could hear raised voices from outside. The arguments were starting – about what had happened, who was responsible, who had done what to whom during the fight, all the usual things.

'Then now is the time to act,' proclaimed the Doctor, already sweeping towards the open hatchway. 'The arrival of the other Makers has speeded up our timetable, I'm afraid.'

'How do you mean?' asked Alec, but the Doctor had already gone.

'I think he's talking about that,' said Gillian, in a small voice. She pointed towards the Brain. It was sweating cold rivulets of metal.

The city was melting. Fitz had noticed it underground but, amid the damage caused by both Rick and the Maker, he hadn't appreciated the full extent of the problem. As soon as he emerged from the rockers' milk bar, though, his breath caught in his throat. The buildings were losing definition, the city's sharp edges and straight lines blurring. He stood, blinking in moonlight that suddenly seemed too bright and adjusting to the unexpectedly bitter cold.

'What do we do now?' asked Vince, hugging himself for warmth.

'I don't know,' said Fitz. Yes you do, he told himself; you just don't want to admit it.

'The Doctor must still be at the Brain,' said Sandra.

'And Davey will be there too, won't he?' said Deborah.

'I suppose so,' sighed Fitz. 'Do you think they've stopped fighting yet?'

'They'll never stop fighting,' muttered Sandra under her breath.

'Looks like we're going to the Brain then,' said Fitz without enthusiasm.

'Shouldn't we do something?' asked Gillian.

Alec just shrugged. There was no more despair left in him. He felt empty and numb. He could hear the Doctor's voice out in the central square. He was delivering a lecture about the futility of violence, the need to work together, and amazingly he hadn't been slaughtered.

'What's the point?' he asked. 'It never makes any difference.'

'Perhaps…' Gillian turned away from him, as if she had thought better of speaking out. Then she composed herself, pursed her lips in determination and turned back. 'Perhaps we've just been doing the wrong thing.' A day ago, Alec would have been annoyed at her cheek. Now he just looked at her blankly. 'The Doctor said something to me before,' she said. 'He said there's more than one way to win a fight.' She nodded towards the hatchway. 'I think I'm beginning to see what he was talking about.'

'What does he know? Things have only got worse since he arrived.'

'That's what I thought at first – but they were getting worse anyway. The city was already dying. The Doctor's kept us alive so far.'

'Since when did you start thinking so much of the Doctor?' asked Alec, sullenly.

'Since I realised we had nothing left to lose,' said Gillian.

At first, Fitz thought he was looking at a horrific sculpture. But a rocker lay at its feet, and another was entangled within it, unable to move and groaning with pain. He hesitated, sensing danger but unsure where it would come from. Deborah gave a sobbing gasp and buried her head in Vince's chest. Sandra rushed forward.

'Well come on, then,' she cried, as she tried to prise the rocker free from his metal bonds. 'Help me!' Fitz could see what had happened now. The tubular framework of an abandoned scooter had been twisted into an almost humanoid shape, which had wrapped itself around its prey and squeezed the life out of them. It was inanimate again now and, like the rest of the city, beginning to melt. Its second victim was fortunate to be alive.

The metal tubes felt clammy beneath Fitz's hands. With an effort, he and Sandra managed to bend them far enough that the rocker stumbled out of the vehicle's deadly embrace. He fell to the ground and coughed up spots of blood.

'Andy,' he gasped, crawling weakly towards his fallen comrade. 'Andy!'

'It's too late for him, Bill,' said Sandra, sadly, reaching down to him.

He knocked her hand away. 'Get away from me, you traitor! Go back to your mod friends!'

'Hey!' protested Fitz. 'She saved your life!'

The rocker's attempt to form a retort degenerated into a coughing fit.

'Who did this?' wailed Deborah.

'Another Maker,' said Sandra, dully.

'What else?' Fitz muttered.

'Why are they doing this to us?' asked Vince, plaintively.

'We destroyed their city,' said Deborah.

'They might only be killing in self-defence,' said Sandra. She was trying to buoy their spirits, despite her own uncertainty. Fitz wished he had thought to do that. Somehow the leadership role in their little group had drifted away from him; he found himself missing what had once been an unwanted responsibility.

'Bill,' rapped Sandra, 'you've got to talk to me. Tell me what happened.'

The rocker called Bill swore at her. 'Not talking to your mod friends,' he wheezed, rolling on to his back painfully and closing his eyes. 'Chest hurts… I think it broke my ribs…'

'Don't try to move. I'll send someone back here with a medical kit.'

'I'm not a mod,' said Fitz, aware that he was still wearing the gang's silver uniform.

'And it doesn't matter anyway,' said Sandra. 'Not any more. You saw a Maker, didn't you?' The rocker's eyes flicked open in surprise. 'We saw one too, under the milk bar. They're killing mods as well as rockers.'

'Good,' said Bill.

Sandra looked up at Fitz, and gave a sigh of despair.

'Davey!' said Deborah, suddenly. 'What about Davey? We've got to warn him.'

She broke into a run, but Sandra leapt in front of her and restrained her. 'Not that way!'

'That's where he'll be. That's where they're fighting.'

'It's where the Maker went,' insisted Sandra.

'No!' cried Deborah.

Sandra shook her head quickly. 'It's all right. It didn't go towards the central square.'

'What are you saying?' asked Fitz.

'I don't know. I can… I can feel it somehow. Like it's pulling on my past. I know that doesn't make sense. I can't explain it. But we can't go down that road. It's waiting.'

'Is there another way to the Brain?'

Sandra thought about it, then nodded. 'One of the elevated roads, down this way. It'll take us over the central square and back into it from the far side. It's the quickest way.'

Fitz started as a blob of cold, liquid metal splashed on to his silver moon boot. He looked up to see that it had fallen from a roadway above him. He wondered if it was wise to trust such a roadway to support four people – they had never looked that safe at the best of times – but, before he could voice his concerns, Sandra set off at a trot and Vince and Deborah were quick to follow her. With a last glance at Bill the rocker, who appeared to have passed out now, Fitz reluctantly ran after them.

The mood of the crowd had changed, an undercurrent of discontent bubbling to the surface. The Doctor frowned and mentally ran through what he had just said, wondering how he had lost them. Then, realising the truth, he swung around to greet Alec and Gillian with a grin as they emerged from the Brain's chamber. 'I'm glad you could make it,' he said.

'Come out of hiding at last, have you?' piped up one disgruntled mod.

'Yeah,' agreed another. 'Get back under your stone, you greaser!'

Alec scowled and opened his mouth to respond, but the Doctor cut in quickly. 'Alec is here because he wants to help.' Forestalling the few shouts of derision, he raised his voice and commanded: 'Listen to me, all of you! Within the hour, this city won't exist, and neither will its oxygen generators. We've all got literally minutes to live!' As he spoke, he pivoted on the spot, making eye contact with as many of his audience as he could. Some returned his gaze with belligerent glares, but most of them were listening, through respect or hope or fear.

'Now,' the Doctor continued in a gentler voice, 'I've already explained to you why you can't afford to waste those minutes fighting each other. Alec is here because he sees the need for us to work together, to show the Makers that we don't deserve to die.' He extended a hand. The crowd parted as Alec walked slowly towards him and took it. The Doctor beamed as they shook hands and he drew the rockers' leader to his side.

'He deserves to die,' came one dissenting voice. 'He's a dirty, stinking rocker!'

The Doctor didn't recognise the man who pushed himself forward at that point. He was younger than most of the inhabitants of the city: a mod, from his uniform, fair-haired and crazy-eyed. His red shoulder flashes would have told the Doctor that he was somebody of import, had the reaction of the crowd not already done so. Some of the mods had raised a half-hearted cheer at his words, but it faded into a heavy silence.

'You must be Rick,' said the Doctor, attempting to defuse the tension with a smile. 'Nice to meet you at last. I'm the Doctor. We have a great deal to talk about.'

Fitz remembered how the city had looked when he had first seen it from the plain: like the future world he had seen in pulp magazines back home. Even for someone as inured to travel as he was becoming, it had felt special. It had been full of promise. Now he looked down upon it as the buildings dissolved into misshapen lumps, and he tingled with an inexplicable sadness. As if his dreams had been stolen.

The sight had halted Sandra, Vince and Deborah too. Fitz could only wonder how much worse they were feeling. This was their home, after all.

They could see about a quarter of the city from up here, all the way to one edge. Not the central square, though: it was blocked by towers and spires. There were few people in the streets, and few Makers now. From what they had seen, the aliens had converged upon the mods' café, killing anyone who got in their way. Which, thankfully, wasn't many people.

Fitz's foot had sunk into the surface of the elevated roadway. Reclaiming it was like fighting clinging mud. He fought off a nightmare image of himself sinking through the road or slipping off its unguarded edge and plunging to his death. Had he realised that it climbed this high, he would have suggested taking an alternative, longer route to the Brain.

He was about to say something, to urge the others to hurry, when Deborah gasped and pointed to another distraction below. It took Fitz a moment to see it, because she was looking beyond the city. But when he did, his heart shivered.

He had almost forgotten about the plain-dwellers, the dropouts, the cannibals. But he saw now that they had assembled in a straight line, parallel to the boundary of the city and about a hundred yards distant from it. There seemed to be more of them than ever: at least thirty, Fitz estimated. They weren't doing anything – just standing there with their animals, watching.

'It's like they're attending a funeral,' said Sandra.

'They're waiting,' whispered Deborah. 'Waiting for the city to die.'

'Waiting for us to lose our protection,' added Vince.

And what, Fitz wondered, were they planning to do then?

Alec and Rick circled each other slowly, the hate in their eyes undiluted. The crowd had pulled back to give them space, and the Doctor withdrew too. He stood beside Gillian and offered her a brief encouraging smile. What happened next was up to the gang leaders. He wondered if he had done enough. He steepled his fingers in front of his mouth and watched with nervous interest, along with everybody else.

For a minute or more, there was silence.

'So,' said Rick at last, 'you've finally plucked up the courage to face me.'

'I'm not scared of you, you little runt!' spat Alec.

Not a good start, thought the Doctor, but perhaps inevitable.

'You should be.'

'What, because you think you've got a Maker on your side?'

Rick paled at that accusation, and Alec grinned through clenched teeth. A murmur of surprise rippled through the onlookers. Rick responded by going back on the offensive. 'Yes, I've got the Maker. It came here over a month ago, and it came to me. It saw what you grease monkeys were doing and it decided to fight with the mods!'

'You forced it, more like.'

'It only had to look at your lot, with your filthy clobber. I bet you knocked it sick!'

'You moron! You've turned the Maker – the Makers – against us.' Alec threw out a hand to point to the melting central tower. 'That's why they're destroying our city!'

'You'd like to think that was our fault, wouldn't you?' retorted Rick. 'But you're the one to blame – you and your deadbeat Technician. We always said we'd all keep away from the Brain, but you – you break in there and you end up shutting it down, you're so incompetent. Well? Can you see now why it was a stupid thing to do?' Like Alec, Rick was playing to the crowd. The confrontation had taken on the air of a title bout, each fighter determined to put on a show that would restore the faith of his followers. 'You've killed us all!'

'No, *you've* killed us all!'

'You couldn't face it, could you? You couldn't face the fact that I was winning!'

'Winning?' scoffed Alec. 'You think a few poxy ray guns would have turned your lot into an army? You'd have to drag them away from their mirrors first!'

'We could take on your rabble any day of the week!'

'Yeah, right. That's why we've got rooms full of mod prisoners back home.'

It was Rick's turn to smile. 'Not any more you haven't.'

'What are you talking about?'

'You don't have prisoners any more. And you don't have a home. I demolished it!'

'You're lying!'

'I told you, the Maker's on my side. It gave me a weapon – and it told me to use it to sort out you scummy rockers good and proper.'

Alec was clenching and unclenching his fists. 'You animal!' he snarled.

'I'm just sorry there weren't more of you in there. I'd have brought your little bolt hole down around your ears. I'd have crushed you – you and your slag of a wife!'

With a furious roar, Alec leapt headfirst at Rick, whose face lit up with malicious delight as he raised his fists and gave a taunting shout: 'Come on then! Come on, greaser!'

They wrestled fiercely, veering backwards and forwards across the limited circle of space, spitting curses at each other, each punching the other repeatedly but neither able to gain the leverage or the distance necessary to gain a decisive advantage. The crowd began to stir again, mods and rockers alike cheering on their respective leaders even if they hadn't yet been galvanised into violence again themselves. It could only be a matter of time, though. The Doctor had hoped for much better than this.

He glanced at Gillian again. She was already looking to him for reassurance that he couldn't give. His smile was weaker this time. But, even as he made to step forward, fearing that he couldn't bring the situation under control after all, another figure intervened.

'Stop that!' screamed Sandra, using her elbows to clear a path to the combatants. 'I won't have this! You're both acting like children! Have you not learned anything?' She gripped the back of Rick's uniform and the collar of Alec's leather jacket, but it was the force of her words rather than physical force that tore the pair apart.

The Doctor caught a glimpse of Fitz through the crowd. He withdrew from the centre again, and this time his hands concealed a tiny smile.

The two enemies glared at each other, but showed no inclination to close again. Perhaps neither was confident of winning a one-on-one fight, although both were determined to mask such insecurities. 'You try that again,' snarled Rick, 'and I'll make mincemeat of you!'

'You?' laughed Alec. 'You're nothing but a scrawny kid. A big baby!'

'And you're well past it. You've got old and lazy and fat!'

'Will you two stop it?' cried Sandra. 'Is this how you want to die? Shouting at each other, making stupid threats, while the air runs out around you?'

'Don't tell me what to do,' snapped Rick. 'You're not my –' He tailed off abruptly, and he and Sandra shared a look of anguish and confusion and unspoken resentment.

Then Sandra spoke, gently but firmly, looking from Rick to Alec in turn. 'This isn't what Jack and Phil would have wanted.' The mention of her older brothers hurt Rick, but she continued before he could say anything. 'They would have done anything – anything, even if it wasn't the right thing to do – to protect their family. Well, we're a family now, the three of us, whether we like it or not. And we're the only family we've got. It doesn't say much for any of us if we'd die rather than put aside our differences for a few hours.'

The Doctor took his opportunity to step forward again. 'This isn't how it was meant to be,' he said, quietly but with enough projection that everybody could hear him through the thick silence. 'This world, this city, might have been how you envisaged your future, but your dreams were based on a flawed premise. You thought the human race would change, that you wouldn't need art or entertainment or recreation or beauty. You imagined that, someday, somehow, your kind would devote itself to intellectual pursuits to the exclusion of all the things that actually make life worthwhile. In time, you would have seen that. You would have seen that nobody could live in the world you were dreaming of. You would have created new dreams. Of course, some of you would have failed. Others would have succeeded, and many of you would have lived with compromises. But all of you would have had a chance to make a life for the people you eventually became. That's what the Makers denied you. They thought they were giving you the future, but they were really stealing it from you. What you need to ask yourselves now is if you have the strength to take it back, with words, not fists. For nineteen years, the Makers have treated you – all of you – like favoured pets. They built you this city, put you in a bowl and watched as you played your games. How are you going to convince them that they've been wrong all this time; that you're deserving of respect?'

Nobody answered that. The Doctor let the question hang in the air for long seconds, before he turned back to Alec, Sandra and Rick. He was gratified to note that there was no hostility in their eyes now, any of them. Just sadness and shame.

'I need you to come with me,' he said to them gently. 'The Makers know you. It was the three of you who started this, on that beach in 1965. I think it's time for you to end it.'

No words were spoken as they crossed the city together. The Doctor took the lead, affecting a casual saunter as Alec, Sandra and Rick shuffled along behind him, studiously not looking at each other. Most of the mods and rockers – and Fitz – followed, knowing that their fates were about to be decided. However, the funereal procession halted outside the mods' café. Even those to whom this building had once been home were reluctant to walk through its doors, to face the godlike intruders within.

The stairs felt almost liquid beneath the Doctor's feet as he descended into the red-tinted gloom of the underground complex. The city had once had a fresh, if sterile, air. Now all the Doctor could smell was the ripe odour of decay. He didn't need to ask where Rick had left 'his' Maker; somehow he felt the aliens looming in his future. He knew where to find them.

They splashed their way along numerous corridors until they reached a set of double doors, which stood open. The Doctor paused for a second, took a deep breath, threw his shoulders back and walked proudly into the long, rectangular room beyond.

The Makers congregated around the rubble at the room's far end. They didn't move. Their huge, yellow eyes were already staring at the Doctor, as if they had been doing nothing but waiting for him, knowing precisely when he would arrive. They probably had. He felt a tingle of fear in the presence of these beings. He was a Lord of Time, but to them time was nothing. In the normal course of things, his path should never have crossed theirs. There were at least twelve of them, probably more in the rooms that led off this one. For once in his lives, the Doctor didn't know how to approach them. A cheery smile and a hand of friendship would probably have meant nothing to them. He ran through everything he had surmised about these beings and found himself wondering to what extent each Maker was an entity in its own right. Perhaps their purple-grey bodies were no more than drones housing portions of a single greater intelligence. Or perhaps the truth was more complex than that.

There was so much he yearned to know.

For now, he contented himself with the relief of the familiar. That cheery smile found its way on to his face after all, as he caught sight of the room's other occupant: the companion he had thought lost out on the plain. 'Compassion!' he exclaimed warmly.

'Hello Doctor,' she said.

'How wonderful! You're talking again.'

'For now. The Maker has shown me so many possibilities. I wish you could see them.'

'You can communicate with, ah, "it"?'

'It already knows why you're here.'

The Doctor pulled a face. 'But I'd like to explain it properly, to put forward our side of the story as it were.' He turned to motion the others forward. They had hesitated in the doorway, the Doctor's infectious confidence unable to carry them further once they had sighted the Makers. Now, Sandra was the first to respond to the Doctor's gesture. She hugged herself as she stepped into the room, and her shoulders were stooped as they had been when he had first met her. Alec and Rick were subdued too, as they summoned the courage to join her, inadvertently walking in step with each other. A bruise on Alec's temple was beginning to turn purple, and Rick's silver uniform was torn and dishevelled. In the presence of the beings who were practically their gods, all three humans were fearful – but also, perhaps for the first time in years, hopeful – for their lives.

'You've done enough already,' said Compassion, a tight smile pulling at the corners of her mouth. She nodded towards Alec, Sandra and Rick. 'You've got them together and you've brought them here. The Maker can't see their futures any more, but it can see their pasts. And it knows the lives they would have led without its interference.

'It can see what it has done to them.'

Chapter Thirteen
Possible Futures

'The Makers have halted the destruction of the city.'

The Doctor's announcement was met with an outpouring of relief. When he had emerged from the mods' café, with Compassion, Alec, Sandra and Rick at his heels, he had found himself facing an expectant audience. Now he beamed with pride as the fear in their faces gave way to joy. He cleared his throat to regain their attention.

'They have also agreed to make reparations for what they have done. Whatever else you may have believed, this is your future. The year, I'm told, is 3012. The Makers will transport anyone who wishes it to Earth. The real Earth, that is, or one of its colonies. Alternatively…' He hesitated, wondering which words to use, wondering how they would take it. 'They could send you home.'

He had to raise his voice and gesture with his hands to quell their excited chatter. It was important that they hear the rest of it. 'Just those of you who weren't born here – and it will be as the people you once were. Nineteen years younger. The Makers can't risk a paradox. It will be as if your time in the city never happened. You won't even remember it. It's up to you. Each one of you has to make his or her own choice.'

In the aftermath of the Doctor's speech, the crowd separated slowly. Many people wanted time alone, to think about the most important decision they had ever had to make. Others wandered off in small groups, to talk it over with friends.

Alec found himself alone in an open square towards the edge of the city, and he sat on a misshapen bench beside a congealed fountain and stared up at the new sky. A cold breeze whistled through his tight jacket, but it felt surprisingly good. The melted buildings stood as a testament to his failure, and his heart ached for that. But increasingly it was also lightened by the knowledge that a burden had been lifted from him. For all that he had liked to pretend otherwise, he hadn't had this much control over his life in nineteen years. Since becoming the rockers' leader, he hadn't even been able to come to the surface and just sit on his own in the fresh air and enjoy this sort of peace and not worry about fighting a war he couldn't win.

He looked forward to getting home, to going back to a place and a time in which his worries would all be trivial ones. He would sell his bike, burn his leathers, buy a suit, knuckle down at work, make something of his life. Make a future for himself. He could do anything.

He started to laugh, almost hysterically, his whole body shaking until his stomach hurt. He didn't know why at first, but it felt good. It was cathartic. And then he identified the giddy sensation that held him in its grip. Pure, powerful relief. It was over at last. He had survived.

'I haven't heard you laugh like that in years,' said Sandra.

She had approached Alec without his seeing her. He tensed as she sat next to him, wondering if there was going to be another row. But her voice had been friendly enough, and there was a gleam in her eyes which, he only realised now, he hadn't seen for years either.

'I haven't had much to laugh about.' The seriousness of his words was belied by the fact that he had to pant heavily to control himself, and by the big stupid grin that he couldn't keep from his face. 'Until now. We're going home, Sandra. We're going home at last.'

'Is that really what you want?'

'Of course it is. Don't you?'

'To go backwards? To forget everything we've been through? Everything we've learned?'

He was sobered by Sandra's words. He couldn't believe she

was saying this; couldn't believe that she didn't see what a fantastic opportunity they had been given. His lower lip curled outwards, sulkily. Why did she always have to pour scorn on everything? 'You heard the Doctor: the last nineteen years were a mistake. They shouldn't have happened.'

'But they did happen. We can't just undo them.'

'Why not?' Alec shuffled round so that he was sitting on the very edge of the bench and staring earnestly into Sandra's eyes. He took her hands, almost reflexively – but, although she was surprised, she didn't pull away, so he kept hold of them. His plea, when it came, sounded more anguished, more pathetic, than he had intended. 'We'd be together again.'

'Only because we wouldn't know any better,' she replied evenly.

'It'd work this time. We wouldn't have the city getting in the way.'

A hint of annoyance entered Sandra's voice. 'It's not just the city, Alec. In case you're forgetting, these stupid war games of yours started before we came here.'

'It would be different this time. I've learned my lesson.'

'But you'd forget! That's the whole point, Alec. If we go back to Earth, to the past, we won't remember anything that happened here. City or no city, we'd go through it again.'

'We wouldn't.'

'We would. Remember what it was like in 1965, Alec? Remember what my brothers said they'd do to you if you came near me? They'll be back, you know. The Doctor said it will be the same for them as for the rest of us: like nothing happened. How will you deal with them?'

'I'll talk to them.'

'No you won't. As if they'd listen anyway. You'll fight them, Alec, like you fought them here. And somebody will end up dying. Next time, it might be you.'

Alec shook his head stubbornly. He knew Sandra was making sense, but he didn't want to believe it. All he could see was a shining path, a way out of all his troubles. He couldn't imagine, couldn't feel, that he could ever just forget, just go back to the way he had been. Surely some memory had to remain? It couldn't be the same again. For nineteen years, he had fought a losing battle. It had changed him. Now he could reverse every setback, counter every piece of bad luck, with one small action. He could start again. He could do it right this time. But he couldn't do it without her.

'Don't you want to see Jack and Phil again?' he tried.

She gave him a wistful smile. 'Not really. It'll be enough just knowing they're alive, that they got home in the end. I can make a life without them. That's what I want.'

'A new life,' asked Alec, tentatively, 'with me?'

Sandra smiled at him sadly. 'I don't know, Alec. I just don't know.'

'So, where does that leave me?'

'Come with me,' she said.

'Where to?'

'I don't know where.' She glanced up at the sky. 'Up there, I suppose. To other worlds. To the future.'

'I've had enough of the future.'

'The real future, Alec, not the city. Let's see what it's like for us somewhere else, somewhere real. You, me and Rick –'

'You want to take that psychopath?'

'He wants to stay, Alec, and I want to stay with him. He's my family. In fact –'

'And you think he won't try as hard as Jack or Phil ever did to tear us apart?'

'Rick needs help. He needs me. I'm not arguing about that. Let's just see if we can all use what we've learned here and move on at last.'

'But what if we can't? What if it doesn't work? What if I end up with nothing? I won't be able to go back then. The Makers won't be around. This is a once-in-a-lifetime chance.'

She pulled her hands away from him, her eyes hardening.

'You're right,' she said. 'A once-in-a-lifetime chance to decide where you want to live, Alec. The past or the future. And we already know what you'll choose, don't we? Because you chose it nineteen years ago.'

She got to her feet then, and she would have walked away except that Alec stood too and blocked her path. 'What are you talking about?' he snapped.

She jabbed an accusing finger at his chest. 'I'm talking about you refusing to grow up. This city could have been a good place – oh, I know there were problems, but we could have at least tried to overcome them – but no, you had to bring your past here. You had to cling on to your gangs and your stupid fights, like you're doing now. You only want to go back home because it's familiar – because you felt you were in control there, like you were a big man. But you're not a big man, Alec. You're scared. You're scared of the future, and I've got news for you: it's going to happen sometime, whatever you do.'

'And what about Rick?' responded Alec hotly. 'You said he wants to stay here. Why do you think that is? This is his world, like 1965 is mine. He doesn't want to leave it, he doesn't want to go somewhere where he's not in control. He's just as scared as any of us.'

'Of course he is. He's just like you, Alec.'

'That's a filthy lie!'

'That's exactly what he said. And yes, he's made his choice for all the wrong reasons – but he's making the right choice. And even if he wasn't, I won't abandon him again.'

'Why not? What's he ever done for you?'

'He's my son, Alec.'

The words came out in a matter-of-fact way, but they struck like a hammer to Alec's ribs – another world-shaking development that overloaded his mind and left him feeling nauseous. He sank back down on to the bench.

Sandra walked away from him then, slowly, as if she expected him to call after her, to stop her. He didn't. He couldn't. He couldn't deal with this on top of everything else.

It wouldn't matter soon, he thought. It would all be over at last. He didn't have to let this problem or any other weigh him down again. He was going home. That was all he wanted now, all he wanted to think about.

He buried his head in his hands and waited for the world to go away.

The Doctor, Fitz and Compassion were reunited at the base of one of the city's spires. By now, of course, it was half its previous height and resembled nothing more than a gigantic, used silver candle. Molten drips of metal had solidified at its base. Fitz glanced warily up at the elevated roadways it had once supported, wondering if they might be about to fall. But like the rest of the ruins, they were frozen into position. There might even have been a drop of metal suspended in midair, but he couldn't be sure from this perspective.

'What do you think they'll do?' he asked eventually, with a tired sigh.

The Doctor shrugged, his hands in his pockets, looking equally weary. 'I don't know.'

'What do you want them to do?'

'That's not really the point.'

'Why can't they go back to their own time as they are now?'

'As I said, the Makers don't want to create a paradox.'

'Not any more,' Compassion chipped in. 'Not since you had me explain it to them.'

The Doctor grimaced, and Fitz couldn't hide a smile. 'I knew it. You want to put everything back the way it was, don't you? The Makers already created a paradox when they brought the mods and rockers here. You told them to put it right. You don't want the Faction gaining another foothold.'

'I simply explained to the Makers', said the Doctor patiently, 'the likely effects of what they had done upon history. You can't just take over a hundred people out of Time and expect it to paper over the cracks, you know.'

'If we had left here without doing anything,' said Compassion, 'we might have found a different universe.'

'Or we might not. But it's not the sort of risk I feel comfortable taking at the moment.'

'In that case,' said Fitz, 'why give them a choice? Why let them stay in this time at all?'

The Doctor was already nodding frenziedly, his eyes closed, having anticipated the question. 'Their memories, their experiences, their lives... I can't take those things from them. They've already lost so much.'

'You'd stay here, wouldn't you?' Fitz realised. 'If it was you, you'd stay here.'

'I'd be true to myself.'

'You wouldn't be tempted to hit the reset switch? Even if it meant, say, getting the TARDIS back or getting Faction Paradox out of your life?'

'You don't learn anything that way.'

'You must be praying not too many of the mods and rockers think the same way.'

'Their futures are in their own hands. That's as it should be.' The Doctor's eyes glazed over and he added wistfully, 'I only wish we had that luxury.'

'The Maker would like to help you,' said Compassion, 'but it cannot. Until you resolve the paradox in your past, your future is uncertain.'

The Doctor nodded again, weakly this time. 'I know. And how about you?'

Compassion looked at him as if she hadn't understood the question. The Doctor turned to her, placed a hand on her hand, and asked softly, 'Do you want to go with the Makers?'

There was nobody in the rockers' milk bar. Rick hurried through it, and into the room that held their antigrav tube. It wasn't working, of course, but he had brought something with him:

something he had salvaged from a mod supply cupboard to which only he had access. The jetpack had been created after the decay of the city had begun. It had been affected, like everything else – it was speckled with silver rust – but it was still usable, even if he had to jump-start its internal power source with a slap.

The jetpack coughed and whined as it carried him down into the complex. He could have used the stairs, of course, but in all likelihood he would have been seen. As his feet touched ground again, he smiled grimly and hurled the pack aside, its usefulness over.

Rick knew the rockers' part of the underground complex almost as well as he knew his own. His knowledge came from long nights spent studying maps that had been drawn up in the early days of the city, before his predecessor had enforced segregation. He knew how to avoid most of the personal quarters – what remained of them – where sentimental fools were likely to be taking a last look at their decimated homes. And, on the odd occasion that he heard rocker footsteps around the next corner, he knew where he could hide.

He also knew where he had left the drill.

His ultimate weapon, he had theorised, would be in even better condition than the jetpacks. He was thrilled to be proved right. He gazed up at the huge machine, as awed as when he had first seen it spring into existence. He ran a hand over its surface, almost lovingly. It felt rough to his touch, and a few flakes of metal peeled away, but the damage bit no deeper than that.

For a time, Rick had been outnumbered. His enemies – Alec, Sandra, the Doctor, the Makers – had had the upper hand. But he had outthought them all. He had pretended to be cowed, to go along with them, until he had what he wanted. The city was no longer dying. But now they wanted to take his home from him, send him back to 1965, to that child's body, to a life over which he had no control. He wasn't going to let that happen.

A fire of determination burned within Rick's chest, invigorating him, as he climbed the rungs on the side of the drill and swung himself into its cockpit. 'Activate,' he rapped, and the dashboard bleeped in response to his voice signature. A grin spread across his face as he started up the machine and felt the throb of its engine, more powerful than that of any motorbike. He clenched his teeth and turned the grin into an angry snarl as the drill bucked beneath him and lurched forward.

He wasn't going to leave the city. It didn't matter that it was a deformed mess now. He would rebuild it. He would make it better than before. The important thing was that he would stay here, and that his people would stay here with him.

He wasn't prepared to relinquish his control. No matter what he had to do.

The trip down to the mods' living quarters had been an unnerving one for Vince and Deborah. The darkness, the precarious consistency of the stairs and their increasing proximity to the Makers had combined to make them almost turn back several times. But they had agreed, without needing to talk about it, that they had had to come here: to a room that they had never entered before. The room that had belonged to their son.

Vince wondered what he had expected to see. It was just like all the other rooms, of course, and in much the same state now. He wondered what he had expected to feel. The half-melted table, chairs, cupboard and bed brought no comfort to him, no sense that Davey had ever used them, ever laughed or cried or danced or talked or dreamed within these four dull metal walls. No sense that he had ever lived here, or lived at all.

He felt tears welling up, demanding release. He tried to hold them in for Deborah's sake. She had hardly shown any emotion, not since they had arrived in the central square with Fitz Kreiner and Sandra, and one of the mods had quietly taken them aside and broken the news. The worst thing was that Davey's wound could have been cured. The city had that technology. But in the heat of battle, no one had seen what had happened until it was too late. He had been laid out in the mods' garage, beside the scooters he had loved so much. His club was still in his hands. Throughout the long walk there, Vince had felt like a zombie, as if someone else were controlling his empty body. He had wept over his son's corpse until he had thought there were no tears left. Deborah had done nothing and said nothing. It was as if she didn't care. But Vince knew better than that.

Now, her eyes flickered from one part of the room to another as if looking for something, anything, to latch on to, and Vince could see the desolation behind them. He wanted to make it better for her, but as always he wasn't up to the task. If he tried to say anything, he knew the tears would come. So he kept silent and hoped that his presence alone would be some comfort, as hers was to him. He took her hand as she reached for him, and he squeezed it tightly as she knelt down, took a deep breath and gingerly opened the cupboard door.

And sagged, defeated, upon finding nothing within.

Nothing but a single black wooden club, which stood forlornly in the furthest corner.

Deborah took it eventually. 'Not much to show for a life, is it?' she said in a hollow voice.

'Possessions aren't everything,' said Vince. 'Davey liked things to be neat, uncluttered. The city gave him food and clothing, everything he needed.'

'The city let him live, that's all. He had nothing, Vince. Nothing of his own. The rest of us – at least we had bundles of clothes and things, things from home. Reminders of where we came from, who we are. There was nothing in Davey's life. Nothing but this.' She nuzzled the club to her cheek as if expecting to feel him on it.

Vince knelt beside her, still clinging to her hand, still struggling for the magic words.

'How did we let this happen?' she asked, almost voicelessly.

'I don't know.' He wondered if it was time. Time to articulate the desperate hope to which he had been clinging, the one thing that made the pain bearable. He almost couldn't stand to do it, couldn't stand the idea of the hope being shot down. Almost as soon as Vince and Deborah had emerged from the garage, they had been told about the Makers' offer, the chance to go back, as if it would make everything all right. But it wasn't that simple.

'I don't know, Deborah, but it doesn't have to happen again.' She swallowed and didn't answer him.

'We've got a second chance,' he said. 'We can go back to the way we were. We can do it right this time.'

'Can we?'

'We've got a lucky break. You were pregnant when we left 1965. You'd be pregnant again when we got back there. We can have Davey back, Deborah. We can have him back.'

'Born again,' she whispered. 'Outside the city. Back home.'

'It was the city that made him what he was. It'd be different next time.'

'And we'll forget...'

'Yes, we'll forget.'

'We'll forget that Davey – our Davey – existed. No one would remember him. No one.'

That was exactly what Vince hadn't wanted to think about. The tears nearly choked him, but he stammered out his plea anyway. 'We'd be giving him a new chance. A new life. Don't you want that?'

'More than anything. But what if we're being selfish?'

'I know. You think we'd be doing it just because we want to forget.'

'Because we can't cope with the grief.'

'But I don't think I can, Deborah.'

And Vince let the tears come then.

'A few days ago,' said Gillian, 'I would have gone home. Even Boredom Village seemed a whole lot better than this.'

'What did you in 1965?' asked the Doctor.

'Oh, you know, worked part-time in my dad's sweet shop, rode with a rocker, waited for someone to marry me and take me away from my parents' home.'

The Doctor pulled a sympathetic face. 'I see.'

'But just two days with you and you've shown me there's so much more out there. If I go back now, I'll never see anything. I'll never learn anything.'

'I'm sure you'll find all you're looking for.'

'I'm sorry I was such a bitch.'

'Were you?' asked the Doctor, in all innocence.

'I resented you at first, coming in and taking over. I mean, I could see you were a better Technician and all that, but... well, I suppose that was the problem. I was jealous. Silly, isn't it? Getting upset over something so petty.'

'When you don't have much, small things mean a great deal. You shouldn't have that problem now. I only wish I could have shown you more.' The Doctor's eyes glazed over and, in a barely audible murmur, he added, 'Perhaps if things were different...'

Gillian waited for him to explain that comment, but his train of thought seemed to have taken him to a cold, faraway place. 'That's another thing,' she prompted eventually, snapping him out of his reverie. 'Life in the city might not always have been a big bundle of fun, but it's made me who I am. I don't want to stop being that person, and I don't want to forget her.'

'I should hope not,' said the Doctor, looking directly, disconcertingly, into Gillian's eyes and beaming at her. 'She's worth remembering.'

She felt herself blushing but, before she could form an ironic, self-effacing reply, the Doctor's expression changed. His eyes widened with alarm. 'Do you feel that?'

'Feel what?'

He whirled around as if trying to get his bearings, his arms and his coat-tails flapping. 'Vibrations. An engine.' He practically leapt at a sudden realisation. 'From underground!' he cried, and he raced pell-mell towards the mods' café.

Gillian thought for only a second before following him.

The Doctor felt a surge of primeval fear as he skidded to a halt in the doorway of what had once been Rick's reception room.

Things were slipping out of his control.

Through a haze of smoke, he saw a hulking shape that could only have been the ultimate weapon of which Rick had boasted to Alec. There was somebody in its cockpit, and as the Doctor narrowed his eyes and looked more closely, he could see that it was the young man himself.

There was no denying what must have happened. He should have kept a closer eye on Rick, should have known he was still dangerous, shouldn't have let him sneak away and do this.

The reception room was a mess. The new hole that Rick had bored into its wall had been the final straw. Most of the ceiling had come down. Between mounds of debris, he could see only five Makers. He needed to know what had happened to the rest.

And then he saw one, pinned to the floor by a solid lump of rock. It wasn't moving – and even if it was alive, its legs must have been crushed. With an involuntary howl of anguish, the Doctor hurled himself into the room and to its side. He dropped to his knees, cradled its head in his lap and felt for a pulse, but he didn't know what he was feeling for. Even so, he knew that the creature was dead. He could feel it.

Other people had responded to the disaster. Most hung back in the doorway, scared to come closer. The Doctor recognised Sandra as she rushed past him.

He realised that Compassion was at his shoulder. He looked up at her, unable to hide the desolation inside him. 'He's killed it. Rick killed this Maker and how many others? They didn't see it coming. They couldn't see it, because of me. Because I was here.'

His voice was stilled as he felt her through their telepathic link, calming him, reassuring him. 'You've saved many lives here,' she said out loud. 'You've made things better.'

'Have I?'

'You keep referring to the Maker in the plural. It's a single entity. Some aspects of it have died today, but not the whole being. It is wounded, but it survives.'

'And what are they – what is it – thinking? Does it –'

'No, Doctor,' Compassion assured him. 'The Maker has learned. It knows that we're different, that it can't blame us all for the actions of an individual. And it accepts its part in shaping Rick into the individual he has become.'

The Doctor exhaled in relief, then felt guilty for it as he turned back to the dead alien. He lowered its head gently, respectfully, back to the floor, and stood. 'And Rick?'

'It tried to communicate with him, as he came through the wall. It was a crude, desperate attempt. It forced him to see the universe from its perspective. Fitz experienced much the same thing, but with far less force – and I was here to mediate for him.'

'It blew his mind,' the Doctor whispered, horrified.

'That would be a colloquial way of phrasing it.'

Across the room, Sandra had extricated Rick from the drill and he was bawling into her chest like a baby. She was crying herself as she cradled him and whispered words of maternal comfort. Despite all he had done, the Doctor couldn't help but feel sympathetic. He wondered what effect this experience would have on the young man. Perhaps he would become more understanding, more sensitive to the effects of his actions on others and on the big picture. He might seek revenge for his humiliation and pain. Or he might have been driven quite mad.

'I don't want to go with it,' said Compassion.

Turning back to her, the Doctor raised an inquisitive eyebrow.

'With the Maker,' she elaborated. 'It opened my mind to so much, introduced me to so many concepts. I'm grateful to it for that. But I'm not lonely, and I'm not unhappy with what I've become. I want to stay with you.'

The Doctor nodded sagely, as one burden at least was lifted from him. 'I'm glad,' he said.

'I need you to spread the word,' said the Doctor. 'Anyone staying in this era should assemble in the mods' old café over the next few minutes. That includes the plain-dwellers. I had a quiet word with them; they know the situation. In fact, most of them were quite pleased.'

Sandra strolled alongside him, her head up. 'And what happens then?'

'The Maker will send you to Earth. The real Earth. It will be quite disconcerting, but a harmless enough process. Apparently it can paste you into this time frame as if you'd always been here. You'll have papers, a National Insurance number, everything you'll need to get started.' His mind drifted off into the theoretical implications of it all; he was vaguely aware that his hands were trying to mime the impossible concept. 'Like cutting you out of one part of the tapestry and sewing you into another,' he muttered. Then, remembering his audience, he flashed Sandra a reassuring grin. 'Then the Maker will –' he searched for the word, indicating the remains of the city with a sweep of his arm – 'unmake all this, and put everyone else back where and when they came from. They won't know a thing about it.'

'Which is how they'd prefer it, I'm sure,' said Sandra, just a little sourly.

'Quite. You're intending to stay, I take it?'

Sandra nodded. 'It's what Rick wants. I don't know if it's the best thing for him – I think it is – but I can't send him back to a life he hates, and I don't want to wipe out everything he's done. Good or bad, it's all a part of him – and he is my son.'

'How is he,' asked the Doctor, 'since…?'

'Subdued,' said Sandra. 'For the first time in his life. We had a short talk, and now he's sleeping. He's exhausted. I don't know what he'll be like when he wakes up, but it doesn't matter.

Whatever happens, I hope – no, I'm sure – we can make things better.'

The Doctor nodded approvingly. 'I think you're making the right decision.'

'Most of the others are going back. There are only a few of us: those who were born here, obviously, and a lot of their parents. And a few more, who just want to see what's out there.'

'Yes, Gillian told me she'd be staying.'

'She actually said hello to me before. She even smiled, I think.'

'The old wounds can heal,' said the Doctor, 'now that their cause has gone.'

'It's not just Rick, you know,' said Sandra, reflectively. 'I want to see the future too.' She laughed to herself. 'Despite everything.'

Their wanderings had taken them back to the mods' café, outside which they were welcomed by a small group that comprised Compassion, Fitz, Gillian and Fitz's two mod friends, Vince and Deborah.

'I wish we could stay to see you off,' said the Doctor, 'but once the Maker reverses what it did, this world will revert to being an airless planetoid. Only the plants and the camel creatures will remain – and it's certainly high time we left them to get on with it.'

'Don't worry about us,' said Gillian. 'I'm looking forward to seeing how the two of you climb inside this woman.'

The Doctor gave her an abashed smile. 'Yes. Quite.' He turned to Compassion and patted her paternally on the shoulder. She didn't respond. She was uncommunicative now, as she had been when they had first arrived. It didn't matter, though. It was what she wanted. And he could feel her in his mind, an ever-present friend easing his loss.

'It is going to be different this time, isn't it?' said Deborah in a small voice.

'We're going back,' explained Vince, with a watery smile, blinking rapidly. 'We want to give Davey another chance.'

'I can't tell you what will happen in your future,' said the Doctor kindly, 'but I can assure you, it won't be anything like this.'

'No servo-robots,' said Sandra. 'No moving pavements, no flying bikes, no space-age food.'

'And absolutely no mad computers,' said Gillian.

'Well,' said the Doctor, 'not many.'

'No,' said Fitz with an impish grin, 'apparently the future is all cyberspace, nanites and the Internet.' The Doctor arched a disapproving eyebrow in his direction.

Compassion opened her arms then, and space-time was distorted. Somehow, against all physical laws, she had become a doorway, from which a blinding light shone.

'Wow,' said Gillian. 'That's not how I'd pictured it at all.'

'Goodbye, Doctor, Fitz,' said Sandra. 'Thanks for everything.'

'Perhaps we'll meet again,' said the Doctor, glancing up to the sky. 'Out there somewhere.' Then, with a smile and a wink, he bustled Fitz through the impossible doors and called over his shoulder, 'Goodbye, all of you!'

As an afterthought, he added, 'And best of luck for the future – whatever you choose to make of it.'

Epilogue

The fire is extinguished and its cause removed. The tapestry is repaired – and, if some details have changed, then they are only minor ones. Just a few small rewrites to the ends of a few small stories: nothing of consequence to the overall picture.

On a grey beach beneath a grey sky tinged with sunset red, in the year 1965, Alec Redshaw and Sandra McBride argue and part company. Elsewhen, they are arguing again on the night of the rumble; she is walking away for the last time; Vince is dragging Deborah out of danger as motorbikes and scooters converge upon them; Alec, hit by fear, turns his bike aside, falls, grazes his arm on tarmac, rips his precious jacket and almost cries at the humiliation.

In time, the moment becomes a memory, provoking a hot rush of blood to his face, which he angrily denies. His mind rewrites the details of that night, exaggerating some, suppressing others. It is early the next morning, and Alec has been too energised to sleep. He rises and dresses, inspecting the bruise around his eye in a grease-streaked mirror and thinking of the few good blows he managed to land before the police turned up and mods and rockers alike scattered. He thinks that, on balance, his gang won the day. But the mods deserve more, and he itches already for the next rumble, the next adrenaline rush.

Church bells ring out on this still Sunday morning, but the tranquil atmosphere is belied by the debris that is still to be cleaned up. The fight was meant to take place on the beach, not in the town itself. Windows have been broken, graffiti scrawled on walls and a few cars vandalised. A shopkeeper with a brush and shovel swears at Alec as he rides past proudly on his bike in full leathers, showing that the roads still belong to the rockers.

There were some arrests. Alec isn't sure, but he thinks he saw

Phil, one of Sandra's older brothers, being hauled into a Black Maria. The recollection emboldens him. He gets closer to her house than usual before he parks the bike and approaches on quieter feet. He is startled when her front door opens and Sandra's fat mum shows a police constable out. Alec leaps into the garden of a stranger and peers over the low brick wall as the copper says a few words to Mrs McBride, then dons his helmet and marches away.

That confirms it, doesn't it? One of her mod sons – both, with any luck – is in the nick.

His heart pounding excitedly, Alec leapfrogs back over the wall and runs along the pavement until he reaches Sandra's house. Nothing stands between them now. Oh, he might have to do a bit of sweet-talking after last night's bust-up, but she'll come round. He is a hero. His gang won the fight. He put her brothers in their place.

He scoops up a handful of gravel and throws it at her bedroom window, as he has done several times before. Even if she is up already, she might be in there with Ricky. Her mother is always pushing the kid on to her, the fat, lazy cow. He should sort her out too.

Sandra doesn't come to the window, but Alec doesn't give up. He needs to talk to her. He picks up more gravel, throws it again and again, hears the pitter-patter of stone on glass. She couldn't be ignoring him, could she? Just my luck, he thinks bitterly. Just my luck if she's gone out. Today of all days.

He realises how careless he has been only when the front door is yanked open. Jack McBride flies out on to the pavement, and Alec is only slightly comforted by the absence of his brother Phil. Jack is broad and muscular, and scarlet with rage. 'What are you doing here, you greasy prat?' he thunders. 'What did we tell you about sniffing around our sister?'

Alec didn't want this confrontation, but his pride won't let him run from it. He puffs out his chest, squares his shoulders, casts a disparaging look at Jack McBride's smart suit and narrow tie and retorts, 'I don't take no orders from you, you big ponce!' even as his feet involuntarily back him away.

Jack reaches out with startlingly long arms, snatches the front of Alec's jacket and swings him around so that the brick wall of the McBrides' tiny front garden presses into the backs of his knees and only Jack is keeping him from toppling backwards on to the flagstones. The huge mod's face is pressed up against Alec's own. 'What did we say we'd do if you came round here again, eh? Eh?' Jack punctuates his threats with a series of little slaps to Alec's face. 'Remember that, do you, grease monkey? What did we say we'd do?'

With a red rush of anger and embarrassment, Alec tries to fight back. But Jack is a good two years older than he is, far heavier and stronger. The more Alec struggles, the more Jack pushes; the further back Alec bends, the wall acting as a fulcrum so that he fears he will end up lying in the garden, his legs slung over it, an object of ridicule.

He is saved by a shrill female voice, coming from the doorway of the house. 'Jack, stop that! Stop that!' Sandra's fat mum is obviously distressed. 'Do you want them to put you away with your brother? Don't you think I've got enough to worry about without that?'

Jack relents a little, but he is reluctant to let go of Alec altogether. Alec takes his chance to push the mod away, hoping it will look as if he has heroically broken his hold.

'And you,' snaps Mrs McBride, waving a nagging finger in his direction, 'I don't want you anywhere near my house, do you hear me? Filling Sandra's head with all your nonsense. I suppose it was your idea for her to run away, was it? Well, was it?'

'Where is she?' demands Alec, defiantly. 'Where's Sandra?'

'At least she's not with you,' snarls Jack.

'You mean she's gone? You mean you don't know where she is?'

'It's none of your business, rocker.'

'It bloody well is my business! You've driven her away, haven't you? You and your stuck-up family. She couldn't stand to be cooped up with you a minute longer.' The realisation of his loss fuels Alec's anger, and his anger drives a fist into Jack McBride's chest. The response is so fast that he doesn't even see it. Knuckles graze his temple, a hammer drives into his stomach, his neck snaps backwards and forwards and Jack McBride keeps punching and, once he has fallen, kicking him, over and over again, until he is curled into a ball in the dirt and all he can see is white flashes in the darkness and all he can hear is the distant distressed shriek of Sandra's fat mum, almost drowned out by the rushing of blood in his ears and the taunting voice that seems to cry out in his mind. Failure. Weakling. Loser.

In days to come, Alec will hear more of what happened. He will learn that Sandra disappeared, along with little Ricky, during the rumble. The police will conclude that she simply walked out of her own accord. He will never find out why or where she went, nor why she took her younger brother with her when she had always seemed to resent his presence. He will always remember those arguments they had, on the last two occasions that he saw her; he will replay them in his mind and think of all the things he should have said instead.

There will be some speculation that she is with Gillian Davis and a handful of others who went missing on the same night; that they cast off their old lives and went exploring together.

She will never come back.

Alec looks in the mirror again. He has fresh bruises and dried blood beneath his nose and no consolation, no way to imagine that he achieved anything this time.

An hour ago, he was happy. An hour ago, he was winning. How could things have gone so wrong so quickly? How could he have lost control?

News will spread, of course. Everyone will know that he was beaten up by a mod, in public no less. He has lost his reputation. He has lost Sandra. He has lost everything.

And he knows whom to blame.

So sudden was Jack's attack, so swift was the fight, that he didn't even think to pull his knife. He won't make that mistake again. He holds it up to the mirror now, and stares at the reflection of its dulled blade. He can feel himself shaking, a delayed reaction to his punishment. He concentrates on the blade, because it means he doesn't have to look at his injuries; because it makes him feel like he isn't helpless after all. It makes him look like a fighter. It reawakens his confidence. He can start to believe that Jack, that Phil, that every lousy mod in town, will regret what they have done to him today; will regret ever messing with a rocker. They didn't learn their lesson last night, but they'll learn it next time.

He'll get the gang together. They'll call out their enemies. There will be another rumble.

The rockers will sort out the mods once and for all.

The Eighth Doctor's adventures continue in THE BANQUO LEGACY by Andy Lane and Justin Richards, ISBN 0 563 53808 2, available June 2000.

About the Author

Steve Lyons lives in Salford and still doesn't regret leaving his job at a large, well-known bank to become a full-time writer. His published work includes half of the best-*selling Red Dwarf Programme Guide*, half of *Cunning: The Blackadder Programme Guide*, plenty of magazine articles and several short stories featuring the Marvel superheroes. This is his ninth *Doctor Who* novel, and he is also a regular contributor to *Doctor Who Magazine*. When he isn't working, he reads *Spider-Man* comics and watches *Prisoner: Cell Block H*. He hates writing these back-of-the-book biographies, which is why he's just copied an old one out of the *More Short Trips* anthology and updated it a bit. He was born in 1969, and the year 2000 isn't at all like he was led to expect.

THE BANQUO LEGACY
by ANDY LANE & JUSTIN RICHARDS

Available June 2000

Banquo Manor – scene of a gruesome murder a hundred years ago. Now history is about to repeat itself.

1898 – the age of advancement, of electricity, of technology. Scientist Richard Harries is preparing to push the boundaries of science still further, into a new area: the science of the mind.

Pieced together at last from the accounts of solicitor John Hopkinson and Inspector Ian Stratford of Scotland Yard, the full story of Banquo Manor can now be told.

Or can it? Even Hopkinson and Stratford don't know the truth about the mysterious Doctor Friedlander and his associate Herr Kreiner – noted forensic scientists from Germany come to witness the experiment.

And for the Doctor, time is literally running out. He knows that Compassion is dying. He's aware that he has lost his own ability to regenerate. He's worried by Fitz's fake German accent. He's desperate to uncover the Time Lord agent who has him trapped.

And worst of all… he's about to be murdered.

PRESENTING

DOCTOR WHO

AN ALL-NEW AUDIO DRAMA – FEATURING THE DALEKS!

Big Finish Productions is proud to present all-new *Doctor Who* adventures on audio!

Featuring original music and sound-effects, these full-cast plays are available on double cassette in high street stores, and on limited-edition double CD from all good specialist stores, or via mail order.

Available from May 2000
DALEK EMPIRE
THE GENOCIDE MACHINE

A four-part story by Mike Tucker.
Starring **Sylvester McCoy** as the Doctor
and **Sophie Aldred** as Ace.

The library on Kar-Charrat is one of the wonders of the Universe.
It is also hidden from all but a few select species. The Doctor and Ace
discover that the librarians have found a new way of storing data –
a wetworks facility – but the machine has attracted unwanted attention, and the
Doctor soon finds himself pitted against his oldest and deadliest enemies – the Daleks!

If you wish to order the CD version, please photocopy this form or provide all the details on paper. Delivery within 28 days of release.
Send to: PO Box 1127, Maidenhead, Berkshire. SL6 3LN.
Big Finish Hotline 01628 828283

Please send me   [   ] copies of *Dalek Empire: The Genocide Machine* each @ £13.99 (£15.50 non-UK orders). Prices inclusive of postage and packing. Payment can be accepted by credit card or by personal cheques, payable to Big Finish Productions Ltd.
Name..
Address..
....
Postcode...
VISA/Mastercard number...
Expiry date...
Signature..

Other stories featuring the Seventh Doctor still available include:
THE SIRENS OF TIME   THE FEARMONGER

For more details visit our website at
http://www.doctorwho.co.uk